# Thisby Thestoop

### AND THE

## Wretched Scrattle

# Thisby

AND
THE

# Thesteop

## Wretched Scrattle

BY ZAC GORMAN

**HARPER**
An Imprint of HarperCollinsPublishers

Library of Congress Cataloging-in-Publication Data

Names: Gorman, Zac, author. | Bosma, Sam, illustrator.
Title: Thisby Thestoop and the Wretched Scrattle / by Zac Gorman ; [illustrated by]
   Sam Bosma.
Description: First edition. | New York, NY : Harper, an imprint of
   HarperCollinsPublishers, [2019] | Sequel to: Thisby Thestoop and the Black Mountain.
   | Summary: "Thisby Thestoop, gamekeeper for all creatures gruesome and uncommon,
   must now win the Wretched Scrattle to save her home, the Black Mountain Dungeon"
   — Provided by publisher.
Identifiers: LCCN 2018021206 | ISBN 978-0-06-249574-7 (hardback)
Subjects: | CYAC: Monsters--Fiction. | Magic--Fiction. | Adventure and adventurers—
   Fiction. | BISAC: JUVENILE FICTION / Fantasy & Magic. | JUVENILE FICTION /
   Monsters. | JUVENILE FICTION / Humorous Stories.
Classification: LCC PZ7.G6695 Th 2019 | DDC |Fic|--dc23 LC record available at
https://lccn.loc.gov/2018021206

Typography by Joe Merkel
19 20 21 22 23   CG/LSCH   10 9 8 7 6 5 4 3 2 1
❖
First Edition

# CHAPTER 1

It was raining, because of course it was. Never before in the history of rain had a downpour been colder, grayer, or drearier than it was that night, and honestly, it was all getting to be a bit much. Even the ravens, who were normally game for the whole "dark and stormy" bit, felt uneasy with the excessive use of clichés, so as the hearse-black carriage rumbled past, they decided to flap from their regular perch atop a gnarled yew tree to what they considered to be a far less derivative spot on the roof of a nearby cobbler's shop.

The coachman blinked his hooded lantern several times at the gatekeepers in a series of dots and dashes, which in turn caused the large, wrought-iron gates to yawn open with the loud squeal of metal rubbing metal. Beyond the gates was a sparkling white castle, or at least what should have been a sparkling white castle had it not been for the gloomy, overcast sky of that particular night, which instead shrouded the building in a sort of bilious green pall. Even the lights that flickered from inside the castle windows—normally so happy and inviting—looked downright macabre, like two candles placed inside the vacant eye sockets of a giant's skull. Nearby, two ravens cawed derisively.

The gates slammed shut behind the carriage as it rattled onward toward the castle, slick cobblestones shining like black marble in the advancing torchlight. It trundled along, until it came to rest in front of the towering drawbridge of Lyra Castelis. The attendants who'd been traveling alongside the carriage climbed down off their horses and opened the carriage door, allowing a very tall, elegant shadow to exit the vehicle.

The shadow's face was indiscernible beneath the upturned collar of a dark, fur-lined cloak and wide-brimmed hat, but whoever it was moved like a ballet dancer. At first glance, it seemed as if the figure was untouched by the rain, simply stepping in between the drops with such ease that it seemed curious as to why everyone else didn't just do the same. Upon closer inspection, however, raindrops could definitely be seen pattering gently on the shadow's wide hat, collecting in small pools before choosing an edge from which to run off in a thin trickle. It was something of a relief to see the figure

*Even the lights that flickered from inside the castle windows
looked downright macabre.*

touched by rain, proof that it was at least real.

Shaking themselves awake from the spell caused by watching the figure, the carriage attendants remembered their mission and ran after the shadow, their mostly decorative swords rattling in their scabbards. The castle guards, looking much more professional than those two struggling to keep up, swung open a set of small wooden guest doors nested within the gargantuan drawbridge and bowed ever so slightly as the shadow whooshed by them without so much as acknowledging their presence.

Inside the castle the world was transformed. The earthy smell of rain was instantly replaced by the scent of warm baked bread and stale floral arrangements, the light transitioned from its uneasy, rainstorm green to the pleasant orange glow of a crackling hearth on the first cold night of autumn, and the rush of rain became a gentle pitter-patter accompanied by the distant twinkling of harp strings. In other words, it was nice. What wasn't nice, however, was the shadowy figure, who suddenly looked extraordinarily out of place where only moments ago it'd looked perfectly at home.

The shadow strode down the hall on long, bowed legs, the dark cloak trailing behind, flapping like an angry bird. Castle guards stared but did not make any motion to interfere as the figure walked right down the vaulted hallway, past the marble statues, the priceless paintings, and the brightly polished suits of armor, through the large oak double doors inlaid with jewels and twirling, decorative golden bands, and right up the dark red carpet to where Parlo Larkspur, the King of Nth, sat upon his throne. Beside the King was a young girl, seated in her own—albeit significantly smaller— throne. They both watched the shadow approaching with rigidly fixed smiles that barely concealed their displeasure at its arrival.

"Welcome to Lyra Castelis, my dear Marl," said the King, beaming. "I trust that your journey here to Oryzia was as comfortable as could be expected, given the weather?"

Marl removed her hat and bowed. "Yes, Your Majesty."

The shadow was suddenly no longer a shadow but a regular human woman; tall and thin and fairly androgynous. If she'd been a man, you would've called her pretty; as a woman you might call her handsome. Either way, it was fair to say that she was striking. Much more than what would've been expected from her entrance. Her green hair cascaded down past her shoulders, her nose was long but pleasantly sloped, and her eyes tilted down gently at the outer corners a bit, creating a sort of charming, sleepy countenance. All these factors combined to create a face that was not so much traditionally beautiful as it was a challenge to ignore. The only thing off-putting about the stranger were the dark purple circles under her eyes, which made them look deeply bruised and tired. They were the eyes of someone who read far more often than they slept.

Marl smiled gently. One of the guards came up to take her cloak.

"Please," boomed King Parlo, who boomed more often than not even when he didn't intend to, "allow me to introduce . . ."

"Your daughter," said Marl with a soft lilt.

With a flick of her wrist, Marl politely waved away the guard, who carried off her sopping-wet cloak and hat.

The King did not look perturbed by the interruption, as perhaps he should have. Rather, he simply beamed proudly at his daughter and then back toward his rather unusual guest.

Beneath her cloak, Marl was wearing expensive robes as black as the night sky; the cloth was black, the trim was black, even the stitching was black. In fact, the only thing that Marl wore that was not black was a golden bracelet that dangled off her right wrist. It was in the shape of a dragon biting its own tail.

Marl smiled again, this time a bit apologetically.

"Forgive my interruption, I only mean that of course I'm familiar with the lovely, brave, and famous Iphigenia Larkspur, Crown Princess of Nth, Chosen Heir to the Throne."

Iphigenia sat absolutely still as she studied the stranger. At last, with great effort spent to show no emotion whatsoever, she nodded curtly at Marl, who returned the nod graciously before continuing.

"I suppose you would like the news, Your Majesty."

King Larkspur nodded. There was an awful lot of nodding going on. With a wave of his royal hand, several guards, including those who had arrived with Marl, excused themselves from the chamber and closed the door behind them with an ominous *ka-chunk!* that resonated throughout the throne room. When at last they were down to the minimum number of necessary and trusted guards—which, it turned out, was exactly four, for some reason—Marl proceeded.

"In Umberfall, they're plotting against you and your kingdom every day, Your Majesty. I hear the whispers in the capital, both in the streets and inside the palace walls. But what they have in ambition, they lack in numbers. Their army is sturdy enough to defend a fortified position but far too small to make the journey south through the mountains. They'd lose too many soldiers in the process, exhaust their resources, and by the time they were on the doorstep of your kingdom, they'd be as good as dead. As long as the Umberfallians are trapped north of the mountains, we can rest easy."

Iphigenia looked over to her father, who seemed pensive as he stroked his salt-and-pepper beard, which, as of late, had become more salt than pepper. Her father was a robust man, but Iphigenia had seen him begin to wear around the edges since last year. Since Ingo's death.

The death of her brother had sent shock waves through the kingdom, but nowhere had it been worse than inside Lyra Castelis itself. Not only her father but everyone who lived within the castle had loved Ingo—*wonderful, brave, charming*

*Ingo!*—and the fact that he'd died a traitor was more than the royal family could bear. For months, her father had lived in outright denial, refusing to admit what Ingo had done, but over time, in the face of no other options, he came to accept the truth. At least, that was what he said publicly, officially denouncing his son and having his name stricken from the Larkspur family history—a punishment reserved exclusively for traitors.

Between Iphigenia and her father, however, things had yet to return to normal. It was likely that they never would. Although it was awful to admit, Iphigenia couldn't shake the feeling that somewhere deep down inside, there was some small part of her father that blamed her for what happened in the Black Mountain. After all, if she'd never been born, things would've worked out just fine. Ingo would've been King and everybody would have lived happily ever after. But she had been born. Much to the displeasure of seemingly everybody.

"Of course, we must consider all possibilities . . . ," Marl said, letting her words hang ominously in the air. The chamber felt oddly colder.

The King leaned forward in his great throne so that it creaked beneath his not insubstantial weight. Along with showing his age, his diet had begun to catch up with him as well. The King's brow furrowed and his eyes widened in a pantomime of worried confusion. Iphigenia was embarrassed for him, that he was playing so easily into Marl's game, letting himself show his emotions like a child. Marl seemed to be reveling in it.

"What do you mean?" asked the King.

Iphigenia rolled her eyes.

Since being back in the castle—and having everyone treat her as if she was somehow responsible for her brother's death—Iphigenia had felt a bit more like her old self again, whatever that meant. All that she knew was that she'd been growing more impatient with people in the castle and their absurd political games lately, particularly since Thisby's visit.

The visit a few months ago had been wonderful. So wonderful, in fact, that the residual happiness had lasted for weeks, even after Thisby's carriage pulled away from the gates of the castle. It was like eating slices of leftover birthday cake: the memories of her visit had sustained Iphigenia for some time, but by now whatever scraps remained had long since gone stale. She'd even gotten to the point where it made her feel slightly sick to her stomach to even think about their time together, not knowing how long it would be until she could see her friend again. Her only friend. Iphigenia chased the thought from her mind.

"There is a chance, however slim, that the Umberfallians could make it through the mountains and into Nth."

The King was eating out of Marl's hands now. His brow was fully knitted, and he tugged at his beard as if in deep contemplation.

"But how?" he asked.

"There is one path in that we haven't considered. One shortcut into Nth. Through the Black Mountain."

The emphasis Marl placed on the words *Black Mountain* made it seem as if she'd expected the King to gasp, but he didn't. Instead his face just sank, and Iphigenia saw the same defeat in his eyes that she'd seen over and over again since she'd returned home from the dungeon. When her father learned about Ingo's death, she'd seen that look on his face for the first time. Now, it happened too often to count. Something about it made her sick. She wanted to feel empathy for her father's suffering, but she had no pity for Ingo, and to see that pity in another, especially her father . . . it was unbearable. A king was meant to be strong, to punish the wicked. And here was her own brother, his own son, more wicked than any, and yet Parlo pitied Ingo. Worse, he pitied himself.

Iphigenia couldn't stand to look at him, so she turned to Marl. She'd had enough of sitting quietly now.

"The Black Mountain wouldn't sit idly by and allow an army to pass through. Especially not an Umberfallian army," she said with what might've passed for a sneer. "Anyone stupid enough to try to pass through the dungeon would be dead before they reached the halfway point . . ."

Iphigenia hesitated.

"I should know," she finished.

It came off as a bit of a boast, and Iphigenia would be lying to say it wasn't intentional. She'd survived the dungeon.

She'd seen the absolute worst that it had to offer and had come out with barely a scratch on her—the scar from where her brother had plunged his knife into her stomach had faded completely over the last few months, thanks to the magic that had saved her. She'd been to the Deep Down, to the place where even the monsters feared to go, and she'd come back to tell the story. No one else in this room could say the same. Probably no one else in the entire kingdom, save Thisby.

Iphigenia could feel her father's eyes burning into her. He hated when she brought up the events in the Black Mountain. He hated it even more when she was proud of what she'd accomplished.

"And what if the dungeon were to let them through?" asked Marl.

"They would never do that!" shouted Iphigenia. "There's no way! I know them! I know—" She stopped.

Marl bowed low, green hair closing like drapes over her long face.

"Forgive me, milady. I didn't mean to speak out of turn, it's only . . . I have reason to suspect we might not be so secure in that belief."

The King woke from his helpless, angry silence and decided it was time to take control of the situation. He righted himself in his chair and glowered in Marl's direction.

"What information do you have? Be quick about it! I respect the necessity for riddles and games in your line of work, spy, but I won't have any more hints and coyness! Come out with it straight!" he bellowed now—his world seemed to make more sense when he was bellowing.

"Your Majesty," Marl said, turning all her attention back to the King, "I have heard a rumor that Umberfallian agents have been in contact with the dungeon, even as high as Castle Grimstone itself. It is possible that the Master of the Black Mountain and Umberfall are conspiring to work together. To turn against the Kingdom of Nth. The Umberfallians may be making promises to the Black Mountain that we cannot make."

With each utterance of "Black Mountain," the King cringed slightly.

"If we don't act now, I'm afraid we might be too late."

The King sat back heavily in his throne. It groaned under his bulk. He looked exasperated. Iphigenia watched him and saw the anger draining from his face, replaced by exhaustion, surrender.

"What would you have me do?" he asked at last.

It was the last question that a good king ever asks of his subjects, let alone a spy like Marl. It was also, quite obviously, the one question that Marl had been waiting for, the one she'd been trying to coax out of the King's mouth for their entire conversation.

Iphigenia looked to her father, who appeared lost behind his own eyes, and then back to the gangly stranger in black who tucked her moss-colored hair behind her ears. She knew exactly what was coming next. As did Iphigenia. It bothered her that her father didn't. He'd spent his entire life in the castle and yet he couldn't see even the simplest patterns of human behavior. Iphigenia was only a quarter of her father's age, but she knew as well as anybody that when you're in a position of power and you ask somebody what they think you should do, they only ever have one suggestion . . .

"Put me in charge of the Black Mountain," said Marl.

There was a well-timed, low rumble of thunder from outside the castle, followed by the cawing laughter of two ravens.

In the courtyard, the rain continued to fall. Beyond the shelter of the veranda, thin rivulets streamed through the gaps between the cobblestones, winding their way through the castle gardens as its well-manicured plants danced in the rain. Where the cobblestone path stopped and the streams pooled was a white marble fountain, flooded to the point where the basin had begun to spill out into the courtyard itself, making it difficult to tell where the fountain stopped and the courtyard began. In the center of the fountain rose a tall pedestal upon which sat a life-size stone lion. Hidden behind its right forepaw was an inscription, crudely carved with a penknife, that read:

THISBY + IPHI = BEST FRIENDS FOREVER

Hundreds of miles away, the girl who'd carved it was already awake, hours before the sun, wriggling her toes in her boots in her particular way so that her pinky toe curled over the toe-which-comes-next-to-the-pinky-toe, shouldering her massive backpack, and getting ready for another day of work down in the dungeon.

# CHAPTER 2

Thisby ducked beneath a low-hanging stalactite and felt the rowboat sway. Across from her, Mingus's jar rocked side to side. It was hung from its usual hook on her backpack, a weathered monstrosity of pockets and stains that looked rather dejected as it sat upright, like another passenger, across from her toward the bow of the boat. It was easy to imagine it as some sort of bloated canvas slug, cast in Mingus's wobbly light, which alternated between mustard yellow and soft blue-green.

"Ugh, can't you keep it steady? You're making me sick!" chided the slime.

Mingus sloshed around, barely able to hold his shape.

Thisby watched as his button eyes drooped lazily down before he was able to pull himself back to his usual shape and viscosity, which was something like a large, wet gumdrop. He produced a brow ridge for the sole purpose of furrowing it at her.

Thisby smiled, revealing a chipped tooth she'd recently acquired during a run-in with an impatient rock golem.

"Oh, yeah?"

Thisby grabbed the sides of the boat and shook it back and forth violently.

"STOP IT! STOP IT! NOT FUNNY!" Mingus screamed, though his laughter undermined his protest.

Thisby stopped, held up her hands in a gesture of mock defeat, and sat back down. She wasn't about to admit it, but she'd actually made herself sick as well. They'd been traveling the river all day, tending to the aquatic residents of the Black Mountain, and spending that much time on the water had begun to take its toll.

There was only one river in the Black Mountain, and it wound its way through every floor of the dungeon, flowing both upward and downward without beginning or end, sprouting off into tiny streams, which fed into larger bodies of water that quite often seemed far too vast for the amount of water being supplied to them. Any attempt to comprehend the physics of the river would drive a sane person mad, as it had done with Cornish Planesse, one of the original thirty-three architects who'd constructed the dungeon. Right up until the day he died, Cornish could not so much as even see a glass of water without becoming irrationally angry.

Common sense and gravity would suggest that the river should have flowed down the mountain from top to bottom, and it did, for about half of it. The confusing part was that somehow, the other half of the river flowed back *up* the mountain until it met with the point where it began, creating a seamless ribbon that flowed counterclockwise around the entire dungeon. More confusing still was that the wizards who examined the river—including the great Elphond the Evil, first Master of the Black Mountain himself—found no indication of magical tampering. The only clue as to something unusual about the river's design was a series of copper pipes discovered beneath the bed of the river in some areas. These were presumably an artifact left over from the Dünkeldwarves, who'd begun construction in the Black Mountain centuries before Elphond the Evil and his team of architects had arrived to finish the job, but the pipes' function had yet to be properly explained, so the mystery of the Floating River—as it had come to be called—persisted.

Due to the river's improbable nature, if Thisby traveled downstream, she could make her way around the entire dungeon from top to bottom in less than two days' time, barely ever having to touch her paddle to the water. It was nice. The Floating River pretty much carried her where she needed to go, and although it was far slower than using her shortcuts on foot, it was also much easier on her legs. It was almost a perfect mode of travel. Almost. Because this was the dungeon, there were, of course, several other complications.

The first of these were the narrow passages. Many of them were so small that Thisby had to cram her backpack way down into the base of the rowboat and hunch over until her back ached, just to squeeze through. These tunnels made moving anything larger than a boat with a single, small passenger a pipe dream. Second, even though the river was basically one long ribbon, that did not mean it was simple to navigate. The river branched off into thousands of fingers both large and small, and if you weren't careful, it was all too easy to get stuck in a dead end—and worse yet, once you were stuck, any attempt to paddle upstream against the strong current was next to impossible. This meant that wherever you ended up, you were more or less stranded. And then there was the third point. The areas surrounding the river—as well as the river itself—were breeding grounds for some of the biggest, wildest, all-around-nastiest monsters in the entire dungeon.

Unsuspecting adventurers who thought they'd found a clever shortcut through the dungeon by navigating the river would all too often be gobbled up by giant albino alligators who lurked just below the surface of the water or dragged under by a horde of angry merpeople. There were countless dangers hidden beneath the black, glassy surface of the Floating River, and if you took a wrong turn, it'd very likely be your last. Even Thisby, with her unsurpassed knowledge of the dungeon, didn't dare travel the river without her supply of meticulously updated, hand-drawn maps. It was for this myriad of reasons that it was typically safer—not to mention faster, if you knew the proper shortcuts, which of course she did—to walk. Which was exactly what she did all but one day of every month, when it was time to tend to the dungeon's aquatic residents.

Thisby and Mingus had already passed the turn at the lowest point of the river when her pocket began to glow. From it, she withdrew what resembled an ornate golden pocket watch with a small, flashing white crystal on the front and flipped it open. Inside, as clear as day, was the Master of the Black Mountain sitting in his study.

"Keeper," he said. The Master never called her by name. Frankly, she wasn't even certain he remembered it—not even after she'd saved the dungeon. "Finish up with your work and meet me in the castle. We have some important business to discuss."

Thisby's mouth opened and shut as she tried to find a response but failed on her first, second, and then third attempt. His request had caught her off guard. Even though the Master had become increasingly reliant on Thisby as of late, communicating with her through her "scrobble"—the nickname Thisby had given the magical device through which she now spoke—she hadn't spoken to him in person since shortly after the Battle of Darkwell, when the entire dungeon had nearly been overrun by Deep Dwellers. She tried not to sound as worried as she felt by the unprecedented suggestion that they meet face-to-face.

"Uh, yes. Definitely. I just need to take care of a few more things. I should be back in a few hours if I hurry?"

"Do," he said.

There was a long pause during which Thisby got it into her head that she was definitely, absolutely supposed to say something. She wrinkled her nose and opened her mouth as if to speak, assuming that maybe the issue was merely that her lips were in the way of her words. She did this a few more times until a few of them finally managed to dribble out.

"I hear the shovelball finals are starting soon. Do you think the Bisby Bigbacks have what it takes? Grunda tells me that sometimes you watch the games from the blackdoor room. So I just, uh . . . well . . . I wondered . . ."

The Master blinked at her a few times.

"Just hurry," he added before the screen of her scrobble went black.

Thisby looked up just in time to dodge a passing stalactite as the boat continued along down the river, carried forward by the endless current.

"What do you think he wants?" she asked.

"Maybe you're finally getting that promotion."

This was Mingus's idea of a joke. Since the Battle of Darkwell a year ago, things in the dungeon had changed quite a bit, and Thisby found herself in an unusual position.

Essentially, she was running the dungeon, and things had never been better.

After the battle, the Master seemed to believe that he'd earned an early retirement, and in short order he'd begun to relegate all his duties to the remaining members of his staff; namely Thisby, who served as gamekeeper, and Grunda the goblin, who was promoted to liaison to Castle Grimstone following the untimely death of the Master's previous liaison, the traitorous Roquat. As it turned out, Thisby and Grunda did a much better job than anybody had previously thought possible.

Under their watch, the dungeon had been running like Dünkeldwarven automata. Everything was cleaner and better organized than it had ever been. The resident monsters were well fed and content, and there'd even been several successful construction projects that restored access to previously unreachable areas of the dungeon, such as the blood bee apiary and the harpy roost. There was even talk about beginning reconstruction on the areas of the City of Night that had been devastated during last year's tarasque rampage. Unfortunately for Thisby, all this extra work came without a promotion (or pay of any kind, it should be noted) and as it was, she'd been having a hard time understanding exactly what the Master was "Mastering" these days.

She rolled her eyes at Mingus.

"I'm not holding my breath."

As much as she hated to admit it, there was a small part

of her heart that leapt when Mingus had suggested the idea. After all, why shouldn't she get a promotion? She deserved it. After saving everyone from Ingo and the Deep Dwellers and then spending the rest of the year making the dungeon better than she'd ever seen it in her time as gamekeeper, why shouldn't she be promoted? Maybe the Master was ready to step aside and name her the new Master of the Black Mountain.

She shook the thought from her head, but it was too late. Even the passing thought had been enough to make her intestines twist up into a knot that would take some time to untie. It wasn't that she didn't feel capable of being the Master; there was just something that felt wrong about the whole idea. Last year after the invasion, several of the monsters had begun to refer to her as *mara'wak kombeh*, a sort of honorary title meaning "Master of the Black Mountain" that was borrowed from the kobolds—and it'd made her uncomfortable in a way that she hadn't expected. Fortunately, she knew there was no reason to get worked up like she had. Nobody simply relinquished the position of Master of the Black Mountain. It just wasn't done. The Master was a position you only left the hard way, traditionally with a knife sticking out of your back.

No. For now, at least, Thisby was happy as gamekeeper. After all, she was still just a few weeks from turning thirteen. There'd be plenty of time to worry about this "promotion" stuff when she was older. For now, all she really wanted was a little help. Maybe she'd bring that up in their meeting.

The boat bounced down the river, and Thisby hurriedly plunged her paddle into the inky water, turning the vessel down the leftmost tunnel. It was hard to tell that they'd rounded the bend near the bottom of the river and had begun their ascension—the angle was subtle here and the tunnel very narrow—but Thisby swore for a second she felt her ears pop as their altitude changed.

When the rowboat emerged from the tunnel, Thisby had Mingus kill his light and leaned forward so that she was almost lying flat on her stomach in the boat, hidden beneath its edge. The boat slid silently out into the open chamber as she lay still, enveloped by darkness, feeling only her heartbeat and the gentle rocking of her boat. In the overwhelming silence of the cavern, she was painfully aware of the sound of her own breathing and fought to get it under control. Once she'd done so, Thisby pressed up into a push-up position, peering over the lip of the boat out into the nothingness that surrounded her.

The rowboat drifted slowly on through the darkness. Without any point of reference, it soon became difficult to tell if they were even moving at all. The feeling was unnerving.

A story sprang to mind. It was one that Grunda had told her before she took her first trip down the Floating River, though it'd happened long before Thisby was born. It concerned the fate of Pedrosa Porret, a famous adventurer who died in Long Lost Lake—the lake at the very bottom of the Floating River, which Thisby always avoided if she could help it, like today—after he ran out of lantern oil. He was stranded, adrift in complete darkness, unable to come to shore because his vessel was surrounded by dire crocodiles, until he ran out of food and perished. Only, when his body was eventually found by the gamekeeper, despite what he'd scrawled in his journal, there were no signs of dire crocodiles anywhere and his body was noticeably uneaten. Had he simply gone mad in the dark? It seemed entirely possible.

Thisby shivered. Why couldn't Grunda ever tell her stories with happy endings?

There was snuffling in the dark. The sound of nostrils the size of grapefruits sucking in long breaths, followed by the gentle splashing of things slipping below the water. The rowboat rocked as if something big had passed underneath.

There was a faint light now from the pale glow of bioluminescent cave mushrooms. It was just bright enough that Thisby could see the outlines of the massive beasts on the other side of the cave, but not bright enough to make out any distinct features. The creatures had bodies like hippopotamuses but necks that stuck out like a giraffe's, which they craned down into the water to root around for plants and algae.

Thisby recognized them as catoblepas. Big, sure enough, but they weren't exceptionally dangerous unless they felt threatened. If that happened, though . . . look out. Thisby had once seen a catoblepas knock a wyvern clear out of the sky with one swing of its massive clubbed tail.

*In the overwhelming silence of the cavern, Thisby was painfully aware of the sound of her own breathing.*

The silhouette of one of the creatures lifted its massive head from the water and sniffed the air in Thisby's direction as her boat glided silently past. She couldn't make out the details of its face in the dark, but she could feel its presence and knew that it was watching her pass. Though it was maybe forty yards from her boat, it was a distance she knew a creature that size could cross quickly if it felt threatened. Thisby watched the outline of its warthog-like head bob up and down as it smelled her from across the water. Thisby nodded silently in the direction of the catoblepas, which snorted once before returning to its business of rooting around underwater. As she steered the boat out of the chamber, she dropped several bags of powder into the river to help facilitate algae growth, and left the catoblepas to enjoy their meal.

After they'd put enough distance between themselves and the catoblepas, Thisby sat up and Mingus began to glow again, faintly, so as not to disturb the light-sensitive creatures in the tunnels and caves along the river. Thisby smiled to herself. Partly from the relief of being able to see where she was going again, and partly from the satisfaction that after so many years, after so much work, the dungeon was finally running more smoothly than it ever had before.

# CHAPTER 3

The dungeon was in the worst shape it had ever been in, and it was entirely everybody else's fault.

This was the sole, miserable thought of the Master of the Black Mountain as he stared out through the window of Castle Grimstone's highest tower—which also happened to be his office—surveying what he could of Nth. It was very little. The sky was completely overcast that day, which, being above the clouds, meant that it was nearly impossible to see through, though occasionally a strong breeze would cause them to stir and through the swirling gray soup he'd catch a fleeting glimpse of Three Fingers and the rolling hills that lay beyond. Straight on from there to the west, at least a week's journey over the hills and through the woods, was Oryzia, the capital city, home to Lyra Castelis and the King of Nth himself.

"King of *pffth!*" spat the Master to himself and the walls.

When the Master was younger, he'd dreamt of being a king himself. Now he just wanted to be left alone. Unfortunately, after the Battle of Darkwell, peace and quiet had no longer been an option. Instead he had to deal with that nosy old bag of goblin warts, Grunda, and the only mildly less annoying gamekeeper. They were both gunning for his job. He knew it. Everyone knew it. At least some small part of him wished they'd just kill him already and be done with it. At least then he wouldn't have to keep hearing endless reports about how the Floating River was getting too dirty for the merpeople, or how the mummies needed fresh bandages, or how the trolls had gotten sick from rancid meat—ridiculous!

Worst of all, however, was that for some reason, the once plentiful stock of brave young heroes willing to risk their lives for treasure or glory down in the dungeon seemed to be at an all-time low. Without adventurers, there was no dungeon. That was something the pesky little gamekeeper girl and the old goblin didn't seem to understand. Adventurers were the lifeblood of the dungeon. Without them—

*KNOCK! KNOCK! KNOCK-KNOCK-KNOCK!*

The Master shuddered. It was a knock he knew all too well. For the last few weeks he'd actually woken up in cold sweats, dreaming he'd heard it.

"Come in," he moaned.

His chamber door creaked open and a wrinkly old goblin trotted in. She was carrying a box that was soaking through the bottom and dripping something gray and oily on his black marble floor.

"Look at this!" she squawked. "Can you believe this?"

Her voice was like hearing fingernails on a chalkboard—no, it was worse than that. Her voice was like hearing fingernails on a chalkboard, only they're your fingernails and they've been ripped clean off your fingers.

Grunda dropped the box at his feet and it landed with a sickening *splortch!* Her thin goblin fingers pulled the flaps open before the Master had a chance to look away, and he found himself staring down at what looked—and smelled—like a box full of spoiled tapioca and ogre snot.

"The new meat supply is way too salty for the slughemoths! They're completely melting! Look at them! It's disgusting!"

The Master agreed but didn't see why it was his problem. He turned away from the box and walked over to his desk, letting out a long, measured sigh as he went.

"I told you not to bother me with this stuff. If *you* have a problem, *you* take care of it."

Grunda glared at him from across the room.

"And what exactly do *you* do?" she asked.

This was it, he thought. This was exactly it. This was it in a nutshell. This was what had been going wrong with the dungeon ever since the gamekeeper—*Thessily? Theremin?*—had "saved" everyone from the deep dwellers . . . nobody was afraid anymore. Not of him, not of one another.

It'd been hard for him to place it at first. He was aware that something had shifted in the dungeon, in the proper order of things, but it took him awhile to figure out what it was exactly. The problem was that once the monsters of the dungeon had united to stop the invasion, they'd become far too friendly with one another. The random violence and chaos of the dungeon had slowed to a crawl and was replaced by a sort of, ugh, cooperation. Everything was "nice." Unfortunately for the Master, "nice" didn't jibe with his management style.

For years, he'd managed to be an effective ruler while doing very little by maintaining an aura of fear throughout the Black Mountain. The creatures were afraid of one another. They were afraid of him, afraid of the Deep Dwellers, afraid of the humans lurking just outside the mountain. But it'd all begun to unravel that one infamous night. When the monsters of the dungeon came together, united toward a single cause, they realized that they didn't have to be afraid, not of him, not of the Deep Dwellers, not of anything. It'd all blown up in his face. After the battle, he'd continued to do very little, only now he was worried that it was beginning to show. Now that nobody feared him, there was no way to maintain order.

Grunda shut the box and trudged over toward his desk, inviting herself to sit down in a chair across from him without being properly asked to do so. The Master bristled.

"You've got to do something," she said.

The Master sat up in his chair, trying to look big despite only being maybe a foot and a half taller than the minuscule goblin.

"No," he said.

"No?" repeated Grunda.

"No, I don't have to do anything."

"And why not?"

The Master grinned. This was the moment he'd been waiting for. A chance to reveal his secret. He'd wanted to just blurt it out the second she'd walked through the door, but he knew that if he could wait for her to bring it up organically in conversation, the moment would be so much sweeter. It was.

"Guards!" he called. "Send in my guest!"

Grunda turned in her chair to see the doors swing open. In strode a tall figure, long and dark, like a shadow cast by firelight.

"Allow me to introduce you to your new boss," said the Master.

By the time Thisby reached the gates to Castle Grimstone, the sun had vanished below the Black Mountain, leaving in its wake swaths of blue to green to pink organized in such a way that the sky resembled the underside of a gigantic salmon. It'd taken longer than she'd expected to get ready, so there was no doubt the Master would already be in a bad mood when she arrived.

She'd only dropped back by her room—just beneath the castle yet still in the mountain—to get changed into something that smelled a bit less like old fish. While she was there, however, she'd caught her reflection in a serving tray that Grunda had left in her room and realized that her hair could use a quick combing. What surprised her most during what was really more of a "hostile detangling" than a proper combing was the moment that—briefly . . . very, very briefly—she'd considered putting a bow in it. It was something she'd done only once, during her visit to Lyra Castelis. Iphigenia had shown her how, and she'd rather liked the way it looked, but for some reason she hadn't been able to bring herself to wear one again since she'd been back in the dungeon. Down here it just didn't seem right. It was a bit like putting on an evening gown to go get your teeth pulled. Regardless, bow or not, she wanted to look presentable. She didn't really think that she was about to be offered a promotion, but she figured it couldn't hurt to look professional anyhow.

Mingus and her backpack had stayed behind. There was no need for them on such a short jaunt to the castle. So, for now, she traveled by simple torchlight, feeling weirdly exposed without her regular supplies and her constant companion. The only items that she'd brought with her, aside from the torch, were her scrobble—which she always carried on her in a small belt pocket as per the Master's demands—and a travel-size notebook designed to fit discreetly in another. This particular notebook was sized more for daily lists than proper recording, and there was no particular reason why she needed it right now, but the thought of going anywhere in the dungeon without something in which to take notes was more than Thisby could handle. If she saw an interesting new mushroom or bug along the way and didn't have the means to quickly sketch it down or describe it, she'd never forgive herself.

At the gates, Thisby was surprised to find there were no guards on duty. Even though entry into Castle Grimstone had been officially opened to the residents of the dungeon following the Battle of Darkwell, there were always a couple of ghouls or skeletons on duty to monitor the comings and goings into and out from the castle, of which admittedly there were precious few. Despite the proclamation, only a handful of creatures actually dared to enter the castle, wary after a lifetime of threats about even venturing too close. The few intelligent creatures that had braved a trip inside had largely been disappointed by what they'd found. It was hard to live up to the hype that the Master had surrounded himself with over the years.

Thisby leaned hard into the gate and felt it move enough for her to know that it wasn't locked. After a hard shove, she managed to open it just wide enough to squeeze through and for the first time found herself grateful that she wasn't wearing her backpack.

It was only Thisby's third time inside the castle. The first had been when she'd shown up to ask the Master to help her stop the Deep Dwellers' invasion, and the second had been shortly after the dungeon's victory. On the second visit, the Master had asked her for a list of demands—anything to stop her from turning her momentary command over the denizens of the dungeon into a full-on uprising—and had been shocked to learn that she had very few. The few demands she did have were simple. At least they'd seemed so at the time.

There were only three demands that Thisby had come up with off the top of her head, although if she'd had time to prepare, she undoubtedly would've come up with more. First, she'd insisted that the gates of Castle Grimstone be kept open to any and all monsters of the dungeon (with the implicit exception of the mindless, eat-first-ask-questions-later types). Second, she'd insisted that Grunda take over Roquat's job as liaison between the dungeon and the Master, effective immediately. And third, she'd insisted on a vacation. She'd wanted to leave the dungeon for the first time and visit Iphigenia. And even though her third demand had felt selfish, it was the one that Thisby relished most of all.

Her stay in Oryzia with Iphigenia had been the most wonderful experience of her life, and for months after, the memory of it sustained her, even on her worst days. Thisby probably would've made a comparison to leftover birthday cake going stale, but she'd never had a proper birthday, much less a birthday cake. She'd tasted some sweets during her time in the capital but found she was more interested in the salty, fried things—especially potatoes.

Thisby placed her torch into an empty nearby sconce and continued down the corridor. The floor, the walls, the tapestries, everything inside Castle Grimstone was some shade of black. The most popular theory as to why this was the case was that it would trick the eyes of potential intruders and thus allow hidden warriors who were also shrouded in black to get the drop on them, but it was just as likely that the man who ordered the castle's construction, Elphond the Evil, simply liked the color—or lack thereof.

The furniture and decorations that adorned the castle were a mishmash of styles that spanned hundreds, if not thousands of years. There was a contemporary chair next to a Gothic end table next to a bejeweled throne paired with a primitive clay footstool. These items had been donated by the various Masters of the Black Mountain who'd occupied the castle at some point in history, and because of this, there was no consistent style to speak of, with the exception of possibly "excessive."

If the Masters of the Black Mountain had one thing in common—aside from a proclivity for murder—it was hoarding, and the halls of Castle Grimstone displayed the accumulated trash of generations. There were suits of armor collected from brave adventurers who'd fallen victim to the dungeon, mysterious artifacts, various monster parts, treasures scavenged from tombs, ancient relics, and even some "dragon bones," which were just as likely to be whale bones sold by a duplicitous merchant. For some, the castle was undoubtedly a treasure trove of untold wonders, but as far as Thisby was concerned, it was a garbage dump of useless bric-a-brac.

It didn't take Thisby long to realize that she had no idea where she was going. It was only once, on her second visit to the castle, that she'd actually come in through the door like a proper guest, and that time she'd been escorted to the Master's chamber. To make matters worse, she'd been so distracted by the castle itself that she hadn't paid any attention to her path. Now that she was on her own, it seemed as if she could wander through the twisted halls of the castle forever and never find a way out. Maybe she'd end up living out the rest of her days among the curios and ephemera until she was just another piece in the collection herself.

She'd been standing at a fork in the hallway for some time, arms akimbo and forehead wrinkled in deep contemplation, when she was startled by a small voice behind her.

"Are you lost?"

Thisby turned to see a skeleton wearing a simple leather jerkin. The skeleton was about her size, maybe an inch or two taller, and had the voice of a young boy. It took Thisby several moments to put this puzzle together, and when she did, it made her heart heavy.

"No, I'm okay."

"Oh, okay," said the skeleton. There was a note of sadness in his soft voice.

"Actually, I don't know why I said that," Thisby recovered

quickly. "I really am lost. Maybe you can help me out. If you don't mind."

She smiled at the skeleton and although she couldn't tell, because he didn't have lips, it felt as if he was smiling back.

"I need to get to the Master's chamber."

"Oh, then you must be important!"

"Not really," admitted Thisby.

"Well, more important than me, at least! Come on, I'll show you! I'd hate to keep a guest of the Master waiting!"

And with that they were off, the skeleton boy keeping a few paces ahead as they went. Thisby couldn't help but notice that his ankle made a sort of snapping sound with every step. Perhaps it'd been broken at some point.

"My name's Jono," he said politely. "You?"

"Thisby Thestoop," said Thisby.

"Wow! Two names! Fancy!" said Jono.

Thisby couldn't tell if this was a joke.

"You just have the one then?" she asked carefully.

Jono considered it for a surprisingly long time.

"Huh! I guess so! I've never thought about it," he admitted cheerfully. "So, what do you do, Thisby?" His mood had quickly improved.

Thisby looked into a room teeming with stuffed monster heads mounted on plaques and felt her stomach turn. Looming in the center of the room was a creature reared up on its hind legs that looked like a cross between an owl and a bear. Its beak was open to reveal a row of sharp fangs, and its hands were raised up threateningly, claws ready to swipe. She thought it was unlikely that the poor thing had actually died that way. More likely than not, it'd been taking a drink from a lake when it was snuck up on by some lousy hedge wizard and zapped with a paralysis spell. That was just the way it was with wizards. Thisby was reminded of a line she'd heard Grunda use more than once, "A true knight keeps his sword in his scabbard, a true thief keeps his dagger in his sleeve, and a true wizard keeps his knife in your back."

"I'm the, uh, gamekeeper here, in the dungeon," Thisby said, finally managing to avert her gaze from the horrible room.

"No way!" Jono yelled so excitedly that it snapped Thisby from her daze. "Do you know Ulia?"

"Sorry, I don't think so—"

Jono stopped, frozen in his tracks. It was almost as if he was a clockwork toy whose key had stopped turning. Being a skeleton, when he stood still, he neither blinked nor breathed, and for a moment, it seemed to Thisby as if he was just another piece of lifeless junk that had been gathering dust in the castle for thousands of years. Maybe she'd only imagined that he was alive to begin with . . .

"Sorry!" he blurted, coming back to life with a jolt. "I don't know what I was saying . . . I just, I just . . . my memory isn't exactly there. Not since . . . since . . ."

He was beginning to fade again.

"Never mind," said Thisby. "It's not important."

"Right," he said.

*Thisby smiled at the skeleton and although she couldn't tell, because he didn't have lips, it felt as if he was smiling back.*

Jono dropped Thisby off outside the large set of double doors that led into the Master's chambers atop the tallest tower in Castle Grimstone. Thisby had nearly gotten winded walking up the steps, and for as good shape as she was in, that was saying something.

"Here you are, milady!" said Jono.

Thisby laughed at that. She wasn't used to being addressed so formally. She did a playful curtsy toward him like she'd seen the ladies do in Lyra Castelis.

"Farewell, good sir!"

Jono gave her an awkward, stiff bow and began to trot off.

"Wait!" she called after him. "If you're ever in the dungeon, feel free to stop by for a visit!"

Jono bobbed his head again and politely took his leave.

Thisby couldn't help but smile. The skeleton boy had left her in good spirits. That didn't last long.

The door cracked open, and from inside she heard a scream.

# CHAPTER 4

"What do you mean, my new boss?" screamed Grunda.

Thisby had opened the door to find the diminutive goblin standing atop an overturned chair and waving a finger in the face of a rather impassive-looking Master. Safely hidden behind his desk, he was joined by a tall, shadowy figure in a floor-length cloak and wide-brimmed hat who stood so still that Thisby almost mistook them for a coatrack.

"I meant exactly what I said. From now on, instead of reporting to me, you'll report directly to our new Overseer. As appointed by the King himself . . ."

"Aw, forget the King!" shouted Grunda. "You think just because you have some bit of parchment you can march in here and start making demands? Since when does the Black Mountain bend to every royal fartin' whim of His Highness? As far as I'm concerned, the Black Mountain is its own sovereign land! Always has been, always will be!"

"And as far as I'm concerned," spoke the shadow, "the Black Mountain falls within the borders of Nth. Correct?"

The shadow removed her hat to reveal a handsome, though long, face framed by green hair. There was no tenor of anger in her voice, only calm reason. The fuming goblin across the desk from her looked childish in comparison despite being at least several lifetimes older.

Thisby edged into the room a bit farther, and everyone craned their necks toward her. If Thisby hadn't been an orphan, she would've recognized this moment as being strikingly similar to walking into a room where your parents have been arguing and didn't hear your approach until it was too late. You could hear a pin drop. Assuming, of course, it was a very large pin and that it landed on the marble floor and not the rugs.

The tension was broken by the mysterious stranger, who casually waved a welcoming, delicately fingered hand in Thisby's direction.

"Thisby, correct? Please come in. Sit down."

Thisby crossed the room and righted Grunda's chair once she stepped down off it. The goblin's nose was bright red, and Thisby could see the fury in her eyes. Grunda had worked her whole life to have some sort of authority in the dungeon, to

*The tension was broken by the mysterious stranger.*

have some means by which she could start to improve things, only to have it taken away from her like it was nothing.

"What's going on?" Thisby asked the Master, trying to conceal her rising frustration as well.

Grunda braced herself against the chair, shaking with anger.

"I'll tell you what's going on—" Grunda began, but the stranger cut her off.

"What's going on is an unfortunate side effect of a necessary change in the day-to-day operation of the dungeon. Please. Sit." The stranger again motioned toward the chairs and Thisby sat down. After a moment or two, Grunda reluctantly did the same.

"Let me start over. My name is Marl. I have been appointed by King Parlo Larkspur to oversee the operation of this dungeon and ensure that everything is safe and well maintained. Frankly, I think you've already done a splendid job, Thisby Thestoop! I daresay you've made my life quite a bit easier!"

Marl said that last bit with an eager smile that Thisby didn't return.

"*Pfft!* 'Splendid job,' my stinking foot!" grumbled the Master, but nobody paid him much attention.

"I haven't come here to fire people or to tell anyone how to do their job. I'm only here to serve my King and my country and to do the best that I can with the task I've been assigned. The unfortunate side effect of my appointment is that now you will report to me instead of the Master himself.

I will in turn report to both the Master and the King himself. It's very simple, really . . . Thisby reports to Grunda, Grunda reports to me, I report to the Master as well as ensure that the dungeon is operating in accordance with the wishes of His Majesty the—"

"Everything was working just fine without any help from you or His Majesty!" snapped Grunda.

"Was it?" asked Marl as if expecting a genuine response, although she didn't wait for one before continuing. "I'm afraid that's not exactly true. For one, as far as what the Master has told me, the number of adventurers visiting the dungeon has severely dropped since last year's debacle. Just how long do you think the dungeon can support itself if that pattern continues, hmm? How long can you keep this place functioning once the gold stops flowing? How long until these beasts of yours run out of food, and when they do, how long would it take for them to turn on each other? Worse yet, how long would it take until they'd break free of the mountain and look to our towns for their next meal?"

Thisby looked to Grunda helplessly, hoping for some clarification, but the goblin was too distracted, too blinded by her white-hot rage to even notice anyone else was in the room.

"We take care of our own, thank you very much!" shouted Grunda.

"Adventurers bring in money. The gold and supplies we get from their remains are what keep this dungeon operational. Whether you like it or not, without adventurers this dungeon would cease to function and become a liability," said Marl.

"Furthermore," she continued, "there have been rumors of Umberfallian spies around the Black Mountain, and we don't believe that you are adequately prepared to deal with the potential threat that could pose to our kingdom."

Grunda shook with anger.

"So THAT'S it, hmm? Is that what you told the King? And you're just going to sit here and let this . . . this interloper worm her way in here with the preposterous claim that the Black Mountain is harboring Umberfallian spies?" Grunda addressed the last question to the Master, and for a second it looked as if he might actually speak out in agreement, but instead he averted his eyes and said nothing.

"I see," said Grunda. Thisby could hear the fight go out of her. The goblin stood up to leave, her chair squeaking against the marble floor as she did. "Well, if that's the way it's gonna be, then . . . I quit."

Thisby's heart lurched in a valiant attempt to escape her rib cage. Blood began to pound in her ears. There was no way this was real. Grunda couldn't be serious. It had to be a bluff. Any second now, this interloper or the Master would crack and drop to their knees, begging her to take it back, and Grunda would laugh and accept. But as the moment dragged on, as the uncomfortable silence lingered, Thisby began to accept the impossible reality that was now staring her right in the face and refusing to blink.

She began to reach out a hand for her friend, but something popped up in the back of her mind telling her that it was the wrong thing to do. Before she could even withdraw it fully, Grunda had moved away from the desk and shuffled toward the chamber door, before stopping at the threshold to speak her mind.

"I'll tell you what. I've been in this dungeon a long time. A long time. We've never had any use for royals no matter which side of our border they fall on. And more importantly"—Grunda looked directly at Thisby now—"this dungeon doesn't *need* adventurers. It doesn't need humans at all."

In the morning, Grunda was gone.

Thisby and Mingus had stopped by with a box of her favorite cave mushrooms only to find her room looking as if it'd been ransacked. Dresser drawers lay overturned on the floor, cabinet doors were swung open. It was a worrying sight at first, but upon further inspection it became obvious that Grunda herself had packed up her belongings hurriedly in the night, paying little regard for anything she couldn't fit into a backpack. She'd been in such a rush that she hadn't even bothered to leave a note.

Despite the likelihood that Grunda had done this herself, it was hard to imagine that after all this time, she could just pack up and leave the dungeon as if it had been an overnight stay at some inn. Thisby remembered Grunda telling her once that goblins had a nose for danger. That the moment they smelled something foul coming, they had an innate ability to run in the opposite direction. Was that what Grunda had done? It was possible, but the thought didn't help settle Thisby's nerves.

After a few minutes spent fruitlessly searching for a note, for anything that might give a better clue as to where she had gone, Thisby gave up hope. It was clear that wherever Grunda was going, she didn't intend for anybody to follow, and that included Thisby. She respectfully put Grunda's room back together on the off chance she might come back and then sat down at the goblin's small kitchen table.

It felt like a moment that would've been appropriate for her to cry, but she couldn't. There were too many feelings all swirled together for her to find one to latch onto. It was like eating a soup where the cook had used every spice in the cabinet. There was no way to pick out what was what. She couldn't tell the sadness from the pity, the anger from the righteous indignation.

She thought about how much she'd hurt when her carriage had pulled away from Lyra Castelis a few months ago and wondered if it was similar to what Grunda was going through. Grunda hadn't known that she'd wanted to be the liaison, but once she'd gotten the job, the pain of losing it had been too much. In a way, that was how Thisby had felt. She hadn't known how badly she'd needed a friend until she'd had one. Now she'd lost somebody again. Only this time she'd lost the closest thing she'd ever had to a mother.

The thought of that cranky old goblin, all warts and pointed ears, being the closest thing she'd ever have to a mother made Thisby laugh, and through the laughter, she managed to fight back the tears that had very nearly escaped her eyes. Finally, when the time was right, Thisby closed the door to Grunda's room and locked it, thinking it wouldn't be right to simply leave it open. Goblins liked their privacy.

On her way back to her bedroom, Thisby passed by the pockmarked rock wall where the mindworm liked to hang out, and as if on cue, the moment she thought about it, the bright red worm wriggled out of its hole, all thick and fat and glistening with worm-jelly. It watched her with some measure of curiosity, studying her with its twelve glittering, jewel-like eyes until she felt compelled to stop and wave hello.

Hello, thought Thisby politely, knowing it was unnecessary to speak aloud to a creature that could read minds.

As if it were being yanked by an invisible string, the worm bolted upright, straight as an arrow, and Thisby heard Grunda's warm, familiar voice echoing in her head.

"Had to go. Will return. Stay safe. Stay strong. Love, Grunda."

Thisby watched the mindworm go wiggly and slink back into its hole exactly like it'd arrived only a moment ago, and before she knew it, one of the tears that she'd tried so hard to deny managed to escape down her cheek.

★ ★ ★

49

Outside the Black Mountain, the warm spring rain had washed away the last traces of winter, but from where Thisby stood inside the mountain, it was impossible to tell. She cupped her hands in front of her face and blew hot breath into them. Curling wisps of steam slipped through the gaps in her fingers, like ghosts fleeing a poorly designed prison.

Thisby paused only briefly to admire her hard morning's work spent chipping open an entry into the ice wraiths' den before shouldering her backpack and hustling on toward warmer climes. There were plenty of miserable jobs around the Black Mountain, but having to pickax through several feet of ice in subzero temperatures while ice wraiths moaned on and on about their former lives as kings and queens of long-forgotten nations had to be near the top of her list. It wasn't quite as bad as shoveling up the nightmares' droppings, but it was probably a little worse than cleaning up the trails of bubbling slime that the acidic oozes left behind.

Thisby walked briskly, and even a few feet out from the ice wraiths' den, the temperature had already climbed enough that she could remove her gloves. She did so carefully. It'd been a long week, and her hands were showing the blisters to prove it. Not even Mingus's slime healing magic had been able to relieve them as quickly as new ones could spring up.

The first few weeks of life under Marl—now primarily referred to as "Overseer"—hadn't been nearly as terrible as Thisby had feared. Monsters were still permitted to come and go freely between the castle and the dungeon, with one small caveat: visitors now needed to provide the guards at the gates of the castle with an Overseer-approved *passage token*—a little gold disk that was stamped with the scowling face of the Master on one side and the silhouette of the Black Mountain on the other. The idea for the passage tokens belonged to Overseer Marl, who thought that the tokens would help "regulate and control the flow of visitors into and out of the castle," despite the fact that an excess of visitors had never actually been a problem to begin with.

By the end of the first week, the passage token system hit some snags. The first was that due to an unforeseen gold shortage, the production of passage tokens had ground to a halt. This resulted in the value of passage tokens among the monsters skyrocketing, which led to their popularity as bartering chips in the dungeon's black markets, which of course led to hoarding and thus, within a short span of time, had conspired to make passage tokens in circulation extremely rare. Somewhat ironically, when Thisby tried to present this issue to the Master in person, she was unable to procure a passage token and couldn't enter the castle. This wouldn't have been an issue if the Master had answered the repeated signals she sent from her scrobble, but getting an answer from him since Marl had taken over as Overseer had been next to impossible. Only once had he deigned to pick up, and Thisby suspected that he'd been inebriated at the time. Needless to say, he wasn't very helpful.

All in all, though, it was a small problem.

On the way back to her bedroom, Thisby took the scenic route. Mingus would've protested if he'd stayed awake long enough to do so, but it wouldn't have mattered. When you're along for the ride, you only have so much authority. Thisby was tired herself, but there was still more work waiting for her when she got back, so she didn't see the point in hurrying. Besides, this was her favorite part of the day, and she was determined to savor it.

Before she'd had mountains of paperwork waiting for her in her bedroom, Thisby had loved the long walk back to her room at the end of the day; her muscles aching, her eyes already growing heavy, knowing that the day was finally behind her. There was something about the feeling that was hard to describe. It felt almost like she was swimming back to her bedroom, carried along by a warm current. Whether it was the beginning of sleep taking hold or the satisfaction of a good day's work or something else entirely, there was an undeniable magic to being in the dungeon while it transformed from a place of work to a place she could simply enjoy. It was like seeing it with new eyes. She noticed things she never would've noticed otherwise: the way that torchlight danced over the mossy bricks, a pair of initials carved into a block of stone by two long-forgotten adventurers, or how, from the right distance, the banshee's wails could sound almost like a song. These were the moments that she lived for, when she could disappear into the dungeon and simply exist as an observer, free of the weight of responsibility. For the duration of that walk, it was just her and the dungeon.

The sight of her door—or more accurately, the mountain of paperwork still waiting for her on the other side of it—sent her crashing back to reality.

Thisby unshouldered her backpack with an aching groan that would've made old Grunda proud and dropped it to the floor. Mingus in his lantern felt like he weighed a hundred pounds as she lifted him off the hook on her backpack and locked the lantern into the fitted brass ring that sat atop the little glass box on her desk. There was a sharp, familiar *klatch!* noise followed by a pneumatic *hssss!* that indicated the slime was hermetically sealed inside the enclosure. Sleepily, Mingus yawned and slid out of the lantern, down through one glass tube and back up through another into his private little bedroom, which hung above Thisby's desk.

His "bedroom" was really no more than an aquarium in size or function. There were some drawings of Thisby's he'd hung on his walls, a little chest for storage of his personal items, and a round bed that'd been stitched together from a multitude of wildly patterned fabrics Grunda found lying around. It wasn't much, but Mingus didn't require much. His bedroom was connected to a series of tubes that led all around Thisby's room, starting from the point where his jar locked into the enclosure on Thisby's desk, then traveling around her bedroom in a circuit. With them he could go wherever he wanted while never being exposed to the outside air he so reviled.

Thisby watched him retreat up to his room, pluck out

his "awake eyes," and put in his "sleeping eyes," upon which she'd painted little crescents to indicate a closed eyelid, and slide into bed.

"G'night," he muttered, half-asleep already.

His glow quickly faded. Mingus never glowed while he slept.

Thisby lit a candle and shuffled through the parchment stacked on her desk. When she reached for her pen, she was so exhausted that she knocked over her inkwell with her elbow, but fortunately the lip of the bottle landed on the edge of a notebook and didn't spill. It was a small victory. She righted the bottle with a sigh and rested her chin in her hand.

"Where do I even start?" she muttered to herself.

Overseer Marl had wasted no time implementing policies designed to make the dungeon more efficient, the most surprising of which was a sudden influx of ghouls, twenty-four in all, who were placed under Thisby's command. Consequently, Thisby was awarded the position of Senior Head Gamekeeper—finally getting the promotion Mingus had so often teased her about—although she found the title itself, as well as the responsibilities that came with it, fairly confusing. Still, she'd tried to focus on the positives. At least, initially. With twenty-four extra workers in the dungeon, she'd thought that she might finally be able to tackle some of the bigger projects that she'd been putting off. She'd even thought, during the brief time when she'd allowed herself to indulge in such fantasies, that with all the new help she might have enough free time to take another vacation.

Her optimism hadn't lasted long.

The first week with her new team had been an unmitigated disaster. By the end of it, she was already down from twenty-four staff to a nice even twenty, after four of them perished in the line of duty. One ghoul had forgotten to wrap a shank of meat and wandered too close to the troll's lair while stinking of raw lamb. Another had been tricked by a monster disguised as a treasure chest that swallowed him whole. And last but not least, two particularly dimwitted ghouls fell off a bridge while roughhousing. Technically, their remains had yet to be recovered, but they were presumed dead. Well, deader than before, at least. And that was just the beginning.

The chaos caused by monsters receiving the wrong food or getting the wrong treatments had spread through the dungeon in record time, thanks to having such a large staff. Thisby shuddered to even think about the amount of work it would take to put everything back to normal. Before, her job had seemed like an endless list of things to do, but at least they were *her* things to do. Now she had to do her own work on top of cleaning up after everyone else's.

Thisby pulled a piece of parchment from the top of the stack, which had grown in height to the point where it was losing structural integrity.

At the top, it said *Ghoul #510* in Marl's big, swoopy handwriting, below which Thisby had added the word *Shivers* in her own messy chicken scratch. The ghouls who worked for the Master were never given proper names, but referring to them as numbers made Thisby uncomfortable, so she'd taken to giving those under her care informal nicknames instead. "Shivers" was so called because he was always shaking, "Blinky" had only one bulbous eye, and so on.

The rest of the paper was organized into a grid, leaving spaces for her to write in a short evaluation. There were fifty-two spaces in all, one for each week of the year, the vast majority of which sat blank. It was almost cruel. Every week since the Overseer had arrived, she looked at that sheet. Every week she had to see that constant visual reminder of how much work there was still left to do.

Thisby stared at the sheet for so long that it put her into a kind of trance. How had Shivers done this week? Who was Shivers again? What had he been assigned to do?

Her eyelids were heavy.

Maybe, she thought, if she just closed them for a minute . . .

In the morning, Mingus rolled out of bed and peered through the glass wall of his bedroom to find Thisby fast asleep on a stack of parchment, ink dried on her face, still clutching a pen in her right hand.

# CHAPTER 5

Iphigenia was alone beneath a blanket of white stars. The grass, still stiff with the memory of winter, pricked at the soles of her bare feet as she craned her neck up, feeling terrifyingly small.

It'd been two months since she'd begged her father not to send Marl to the Black Mountain, which also marked the last time they'd spoken. She'd protested against the interference of the kingdom in the dungeon. Only a little more than a year ago, she wouldn't have batted an eye if they'd blown the entire thing to bits, but after spending some time in the dungeon, she'd begun to see its value. The dungeon was more than a place for thrill-seeking adventurers to test their mettle for treasure and personal glory. It was a home for all the creatures who had no other place to go. And it was a good home, too, because they had Thisby.

She left the lawn and walked down the path, balancing on the balls of her feet so that less of her bare skin had to come into contact with the cold stones. A breeze washed over her face. She drank in the night, inhaling deeply. It reminded her of being a little girl, catching fireflies in the courtyard with her brother. She remembered how they'd raced around the fountain for hours. Not a care in the world. Back then she still loved him. It felt like a lifetime ago.

More recently, she'd been here with Thisby. It was Thisby's last night at the castle, and they'd wanted to commemorate the occasion. So Thisby had rolled up the cuffs of her pants, splashed through the fountain as if it were a perfectly normal thing to do, and climbed up the pedestal to carve their names in a well-hidden spot at the base of the statue, near the lion's paw. Later that night, neither of them could sleep. They stayed up talking all night until the sun rose pink and happy, betraying the sadness Iphigenia felt within.

Iphigenia had never shed a tear for her brother, but when that girl's carriage had pulled away the next morning, she'd had to dig her fingernails into the palm of her hand to fight them back. Eventually her fear of embarrassment bested her sadness, and she shook the feeling away. There was always a sense of pride in not letting her emotions get the best of her. Her father had told her years ago that a good leader never cries. Not in front of his subjects, not even in private. She asked him if he'd cried when her mother died, and he'd told her no. Iphigenia had wished it was a lie but knew that it wasn't.

She had a new mother now; well, her father had a new wife, at least. But she was barely older than Iphigenia herself, and they had so little in common that aside from being part of the same family, the only thing they shared was a fondness for her father. Now, Iphigenia wasn't even so sure they shared that anymore.

Her father's refusal to listen to reason about the Black Mountain had driven a wedge between them that Iphigenia wasn't sure could ever be removed. She wasn't one to beg. She'd never done it before. She'd always taken her disappointments in stride. But this time she'd pleaded with her father, absolutely certain he was making a grave mistake by interfering in the dealings of the dungeon, and he'd simply shut her out. It wasn't a surprise. Iphigenia knew the real reason. And it wasn't because her father honestly suspected that Umberfallian spies were having secretive dealings with the Master of the Black Mountain; it was because her father hated the dungeon with all his heart. He blamed it for the death of his son. Although he never would've admitted it, perhaps not even to himself, Iphigenia suspected that her father would gladly see the dungeon destroyed along with every creature that lived within its walls if it meant a fleeting moment of vengeance for his beloved Ingo. Unfortunately, destroying everything in the dungeon included Thisby.

For the first time since her experience in the Black Mountain, Iphigenia felt helpless.

She dangled her fingers in the fountain water. It was warmer than she'd expected. Without realizing why she was doing it, Iphigenia hiked up the bottom of her dress and began to splash out toward the center of the fountain. When she reached the pedestal, she placed her hand on the cold marble and began to climb up toward the statue, just as Thisby had done on her last night at the castle. She wasn't as good at climbing as the nimble gamekeeper, but after some effort and a few false starts, the Princess managed to climb high enough to swing her leg up over the lion's back and sit upon it to gaze out at the stars.

The air turned her wet legs to ice, and she laughed at her lack of forethought. Below her dangling feet, she could read Thisby's inscription. She hoped that no one else would ever find it, at least not in her lifetime. Maybe thousands of years from now, it would be okay if some white-haired historian read it and wondered over what it meant, but for now she preferred it to be their secret.

She looked up. The Black Mountain was hundreds of miles away, but somehow it felt extremely close. When she squinted, she imagined that she could faintly see its jagged outline looming over the horizon. As she watched the edge of the castle grounds where the darkened tree line met the sky, Iphigenia could feel her heart swell, and suddenly, with great clarity, she knew what needed to be done. There, awash in the night sky, the Princess set her resolve and made a silent promise: somehow, some way, she was going to protect the Black Mountain and every creature within it. From Thisby to the smallest, cruddiest imp. Even if it meant defying her father and her kingdom.

She wondered if Thisby had made a similar pledge, and it made her feel closer to her friend despite being separated by an entire country. Somebody had to look out for the creatures in the Black Mountain, and Thisby shouldn't have to face that challenge alone. There were some things that were worth risking everything for, and as Iphigenia understood in that moment, friendship was one of them.

*KNOCK! KNOCK! KNOCK-KNOCK-KNOCK!*

Thisby awoke with a start to Grunda's familiar knock.

Jumping up from her desk—this time managing to successfully tip over her inkwell—Thisby raced to her bedroom door in a mad dash and flung it open.

"Grunda!" she shouted.

But it wasn't. The creature at the door was a bit too thin and far too dead to be her former mentor.

"Hello," said the skeleton. "Remember me?"

Thisby stared blankly as her groggy brain tried to parse the question. She rubbed her right eye with the palm of her hand, as if not seeing clearly had been the problem.

"We met in the castle. Castle Grimstone," he added, as

if there were another castle with which she might be confusing it.

*Oh, THAT castle! Castle Grimstone! Now I remember! I thought you were referring to the cotillion last week at Castle Montgrave! You remember, right? I had the lavender ball gown and you made a joke about how the caviar was "egg-cellent"?*

Thisby cracked the door wider and waved for the skeleton to come into her room. Feeling something caked on her face, she touched her cheek as he passed and realized that there was dried ink on it.

"Jono, right? Can I help you?"

The skeleton rattled into her room and gazed around in wonder.

"Wow! This is so nice! I love what you've done here!" His voice was gentle and earnest.

"Thanks, but, um, why're you here?" she mumbled.

"Oh!" he said, grabbing a bit of parchment from his pocket. It was folded up into an uneven little square, several more times than seemed necessary. It looked as if he'd been folding and unfolding it all morning.

Jono handed it to Thisby, who opened it.

"I've been assigned here, you see? With the recent, uh, messiness of this whole transition, Ma—I mean, Overseer Marl, believed that it might be best if you had a personal assistant. You know, somebody to take care of your day-to-day stuff!"

Thisby stopped reading the parchment, which was mostly

just foil stamps and insignias anyway, and looked at Jono. He'd picked up a notebook by its edge in a way that made Thisby's stomach twist as she imagined the pages ripping free from their binding.

"Put that down!" Thisby said as politely as she could—which was not very.

Mingus, who'd remained silent until now, possibly asleep, joined in the conversation. "Thisby doesn't need an assistant! She already has me!"

"Yes, but the letter . . . ," said Jono.

Thisby felt sorry for him. Whoever this skeleton was in his past life had clearly only been about her age when he'd died and now here he was, a resurrected skeleton brought back from beyond the grave by whatever stupid dark magic some arrogant wizard had dreamt up, and somehow, he'd managed to stay positive despite all that. It was an impressive level of optimism that Thisby found charming. And he did seem eager to help . . .

"I don't see the harm in having *two* assistants," Thisby offered, refusing to look at the angry slime, who was staring at her, mouth agape.

"Oh! Great! That's great!" said Jono excitedly. "Is there anything I can do for you right now?"

Thisby scooped up the partially finished weekly staff reviews from her desk and handed them over. They'd have to do. She suspected nobody was really reading these things anyway.

"You can take these up to the Overseer," she said.

"Yes! Right away!" he replied, and was out of her room in such a hurry that he didn't even bother to close the door behind him. The moment his bony frame had disappeared behind the doorway, Mingus let out a pained groan.

"Come on! You can't be serious!"

"What choice do we have?"

Mingus slid down into his jar. He'd already begun to glow a dull red, which Thisby knew meant he was annoyed. She unlocked the lantern and lifted Mingus from her desk, hanging it on the hook on her enormous backpack, which she then slid on in her usual way—both arms through and lift with your legs. Her bag rattled like an overstuffed kitchen cabinet as its contents settled into place, and she instinctively reached up to steady Mingus's jar and stop it from swaying.

"It won't be so bad," she said, "and besides, we could use all the help we can get."

Mingus's color didn't change.

"And how has that 'help' worked out so far?" he asked.

Thisby didn't respond. It was usually best not to say anything when he got like this.

They walked down the hall, past the spot where the mindworm liked to hang out. She glanced expectantly over at the pockmarked wall, the same as she'd done every day since Grunda had left, but there was no sign of life. The mindworm's message had been weeks ago, and it was still the last she'd heard from her former mentor.

Thisby reached the ladder and was surprised to find a familiar bony face waiting for her.

"How'd you get back so fast?" she asked, genuinely impressed.

If Jono could have blushed, he probably would have.

"It's easy to run fast when you don't run out of breath, boss."

"Huh. I never thought of it that way," said Thisby as she passed him and began to descend the ladder. "Well, c'mon, I guess! We've got a busy day ahead of us!"

"See? Maybe this won't be so bad after all," she whispered to Mingus as he dangled over her shoulder, trying his best to look sullen. Nuanced looks were difficult for him, but Thisby got the gist.

Mingus snorted in reply and began to glow a fiery, contemptuous red. He wasn't about to give up pouting easily. Thisby sighed. It was going to be a long day.

And with that, the three of them descended the ladder, three hundred and four rungs in all, down into the yawning mouth of the dark dungeon.

# CHAPTER 6

It didn't take long for Thisby to realize there was trouble in the dungeon. The fire bats were out of their cave, the trolls were wide awake when they should have been sleeping, and—most tellingly—the dire rats were acting strange. They scurried from their holes, running this way and that, paying no mind to Thisby and the others. She was nearly bowled over when a pack of the barrel-size rats surprised her by bursting from behind a closed door the moment she'd opened it.

Inside the room, they discovered that the poor things had been trying to gnaw through the solid oak door for hours in a desperate attempt to escape. It was a bad omen. Dire rats were one of the first indicators of any serious trouble in the dungeon. If the dire rats were trying to get away from something, it was often best to follow suit. Unfortunately for Thisby, her job was to head toward trouble, not away from it.

They'd been walking for an hour or more when Thisby heard a strange cry from up ahead, followed by what was quickly becoming an all-too-familiar *shiiing!* from behind her. Thisby turned sharply.

"Put that thing away! I'm not going to tell you again!" said Thisby.

Jono sheepishly tucked his short sword back into its rusty scabbard.

"Sorry, boss. It's force of habit. Like a sneeze or something."

Thisby rolled her eyes. She hoped his bravado wasn't intended to impress her. She abhorred the use of violence against the monsters of the dungeon. It was the primary reason she never carried a weapon herself, the secondary reason being that she didn't have one. Either way, she'd always considered violence to be an absolute last resort.

She thought about her former boss, Roquat, and how much he'd enjoyed doling out beatings for misbehavior. His idea of discipline wasn't so much, "Spare the rod, spoil the child," as it was, "Spare the rod? Why? We've got plenty of rods! In fact, this one has barbs on it. You hit someone with this rod and they won't be sitting down for a week!" And what had it gotten him in the end? For all his posturing, for all his brutality, he was gone, and Thisby, armed only with her lantern, was now the Senior Head Gamekeeper—whatever that meant.

"If you go in there with your sword drawn, it's like you've already made the first attack," Thisby reminded him.

Jono nodded in agreement, but Thisby had a sneaking suspicion it wouldn't be the last time they'd have this conversation. Some habits are hard to break.

"Just be calm, okay? Relax," she added.

Thisby wished she could follow her own advice.

The same awful cry rang out again. It was a strange, otherworldly sound. A bit like mashing every key on a pipe organ at once. Thisby couldn't place it. Before that morning, she had been sure that she knew every noise in the dungeon, from the rhythmic drip of a stalactite to the frenzied bark of a gnoll during mating season, but this was something new. Crouching down, she followed the noise carefully, slinking through a tight passageway and at last peeking her head around the corner. Thisby immediately felt sick.

In the middle of the room was a rock golem—for all she knew it could have easily been the one who'd chipped her tooth several weeks back—or, more appropriately, it was what was left of a rock golem. Its body had been smashed into pieces, torn apart at the waist, its legs crushed to rubble, and a yellowish, acrid smoke streamed from its wounds. Prior to this moment Thisby had thought rock golems were made up entirely of solid rock, but now, horribly, she could see that they were actually filled with a sort of ooze, something almost like molten lava, that spilled out onto the ground and burned the floor where it fell.

Thisby stepped into the open chamber without thinking. The horror of the scene had clouded her mind to even the obvious thought that whatever had done this might still be in the chamber with them.

"Thisby, wait," whispered Mingus, but it was too late. She was already approaching the wounded golem, moving as if in a trance.

The poor creature cried out again, and Thisby shuddered. She realized why she'd never heard the noise before—up until now, she'd thought rock golems were mute. She'd never heard one make any sort of vocalization. Not so much as a grunt or whimper. She didn't realize they could. Now that she'd heard it, she was certain it was a sound that she'd never forget.

The rock golem turned its head, which was thankfully still attached to its neck. Below that, however, just below where the creature's ribs would have been if it'd had bones, the rock golem had been torn clean in half. There were rending marks in the stone that looked as if they'd been made by impossibly sharp claws. Claws capable of cutting stone with a single swipe. The golem stared at Thisby with its black onyx eyes.

"Thisby . . . ," started Mingus, but words failed him.

The rock golem convulsed and more of the burning ooze

spilled from its torso like lava erupting from its volcano of a chest. Thisby watched the ooze fall to the ground, where it immediately hardened into delicate crystals as it rapidly cooled on the limestone floor. It was both beautiful and sad.

"Who did this?" she asked softly.

The creature gave no response, which wasn't exactly a surprise. Thisby had only just learned that rock golems could make any noise at all, and this one wasn't in much shape for conversation, even if it could understand her.

Jono approached and laid a hand on Thisby's shoulder. She jumped.

"Can you do something?" he asked.

Thisby tried to stop her heart from pounding and shook her head. Even if she'd wanted to put the poor creature out of its misery, she had no idea how, and this was a bigger job than Mingus's healing magic could handle. Thisby walked closer to the monster's massive boulder of a head and placed her hand on it.

The golem blinked its stony eyes impassively, and when it did, Thisby could see little clouds of dust rise from where its eyelids rubbed against the sockets. She wondered if anybody else had ever been close enough to a rock golem before to notice.

Thisby slid her backpack off her shoulders and withdrew a notebook. Sitting down only an arm's reach from its face, she began to sketch. The beast sighed. She could smell its breath, like a mixture of copper and wet bricks drying after a summer rain. She made a note of that. It was nearly two hours later that the rock golem closed its eyes for the last time, but since the moment that Thisby sat down, it had never cried out again.

In the end, there was nothing to do but stand up and leave. The three of them—Thisby, Mingus, and Jono—walked for some time in silence, not knowing what to say.

"Jono," said Thisby at last, breaking the long silence.

The skeleton turned to her with his empty eyes.

"Yes, boss?" said Jono quietly.

"Two things," said Thisby. "First off, I don't like 'boss.' It's weird. We're basically the same age. Call me Thisby, please. Second, I need you to do something for me . . ."

"What's that, b—Thisby?"

"I need you to find out exactly what the Overseer has set loose in my dungeon."


Overseer Marl paced in her chamber, too excited to sleep.

Her long evening robe whipped darkly as she paced, making her look a bit like a raven caught in a snare trap. Her green hair was pulled up into a loose bun on the verge of coming undone, and for some reason she was wearing all her jewelry, as if she'd been sleeping in it. There'd be no more sleep tonight, though. No one could be expected to sleep with an idea this good. The idea had come to her all at once, like a lightning bolt, but after it'd shocked her out of bed, she'd begun to see it for what it really was: a ball of yarn wrapped around a diamond. The idea was pure and beautiful but surrounded by an absolute knot of details, exactly the kind that Marl loved to unravel.

Since she'd arrived at the Black Mountain, these kinds of ideas had been coming to her at a record pace. Marl had always been clever; it was why she'd been assigned to work undercover in Umberfall to begin with, but these ideas weren't just clever, they were positively inspired. It was tough to keep up with them. At times, it seemed like a small voice was whispering in her ear, providing her with constant inspiration for how to run the dungeon better. Actually, that was exactly what was happening.

The voices had started innocently enough. *Replace the loose tiles in the hallway. There's a dead mermaid stinking up the lake on level two.* That kind of stuff. In the beginning, Marl had mistaken the voices for her own inner monologue, but lately the thoughts were getting a bit more invasive. It was somewhat troubling, sure, but good ideas were good ideas, regardless of the source. She'd studied psychometry at the Grand College of Arcanology—*go, Werewolves!*—and knew that being in a place with as much latent supernatural power as Castle Grimstone, it wasn't uncommon to encounter ghosts and spirits who wished to communicate from the Other Side. If Marl had instead studied the history of the Black Mountain, the voices likely would've been a bit more disconcerting. However, as it was, she knew there were no bad ideas in brainstorming and took all suggestions—whether they came from the living, dead, or otherwise—under advisement.

She knew about the Eyes in the Dark, of course. She'd learned all about him in school, and her opinion was the same as that of all her professors and grand mages: the Eyes in the Dark was just a boogeyman to scare people into behaving. Whether or not the Eyes in the Dark was real—she suspected he might be—she believed what she was taught, that the concept of the Eyes in the Dark as the source of all evil in the world was patently absurd. Old, superstitious wizards loved to speak about things that way. Everything was a duality; light and dark, good and evil. But that way of thinking had gone out of style long ago in popular wizard education. As far as Marl was concerned, the Eyes in the Dark was just a nuisance. Like a rat that lived in her basement and would occasionally get into the food. There were far bigger problems to worry about, like the threat of Umberfallian spies and, perhaps worst of all, the general condition of the dungeon itself. Thankfully, her new idea was going to change everything.

In the weeks since her appointment, Marl had been desperate to find ways in which to revitalize the flagging dungeon. When she'd first been appointed Overseer, the dungeon had seemed an impossible mess: monsters governing themselves, a Master who'd handed over power to his subordinates, and a severe drought of adventurers had all combined to bring the dungeon close to the brink of obsolescence. But in only a few short weeks, Marl had managed to reestablish a sense of order that worked from the top down—with her at the top, naturally. She'd even begun a promotional campaign aimed at attracting young people from all over the kingdom to the dungeon by bringing the newest, most exciting, most dangerous monsters to the Black Mountain. After all, who really wanted to fight a troll for the zillionth time? But this latest idea, the idea that had the Overseer pacing back and forth in her office, laughing to herself and writing feverishly on a scrap of paper, was going to make all her other ideas look uninspired by comparison.

The door to the Overseer's office swung open without so much as a single knock to reveal a rather scruffy-looking Master. He was wearing purple silk pajamas that barely contained his belly, which had grown rather prodigiously in the last year, and his beard was bound with several small rubber bands. An obedient ghoul, stationed in the hallway, closed the chamber door behind him.

"Marl," he said.

"Please, please, sit down," said Marl.

"Do you know what time it is?" asked the Master. "Sending for me in the middle of the night! You ruined an incredible dream, I'll have you know."

"Can I get you some tea?" asked Marl.

She was already pouring herself a cup of some sort of steaming, violently red liquid. It looked a bit thick for tea.

"Uh, no, that's okay," mumbled the Master. "What kind of tea is that anyway?"

"You know, I'm not sure. I've only started drinking it since I've been here, but it's fantastic. My assistants bring it to me. Twice a day. Morning and night. You sure I can't get you some?" Her voice was trembling with anticipation.

"Is it . . . caffeinated?"

Marl paused, but not to consider his question. She set down her tea and gathered herself. It took all her focus to quell the storm of excitement raging within her chest, desperate to get out. She knew now was not the time to be bouncing around like an excitable child. This was serious business. Her mind skittered back to his question. Perhaps the tea was caffeinated.

Marl turned her back to the Master and composed herself. She folded her hands behind her back and took two deep breaths. Then she turned slowly, with purpose.

"Have you heard of the Wretched Scrattle?" she asked dryly.

The candles that lit the darkened office cast a dancing glow across Marl's face, adding an eerie punctuation to the question. Despite being annoyed, the Master had to admit he liked the effect. This whole presentation of whatever it was the Overseer was getting at was quite nice. Pulling him from sleep in the middle of the night, asking cryptic questions by candlelight. It was all very dramatic. He made a mental note to hold more of his own meetings in the middle of the night by candlelight.

The Master tugged thoughtfully on his rubber-banded beard and scanned his memory. He'd never heard of any

"Wretched Scrattle," and history had always been his strong suit.

"It sounds familiar, but I'm afraid I can't remember it exactly," he lied.

Marl smiled. It was obvious that she was hoping to have a chance to explain it.

"In the five-hundred-and-fifty-second year of the dungeon, its Master at the time, Celes the Clever, faced the worst downturn of adventurer activity in the history of the Black Mountain. The Black Mountain was on the verge of bankruptcy. The kingdom of Nth was still young then and had, for the first time, fully recovered from the hardships of the war from which it had been born. The people of Nth were fat and rich and lazy from the spoils of their victory over the fledgling kingdom of Umberfall. There was no drive for adventure, no thirst for fame, no desperation for money. It was a time of peace and prosperity and also one in which the Black Mountain nearly ceased to exist."

Marl took a sip of the tea and smiled at the Master through ruby-red lips.

"The thing that people like you and I understand but that the people of Nth will never get is that the Black Mountain is a business, first and foremost. Adventurers come here seeking their fortunes, imagining the treasures they'll acquire, but what else do they come with? They come with their pockets heavy, jingling with gold. They come with their backpacks laden with goods. They come with their brand-new armor and swords strapped across their backs. But they never leave, do they? And with the money we collect from their remains, we arrange deals, we buy provisions, we trade with the King of Nth himself. Everybody wins."

The Master gave a conspiratorial nod, the kind that wizards often made to each other, much to the annoyance of those around them. Marl was a wizard of a very different breed than the Master. She was an Arcanist, while the Master was more of a . . . something else. Still, they both spoke the language of secret nods and winks that all wizards shared.

"During the downturn, Celes wasn't discouraged, however," Marl continued. "Instead she put her formidable intellect to good use and came up with an idea that not only saved the dungeon but went on to ignite what was perhaps the most successful period in its history. She created the Wretched Scrattle."

Marl moved over to the window and gazed out thoughtfully before turning back to the Master. She took a long pause to let her words hang in the air. The Master sighed. Marl's flair for theatrics was growing tired now, as was he.

"Strange that something so successful would be so easily forgotten," sneered the Master.

Marl brushed her green hair away from her eyes.

"Oh, but it was no accident! You see, Celes the Clever was replaced by Gambol the Gutless. Gambol was by all accounts a relentlessly arrogant man. It's likely that he not only buried

Celes but her legacy as well, wishing to take credit for saving the dungeon himself. During his reign, all mentions of the Wretched Scrattle were removed from the history books."

"Yet somehow, you know all about it."

"Well, I did my research," Marl lied.

It didn't seem prudent to mention that the mysterious voices Marl had been hearing had pointed her to a long-hidden volume containing the secret history of the Wretched Scrattle. The relationship between Marl and the Master was a carefully constructed house of cards, and revealing her access to ethereal voices could be enough to topple the whole thing. The Master had been eager to have Marl here at first, and the comeuppance of Grunda had been a treat for him, but over the past few weeks the Master had begun to wonder if he'd possibly gone from bad to worse.

"Well, don't keep me in suspense! It's far too late for that. Out with it! What is the Wretched Scrattle?"

Marl grinned, revealing a row of perfectly white teeth there, which were rarer around Nth than the opals they resembled.

"There was a proclamation made throughout all of Nth that a tournament would be held in the Black Mountain. That it was open to the public. So adventurers from all across the country could come and test their luck against the dungeon and see if they could escape with however much treasure they could carry."

Marl paused, and the Master took the bait.

"That's it? That's your brilliant idea? Sending out invitations?"

"There's more," Marl cooed. "Celes the Clever's *real* idea."

The Master shifted uncomfortably in his seat. Marl was practically salivating.

"Every entrant in the tournament was charged to compete. Celes charged three gold a head, but I'm asking twenty-five. We win twice. Once when they enter and again when they die. By the end of it all, we'll be wealthier and more powerful than the King himself."

"Twenty-five gold is more than most Nthians make in a year! No one will come!" the Master scoffed.

"They will once they discover . . . *the grand prize*."

Marl walked over to the bookshelves that lined the walls of her office and ran her thin, pale fingers over a row of leather-bound volumes. The Master clenched his teeth to prevent himself from asking the inevitable question but only managed to hold out for a few seconds before blurting it out almost involuntarily.

"And what is *the grand prize*?"

Marl turned slowly away from the shelves and eyed the small, frail man in the chair.

"The first one to make it to the top of Castle Grimstone would become the new Master of the Black Mountain."

# CHAPTER 7

Thisby stood on the edge of the Darkwell for only the second time since last year's battle. The other visit had been to inspect the work that Grunda and the other goblins had done on repairing the gate, and once Thisby had given it her unofficial stamp of approval, she was off, as quick as humanly possible.

It wasn't that she was afraid of the Deep Down. Not anymore. Not like she used to be, at least. She knew the Eyes in the Dark was still down there, waiting for its opportunity to strike again—which was terrifying in its own way—but once she'd been to the other side of the gate, something within her had changed. It was no longer fear that she felt when she thought of the Deep Down beneath the mountain and the Deep Dwellers who lived there, it was something else entirely. Something even more unpleasant.

When the dust had settled after the battle over the Darkwell and the Deep Dwellers were driven back below again, Thisby couldn't help but think that none of it really seemed fair. The Deep Dwellers were pawns. They'd been used and tossed aside by the Eyes in the Dark, by Roquat, by Ingo. Their only sin was their anger over being stuck down in that horrible place for all those years. Spending millennia in the darkness with a force of pure evil warping them, coercing them, infecting their minds with its awful thoughts . . . Who could blame them for wanting to escape? And yet, Thisby herself had been party to driving them back below the mountain. She'd sent them back to the eternal darkness, back below the gate at the bottom of the world. Up until that point, Thisby had seen the Darkwell as a fence to keep the bad creatures out, but since that day, she'd seen it more as it really was . . . a prison to hold them in.

As she stood at the edge of here and there, Thisby was happy to have Mingus with her, especially since he'd relaxed his previous stance on hiding in her backpack during their trips to the Darkwell. It seemed that after all they'd been through, he'd gotten braver as well, and as a result, his presence was all the more comforting. His soft sea-foam-green light and the gentle sway of his jar steadied her nerves.

Thisby had instructed Jono to take the afternoon to

continue training the rest of her team. As her apprentice, Jono was far exceeding Thisby's expectations. For someone who had no memory of his prior life, Jono's short-term memory could be quite impressive. It was certainly better than Thisby's had ever been. Her inability to recall recent goings-on was more or less why she'd started using notebooks to begin with. Jono seemingly had no use for them. He could recall with great detail whatever Thisby taught him, and what she didn't, he acquired for himself by staying up all night and reading through her old notebooks. She supposed it helped that he didn't need to sleep. Since he'd been accelerating so quickly through Thisby's lessons, she'd appointed him to the task of training the ghouls who'd been placed in her care, and in that, it seemed that Jono had found his true calling. He loved to teach, and Thisby was glad because she had nowhere near his patience for it.

Thisby crept closer to the edge of the Darkwell, and some loose gravel slid beneath her feet, causing her to nearly lose her balance. She regained it only to realize how fast her heart had started beating.

"Maybe he's not home," she said.

She hadn't seen Catface since last year, and it was yet another ball of guilt that sat heavily in Thisby's stomach. Grunda had taken over bringing Catface his reports from the castle after she'd sensed Thisby's deep reluctance to return to the gate of the Darkwell. But now, with Grunda gone, there was nobody else to do the job. Thisby considered sending

Blinky, the one-eyed ghoul who was the most competent of her current underlings (aside from Jono), but the truth was that Thisby had grown quite fond of her and was afraid that Blinky wouldn't survive the trip.

"We should just go," said Thisby.

"Thisbyyyyy . . . ," said Mingus, letting the *y* sound drag on in a sort of gentle reprimand.

"Yeah, yeah."

Thisby walked slowly down the remainder of the incline toward the Darkwell, taking care not to slip. Once she reached the bottom, she went the long way around the gate instead of walking over it. She knew Grunda had done a thorough job with her repairs, but once she'd seen the Darkwell flung wide open with Deep Dwellers crawling out of it, it was hard to imagine willingly setting foot on it again unless it was absolutely necessary.

Something stirred in the darkness, and Thisby froze in place, holding her breath.

Over the past week, she'd been tracking the mysterious new monster who'd been responsible for the attack on the rock golem. She'd dedicated a notebook to the creature, but so far, aside from the trail of carnage left in its wake, there wasn't much to go on. And every day more and more monsters turned up dead—from tiny imps, to banshees, to a full-grown wyvern. Most frustratingly of all, there was no discernible pattern to the attacks. This creature, whatever it was, was moving through the dungeon at an alarming rate, killing monsters seemingly at random.

And now, despite knowing full well that it was just her mind playing tricks on her, it was easy to imagine that it was here with her in the dark.

"Little Mouse," a familiar voice purred. "It's been a while."

Catface, the Sentinel of the Darkwell, emerged from the pool of inky black shadows that lay beyond Mingus's glow, the darkness practically dripping from his fur as he stalked toward her. Thisby exhaled, feeling something that she'd never felt before upon seeing the gigantic cat . . . relief. He hadn't changed much over the past year, with the exception of perhaps a few more gray spots around his muzzle.

"Sentinel," she said with a verbal curtsy.

"Ugh! How formal! Please, it doesn't suit you!"

Thisby laughed, "Right. Catface then."

"Catface is much better, I think." He grinned.

Unlike her, Catface had no problem strolling out onto the edge of the Darkwell as if he owned the place, which in a sense, he did. At least as much as anyone could claim to.

"To what do I owe the pleasure?" he asked, sitting down.

Thisby considered making small talk, figuring she owed the cat at least that much courtesy, but nothing came to mind. After dismissing several potential conversation starters like, "Has it been cold down here?" and "Any good hairballs lately?" Thisby decided to get straight to the point.

"Something in the dungeon has been killing at random.

It's like nothing I've ever seen before. Probably a new addition of Overseer Marl's."

"*Tss!*" Catface hissed at the mention of her name. "'Overseer,' hah! Marl can barely see over the end of her nose!"

Thisby laughed. Most of the goblins who worked in the dungeon didn't dare complain about Marl, not after a lifetime of fear and obedience had been drilled into them the hard way by Roquat and the Master. It was nice to hear from someone who wouldn't be bullied by any so-called authority in the Black Mountain.

"Well, I don't suspect she released something this terrible on purpose," Thisby added, a bit surprised to hear herself defending the Overseer.

Catface scowled. "I could be wrong, but it seemed to me as if things were running just fine before the Overseer arrived."

Thisby couldn't argue with that. She almost spoke, but it was obvious that Catface wasn't done yet.

"The King of Nth has no business interfering in the day-to-day operation of the dungeon!" he snarled. "There's always been an understanding between the Black Mountain and the royal family. Why do you think the Royal Inspection was created in the first place? The kingdom never cared about the operation of the dungeon; they only wanted to make sure we weren't building an army. Make no mistake about it. The capital has always been afraid of the power we wield, as they should be, but the appointment of an Overseer?

This is a bad omen, Little Mouse."

Catface paused and looked at the diminutive gamekeeper standing before him. Next to him, she was indeed the size of a mouse, and a little one at that. His face softened, allowing his whiskers to droop.

"Excuse my rambling. I've been at this job for too long. I've seen too many Masters, too many gamekeepers come and go."

In years past, that line would have sounded like a threat. This time, however, there was a barely concealed hint of sadness to it that Thisby found perhaps even more unsettling.

"So, you haven't . . ."

"Seen your monster? No. I have not."

There was a long pause before he added, "Is that all, Little Mouse?"

Thisby nodded and watched him slink away, his powerful shoulder blades rising and falling, and he receded silently back into the darkness.

"Catface?" she called out when he'd at last traveled beyond the edge of Mingus's light.

There was a pause, and then two round eyes appeared like moons floating in a starless night from the darkness beyond. He stared at her, unblinking.

"Yes?"

"Be careful," said Thisby.

Catface laughed.

"There's nothing in the Black Mountain I fear. Not

within it, not below it," he purred from the dark.

"And outside it?"

The eyes floated in space, considering.

"We'll see."

And with that the eyes were gone as quickly as they'd appeared.

Iphigenia slept peacefully in her overlarge, fluffy bed until the exact moment she didn't. She'd awoken to the sound of somebody clearing their throat to find a haggard old goblin sitting on her footboard, holding two silver daggers, glinting dangerously in the moonlight.

She screamed.

"I'm sorry," said Grunda, setting down her knitting needles. "I didn't want to be rude, I just couldn't wait any longer. I thought you'd never wake up!"

"G-Grunda? W-w-what are you doing here?" Iphigenia asked, waiting for her pulse to return to normal before she dared move. The moment she could, the first thing she did was gather up her sheets around her.

"I was in the neighborhood."

"R-really?"

"No, of course not."

The goblin stuffed the scarf she'd been knitting—and her needles—into a little leather bag she'd left sitting on the bed.

"Thisby's in danger. The Black Mountain, too. We need your help."

"What can I do?"

"You just need to trust me. There are things at play here, powerful things. Things more important than what king or queen you bow down to, no offense. The Overseer your father appointed is upsetting the balance of the Black Mountain. There's only one way to set it right. It all comes down to the Wretched Scrattle."

"The what?" Iphigenia wrinkled her nose at the words.

"The Overseer—Marl, as you know her—is planning a tournament in the Black Mountain. I just heard about it this morning from a contact inside the dungeon. The prize is that the first person to reach the top of Grimstone Castle will be named as the new Master of the Black Mountain."

Iphigenia was stunned. A new untested Master would mean chaos not only within the dungeon but everywhere. The complications of having some Three Fingers townie take over control of one of the most dangerous places in all of Nth was a terrifying prospect for the entire kingdom.

"And the Master is okay with this?" asked Iphigenia.

"Of course not, but he's too stupid and helpless to do anything about it. The important thing now is that we don't let the mountain fall into the wrong hands."

"Whose hands are the right ones then?" asked Iphigenia.

She had a sneaking suspicion the goblin meant herself, but Grunda shook her head, seeing the gears turning in the Princess's head.

"No. Not me. You think your daddy wouldn't storm the

gates in an instant if a monster was placed in charge of the Black Mountain? Use your head," she grumbled.

"Then Thisby," said Iphigenia.

Grunda smiled, showing a row of jagged yellow teeth.

"Now you're thinking," said the goblin.

"She'd never do it," said Iphigenia.

If she knew her friend as well as she thought she did, she was sure there was no way Thisby would ever go along with this plan.

"She'll do what needs to be done if there's no other choice. Thisby cares about the dungeon. She cares about the people who live there. Just like she cares about you," said Grunda.

"But what can I do?" asked Iphigenia again.

"I was just getting to that. It's really very easy. All you need to do is sign this piece of paper."

Grunda reached into what Iphigenia hoped was a hidden pocket inside her robes and not her underwear and produced a folded-up square of paper.

"That's it?"

"That's it."

"Oh," said Iphigenia.

She had to admit that part of her was a bit disappointed. As a princess, she spent all day signing royal decrees. She didn't necessarily want to ride a steed into battle, but signing a piece of paper was fairly underwhelming as far as late-night calls to adventure go.

"Okay, let's see it then," she said as she lit the candle on her bedside table and began hunting for a pen and inkpot.

Grunda just blinked at her, her eyes adjusting to the light.

"Oh, you can't sign it here," said Grunda.

Iphigenia felt her pulse start to quicken again. And just as she'd finally gotten it settled, too. Only this time it was speeding up in the good way. The way that felt like it was pulling her toward something.

"Oh?" asked Iphigenia.

"The forms are magically protected. Both parties must be present at the signing. A member of the royal family or a duly appointed official has to be one of them. It's to protect against forgeries. You can never be too safe with the world as it is. You'll have to sign it in person."

"And where would that be?" said Iphigenia, unable to contain her smile. Her heart was practically dancing in her chest.

"Take a guess," said Grunda.

It would be hours before Iphigenia's pulse would settle back to its normal rhythm.


By the time Thisby finished her ascent up the three hundred and four ladder rungs that led back up to her bedroom, she felt as if her legs might give out. She'd spent the entire day searching for something, anything, that might give some clue about the mystery monster, but had come up empty-handed. An ice wraith had seen something big lurking around the outskirts of its den, but it was probably just a yeti trying to cool off without being seen.

Near Giant's Crossing—the spot where dozens of thin stone bridges met above a rather significant chasm—Thisby found some strange scratch marks that looked similar to the ones left in the rock golem's torso, but they were too faint to be certain. They could just as easily have been left there years ago by a pterodactyl who'd stopped by on his way to go fishing in the river. It was the only other lead she'd found all day.

Thisby held out her hand and ran her fingers along the wall as she walked back to her bedroom. She wasn't entirely sure why she did it, but something about the sensation of the cool stone bumping against her fingertips relaxed her, even if it felt a bit childish. If anyone aside from Mingus had seen her doing it, she would've stopped. She was almost thirteen now, which might not seem like much to the outside world, but in dungeon years it meant she was definitely too old for such childish behavior.

Thisby had never had a proper childhood. She wasn't sure she'd missed anything—how could she be—but there was a nagging feeling in the back of her mind that she wasn't exactly an adult, not like the rest of the "adults" she knew. Grunda was an adult. The Master was an adult. Thisby was something else. Not quite a child but not exactly like them, either. Ultimately, all she knew was that she preferred to be treated like an adult, so she presented herself as one. And when little reminders of her true age—for example, running her fingertips along the wall—popped up like gophers through the holes of her confident and capable facade, she was typically waiting there, mallet in hand, ready to smash them right back down to where they belonged. For the moment, she let herself have this one minor indulgence. She needed it.

Catface had been her last hope of a shortcut to finding the monster, and now she was on her own again. Not much went on in the dungeon without Catface knowing, so the fact that he hadn't even caught wind of this new killer monster was troubling. If the introduction of this creature had been the work of the Overseer, which Thisby was beginning to suspect it was as she had no other leads, then Marl must have smuggled it into the dungeon herself without anybody knowing. Perhaps not even the Master.

If Grunda were here, she'd know what to do. Thisby was sure of it. She tried to force the thought from her mind. It was, at best, an unhelpful thought, and at worst, it stirred up some resentment that she'd been trying her best to ignore. Her mentor had abandoned her and the entire dungeon in their time of need. She'd sensed danger and simply fled. Just like that. For as long as she'd known her, Thisby had considered Grunda a close friend, a guardian, even at times almost a mother of sorts . . . Thisby shook that thought from her head the moment it appeared. The word *mother* itself had sat for years like a loaded bear trap in the back of her mind, and she did everything she could to tiptoe around it.

As far as the monster went, maybe there was something obvious she'd been overlooking, a clue in one of her old notebooks, or an entry in one of the few incomplete bestiaries she'd managed to get her hands on over the years. Once back to her room, she figured she might be able to sneak in an hour or two of research before completely collapsing from exhaustion. It was an optimistic estimate.

Trying to track down the monster on top of all her other duties was taking its toll. The good news was that she'd been able to assign her new workforce to do some extra chores while she was off playing monster hunter; the bad news was that far too often their inability to complete these chores demanded her immediate attention, more so than if she'd just done them herself. Every morning there were fires to put out, and quite often that was literal, as ghouls with missing fingers—most of them were missing at least a few digits— were rather prone to dropping torches.

Thisby opened the door, and the familiar smell of her bedroom wrapped around her like an old blanket. She unshouldered her heavy backpack and placed Mingus into his spot on her desk. He'd fallen asleep on their walk back, and she was careful not to wake him now. She ran her index finger across the shelves containing volumes of her carefully handwritten notebooks and pulled one out seemingly at random. She took the book with her into bed, where she lay down to read.

She flipped open the dusty cover, which had been stained with ink, and turned to a random page. At the top of the page was *DAY #3147* in her familiar, sloppy handwriting. There were lists of crossed-off chores, reminders, a drawing of Mingus she'd made while he was sleeping, and an illustration of some fresh herbs she'd gotten from Shabul, who it seemed that she'd only met fairly recently, based on her description of their encounter. The last thing on the page was a note that the spectral goat seemed partial to mint.

She turned the page.

Then another.

*DAY #3148* was nearly indistinguishable from *DAY #3149*, which was, in turn, nearly indistinguishable from *DAY #3150* and *DAY #3151*. Thisby flipped several more pages and yawned so loudly that Mingus turned over in his jar, momentarily glared at her, and then immediately fell back asleep.

Thisby stared at her notebook, not so much reading the words as looking through them, until they all began to morph into a single grayish blur, and she could no longer fight to keep her eyes open.

*KNOCK! KNOCK! KNOCK-KNOCK-KNOCK!*

Thisby awoke to the sound of Jono's bony hand rapping on her door.

"Hunh?" said Thisby, lifting her head and taking a page of her notebook with her. She peeled the page off her cheek and wiped the drool from her mouth.

"I said, 'Come in!'" Thisby lied.

Her door was flung open before she could even finish speaking, and a harried-looking Jono came tumbling into her bedroom. She knew that it was impossible for something that didn't breathe to be out of breath, but she swore she could see his chest heaving up and down. Maybe it was just an old habit.

Thisby sat up, wrapping herself in her quilt.

"Th-th-th-th . . . ," he stammered.

"Thisby, yes. What's going on?"

"Come! Come with me!" he said, reaching for a free hand that was poking out from beneath her quilt.

Thisby yanked her hand free of his cold, bony one.

"I'm not even dressed yet!" she said.

"Well, hurry!"

She could hear Jono's impatient foot tapping outside her bedroom door as she scrambled to get dressed, grabbed Mingus and her backpack, and rushed out to meet him in the hall. He stood leaning against the wall opposite her door and actually jumped up when he saw her. He looked practically frantic. It was amazing how many looks Jono could convey without a proper face.

"Thank you for your patience," said Thisby with a bit of sarcasm that was completely lost on the skeleton boy.

Jono nodded and waved for her to follow.

Thisby chased after Jono as they raced down the hallway outside her bedroom and toward Castle Grimstone. As they ran, Jono's left ankle bones snapped and clacked loudly, the way they always did. Thisby had nearly been driven crazy by the sound on their first day together down in the dungeon.

Over time, though, as the noise became more familiar to her, it began serving as a sort of foretelling of his coming, sort of like the jingling collar of a friendly dog, and in doing so, it transitioned from annoying to endearing. "Here comes Ol' Snappity Clackers!" she'd jokingly say to Mingus when they heard him approaching from a distance.

Jono snapped and clacked across the bridge and took a sharp right. The left at the junction held the ladder leading down into the dungeon, while the right path ended in the far shorter ladder that led up into the corridor that terminated at the castle gates. There were two ghouls on guard duty today, who recognized Thisby instantly.

"Hiya, kid. Goin' up to see the excitement?" grunted the bigger one.

"What's going on, Pox?" Thisby asked.

The large ghoul scratched his beard and grinned.

"You don't know? Really?"

"It's the Wretched Scrattle," wheezed Larson.

Larson was much smaller than Pox, bald, and his skin was far rottener. He also had a rather large horn jutting out of his forehead, which was not a common feature among ghouls. He was quite proud of it.

"The what?" asked Mingus.

"It's what I was trying to show you!" shouted Jono.

"Why is he shouting?" asked Larson, pointing his thumb toward the skeleton.

Jono paced back and forth impatiently.

"What's the Wretched Scrattle?" asked Thisby.

"Wow! I can't believe they didn't tell you," said Pox. "People are coming from all over Nth. I mean from everywhere. North. South. East . . ."

"West! Yes, we get the picture," said Jono.

"Can we get through?" asked Thisby. "We don't have any passage tokens. There's a shortage of them right now, and I just used my last one to get into the castle library a few days ago. I'm sorry. I hate to ask you to do this, but can you help me out?"

Pox stroked his beard thoughtfully.

"I'm sorry, Thisby. Master would . . . you know."

She didn't know but she had some idea. At least, she had an idea of what Pox *thought* might happen. It was why she hated asking in the first place. For the monsters who worked closest to the castle, the fear of retribution for disobeying orders was scarred too deeply in their minds to ever really fade away completely. Even though Roquat was dead, his legacy of fear lived on. How much of it had been the Master and how much of it had been Roquat? It didn't matter. Most monsters in the dungeon weren't about to go out of their way to find out. When you've spent your whole life being afraid of something, it's not as easy as just flipping a switch to turn it off.

"I understand," said Thisby.

As she went to turn away, Pox coughed, and she turned around.

"I don't know about you," Pox barked to Larson. "But I

think we could use a quick break!"

Pox gave an exaggerated wink to Larson, who seemed a bit confused.

"What? We just took our break!"

Pox winked harder.

"But maybe we should take another! Why don't we just go over there for a minute?"

Pox wasn't a very good actor, and Larson was an even worse audience, yet despite his performance going completely over Larson's head, the smaller ghoul was intrigued enough by the idea of another break that after a moment or two of consideration, he shrugged and followed the bigger ghoul down the hall. He might not have understood what was happening, but he wasn't about to pass up a chance to sit down. As Pox passed Thisby and the others, he gave a little nod.

"Thanks," said Thisby under her breath.

Once the ghouls were out of sight enough to ensure that she wouldn't get them into trouble on the off chance somebody was actually watching—you could never be too careful in the dungeon—Thisby pushed open the heavy oak doors to Castle Grimstone and the three of them ducked inside.

# CHAPTER 8

The castle was dark and quiet, only not in a nice way. Even people who like things dark and quiet would probably suggest, if they'd walked into Castle Grimstone at this moment, maybe lighting a candle and playing some music.

Given what Pox and Larson had said about the commotion, Thisby was surprised to find the castle so empty and undisturbed. She listened for the sound of footsteps, but all she could hear was the faint buzzing of flies struggling to flap their wings in the thick, dusty air.

They walked together briskly through the black halls of the castle, Jono leading the way. As they moved closer to the courtyard, the buzzing of the flies grew louder until she could hear the sound for what it really was, not flies at all, but voices, which were steadily growing louder. When they finally emerged out into the fresh air of the breezeway, Thisby realized why the castle had been so quiet. Everybody in Castle Grimstone was here.

The breezeway was packed full of ghouls and skeletons who worked in the castle. Thisby scanned the crowd for signs of the Master or Overseer Marl but couldn't find them. It seemed unlikely that they'd be down here milling about with the common folk, but it didn't hurt to look. She and Jono squeezed through the crowd. Jono flung "excuse me's" and "pardon me's" every which way, while Thisby tried not to bump anybody with her backpack, until they managed to reach the front end of the courtyard, which had an overhang where you could look clear down to the bottom of the Black Mountain. Here the crowd was thickest—and with good reason . . . the real show was happening down below.

Thisby shouldered her way between two sweaty ghouls and gazed down the mountainside. There, way, way down at the base of the mountain, hundreds, perhaps thousands of people had gathered. Tents of all shapes, colors, and sizes dotted the landscape, like somebody had dropped a bag of multicolored sprinkles from on high and people were swarming like ants between them.

"What's going on?" Thisby shouted over the thrum of the crowd.

A few ghouls down, Jono's bony head squeezed through

the tightly packed wall of onlookers to answer her. "It's the Wretched Scrattle!"

Thisby cocked her head toward him.

"People keep saying that! But what is it?"

A ghoul whose armpit was far too close to Thisby's face chimed in, "It's like a contest. The Overseer has invited adventurers from all over Nth to test their luck in the dungeon! There's going to be new monsters, fabulous prizes, the whole deal! Isn't it great?"

Thisby turned suspiciously toward the ghoul.

"What's the catch?"

"Catch? There's no catch."

The ghoul paused to rethink his statement.

"Oh, well, there is this one thing . . . If you somehow make it to the Master's chamber in Castle Grimstone, you become the new Master of the Black Mountain. But I can't really see that happening, can you? I mean, what are the odds?"

Thisby sighed.

What were the odds?

What were the odds that she would be the one to clean up the mess? What were the odds that after this all was said and done, the dungeon would never be the same again? What were the odds, indeed.

Ever since Thisby's run-in with the Eyes in the Dark, she'd been certain that the end of the dungeon would be his doing. That the mountain would crumble to dust beneath his massive claws, that his flaming breath would melt Castle Grimstone into a roiling, acrid pool of liquified stone and iron. The last thing that she'd expected was some green-haired woman with a penchant for unnecessary rules and bureaucracy to be its downfall. Even if Thisby had been warned, she never would have believed it. After all, what were the odds?

Thisby retreated into the crowd and walked back through the castle without saying another word to Jono, who muttered something to her about meeting up later to help clean up a mess some bugbears had made near the crystal caverns. She was barely listening, anyway. Thisby left the castle through the gates through which she'd entered and made her way to the long, familiar ladder into the dungeon. Regardless of whatever insanity was going on in the dungeon tomorrow, there were still chores to be done today.

The camps at the foot of the Black Mountain stretched out for miles in every direction, forming a semicircle that wrapped around the base of the central peak until the tents bumped up against the smaller foothills that surrounded it. Most of the campers settled on the softer grassy fields to the southwest, not wishing to sleep on the rocky terrain of the mountains or eager to take their chances with Umberfallian raiders, who liked to murder and rob unsuspecting travelers who traveled too far east of the Black Mountain. The mountain range technically belonged to the kingdom of Nth, but Umberfall

*The carousing and storytelling had become quite the lively party in and of itself.*

butted up against the back side to the northeast, and raiders weren't always great at recognizing borders. It wasn't entirely their fault. In the real world, it wasn't as if there were solid white lines drawn on the ground, despite what maps would have you believe.

The tents stretched from the base of the Black Mountain all the way to Three Fingers, which had been enjoying the most prosperous few weeks in the history of the chronically downtrodden village. For the first time in a century, the inns were full, the bars were packed, and the merchants couldn't restock goods as fast as they could sell them. At first, it'd been hard to convince people to stay overnight in the village until somehow, mysteriously—in what would eventually go down in history as the smartest decision the Three Fingers city council ever made—the Beware Huge Rats sign vanished from the front gates in the middle of the night and was replaced with one proclaiming Normal-Size Rats. It was a stretch of the truth, to say the least. The city council, however, slept easily knowing that they had a fairly secure loophole in that "normal" was a matter of opinion, and the people of Three Fingers had lived with rats the size of dogs their entire lives.

The Wretched Scrattle wasn't set to begin for several weeks still, but news of the event had traveled like wildfire throughout the country. Out in the field of tents were people from all walks of life: professional adventurers with scars and dented broadswords, hunters with crossbows and dogs, farmers who'd scraped together their life savings for a chance to hopefully steal a little more treasure than it'd cost to enter, and opportunistic merchants selling and trading goods with anybody who'd give them the time of day. There were large, ornate tents with well-armored guards stationed around them, housing lower-tier nobility and other upper-class people who'd come for the sport of the whole thing, and these luxurious tents sat right alongside the lean-tos and ragged blankets of Nthians desperate for an opportunity to turn their lives around.

Men in black cloaks wove through the sea of tents, ringing bells and collecting the twenty-five gold fee in exchange for entry forms. They were accompanied by an envoy of soldiers carrying tall flags that bore the sigil of the royal family of Nth, both to foreshadow their arrival and to symbolize that they were indeed authentic collectors who'd been hand-selected by the royal family itself. The men in black, or "buzzards" as the crowd had taken to calling them, were low-level hedge wizards in the employ of the crown, there to ensure that only those who paid through the proper channels were admitted into the Wretched Scrattle by cosigning the magically protected entry slips once sufficient gold was provided. Though they did little more than sign a piece of paper and collect money, it was a service for which the King insisted on a payment of five of every twenty-five gold collected and to which Marl ruefully agreed.

Through the middle of the camp ran one long strip of

unoccupied road down which the dungeon could move supplies into and out of the Black Mountain. Marl had ordered the construction of a stone arch that sat against the side of the mountain at its base and looked something like a doorframe in which someone had forgotten to place a door. The arch was tall enough for a giant to walk through without crouching and twice as wide, and once per day, typically in the very early hours of the morning, a team of wagons would come down the road and stop before it. The wagon master would shout up his command, and as if by magic—which, of course, it was—the empty doorframe would fill with a glowing blackdoor portal that allowed the wagons to pass through. The moment they were inside the mountain, the portal snapped shut behind them.

People camped near the base of the mountain occasionally attempted to sneak through the blackdoor before it closed in hopes of getting a head start, but the guards who accompanied the wagons usually caught them before they got very far. The few who did manage to slip through the cracks were never heard from again. The dungeon was fairly self-correcting that way.

It was also common for people to attempt to sneak a peek into the wagons as they came and went from the mountain, in hopes that if they could only get a glimpse of what sort of monsters they might be dealing with inside the dungeon, or what sort of traps might await them, they would have an advantage. The guards, however, were extremely vigilant, and only once in the month that led up to the Wretched Scrattle did a woman manage to outfox them and sneak a peek beneath a tarp. When she returned to her campsite, she was ghostly white and barely able to speak. Without another word to her fellow adventurers, she packed up her tent and went home. Nobody ever found out the truth about what she'd seen.

Still, the mood in the camp was optimistic. At night, the crackling campfires were alive with stories of adventures past. People sang songs and laughed and strategized as to how they planned to conquer the legendary Black Mountain once and for all—not to mention what they'd do once they became the new Master of the Black Mountain. It was the sort of revelry that adventurers truly lived for, despite what they might claim.

Adventuring as a lifestyle—and it was, in fact, the fifth most common profession in all of Nth[1]—was very different from the common perception. The average adventurer spent far more time sitting around campfires and inns telling stories than they did out in the world coming up with new ones. Most of the adventurers in Nth could've done without the actual adventure at all. The sharing of stories was what drove them, what made them feel alive. If it'd been about the money, they'd have become thieves. If it'd been about the thrill of battle, they'd have become soldiers. No, adventurers

---

1 The top ten most common professions in Nth were as follows: 1. Gravedigger, 2. Farmer, 3. Soldier, 4. Merchant, 5. Adventurer, 6. Servant, 7. Town Guard, 8. Outlaw/Scofflaw/Rake, 9. Innkeeper, 10. Gravedigger's Assistant.

lived for the time spent telling stories, so naturally, when you got a crowd of them together as large as there was at the base of the Black Mountain, the carousing and storytelling had become quite the lively party in and of itself.

Inside the dungeon, however, the mood was quite different.

There was no time for frivolity in the dungeon. From the day that Thisby first saw the crowd at the foot of the Black Mountain, the dungeon had exploded into a frenzy of activity that never seemed to stop. Ghouls, goblins, and skeletons worked all through the night, taking shifts and picking up where the others left off: building traps, placing treasure, moving around monsters, introducing new ones, cleaning certain rooms while messing up others; it was a complete overhaul of the dungeon, and Thisby had never been present for anything more upsetting in her life.

For one thing, they were doing it all wrong. Perhaps more frustratingly, nobody wanted to listen to her. Before Marl's interference, despite its rather haphazard appearance, the dungeon had been a well-oiled machine. It may have seemed coincidental that the ogres were next to the fire bats or that the mermaids were cordoned off from certain sections of the river, but it was those fine details that maintained the delicate balance of micro-ecologies and biomes necessary to keep the dungeon from flying entirely out of whack. Now, thanks to Marl, everything was falling apart. The gears were coming loose from the great big machine, and there was nothing Thisby could do about it.

She tried to get in to speak with the Overseer in person, but it was no use. Pox wasn't watching the gates anymore, the guards changed every day now, and the passage token situation had gone from bad to worse. Nothing short of a blackdoor bead was going to get Thisby into the castle, and even if she'd had one, she wasn't sure it would've mattered. Marl was seemingly wholly unconcerned with the dungeon in the long term. As long as the Wretched Scrattle brought in more adventurers, who cared about the future of the dungeon? More often than not, it seemed to Thisby as if she was the only one.

Furthermore, the more she tried to correct the problems Marl was causing, the more she found herself being pushed out. The vast majority of her duties had been reassigned to untrained ghouls who no longer seemed to serve under her authority but under Marl's—or at least under whomever Marl had appointed as their authority for the time being. Marl's version of the dungeon consisted of layers upon layers of bosses and mid-bosses and under-mid-bosses to the point where Thisby could no longer tell who worked for whom or why anybody was doing whatever it was they were doing. When she confronted a ghoul who was digging a pit in the gnoll den and asked him why he was doing it, he could only shrug. Somebody had told him to. Why? Another shrug. It was absolutely infuriating.

The only person who seemed to listen to Thisby anymore was Jono, and it was through him that she obtained all her information about what was happening inside Castle Grimstone. As a skeleton who primarily worked in the castle, Jono had been granted a sort of permanent passage token that he wore around his neck, which allowed him to come and go as he pleased. Most nights, he would stop by her room and report any rumors he'd heard that day. As much as she came to value Jono's company, their meetings were getting more frustrating every day as she'd become a passive observer to the gradual dismantling of her home.

Thisby's door was locked now. Over the last few weeks there'd been more than one confused ghoul who didn't know up from down, barging into her bedroom in the middle of the night looking for a bathroom.

Mingus was fast asleep in his small glass aquarium. It seemed that no matter what sort of disaster was going on around him, he could always sleep through the night. Last year, when the three of them, Thisby, Iphigenia, and Mingus, had been wandering through the dungeon, she remembered how easily he'd slept even in the face of certain doom. Even in the Deep Down, Mingus had never gotten less than a full nine hours of sleep each night. She envied that about him. It always seemed to her that good sleep was a privilege of people—or in Mingus's case, slimes—who felt comfortable with their place in the world. Before last year, before Iphigenia and Ingo and the Eyes in the Dark, she'd slept pretty well herself. Now it was all she could do to keep her eyes closed for more than a few minutes before her mind started racing.

Thisby crawled out of bed and went over to her desk.

By candlelight, she began to flip through her last notebook where she'd left off, cross-referencing her notes with one of the few damaged bestiaries she'd inherited from Grunda back when she was still learning the ropes as gamekeeper. With the Wretched Scrattle looming, there were so many new monsters in the dungeon that she couldn't keep up with them all. Just two days ago, she'd had to rush in at the last moment to stop a group of overworked ghouls from freeing a gorgon too close to a basilisk nest. Either they hadn't realized that the two were natural enemies or they were too tired to care. That was far from the worst of it.

At least Thisby knew what a gorgon was, even if she'd never seen one before in person. What frightened her more were the monsters being released every day that neither Thisby, nor anybody else, seemed to know anything about at all. Wandering the halls of the dungeon over the last few days, she'd encountered a group of sentient mushrooms with legs and fangs, a very angry crab the size of a horse, and a particularly frustrating monster who had camouflaged itself to look like a wall and insisted on using this power to hide doorways from her, causing what should have been a simple excursion to take hours longer than it should have. These creatures were like nothing she'd ever heard of, and she suspected that there was a good chance they'd either been shipped in from across the Nameless Sea or smuggled in from Umberfall.

She thought it was likely that the dungeon's mystery killer

also fell into that category. The killer was still on the loose and claiming more victims with each passing day. The good news was that since she'd been stripped of most of her other responsibilities as gamekeeper, Thisby had had plenty of time to investigate the mysterious creature. The bad news was that she'd made absolutely no progress whatsoever.

There was a knock on the door.

"Bos—Thisby? It's me."

Thisby answered the door to see a filthy-looking Jono, smiling his perpetual, toothy skeleton smile.

"You're a mess," Thisby stated bluntly, as if there were some chance he wasn't aware of it himself. "Don't you know what time it is?"

"No," he said, ignoring the implication. "Can I come in?"

"What are you doing here? Can't this wait until tomorrow? It's late."

"Hmm. Right. Okay."

Jono turned and began to walk away.

"Jono, wait," said Thisby.

He stopped.

"Just tell me. I'm already up."

With that, she waved the skeleton into her room and closed the door. Jono yanked a roll of parchment free from his belt where it'd been tucked—and smooshed more than a little—and handed it to Thisby.

"I found this letter on my walk back through Castle Grimstone after speaking with the Overseer tonight. It was addressed to me, but it's clearly intended for you. Here. Read it," he said.

Thisby unrolled the parchment and furrowed her brow at what had to be the tiniest handwriting she'd ever seen. The writing was an alternating combination of tight cursive script and choppy, messy scribbles, which did itself no favors in the legibility department.

"What is this?" she asked.

Jono grinned, which, to be fair, he always did.

"Don't just look at it! Read it!" he blurted.

Thisby held the note an inch from her nose, but she could only make out every other word. *Jono. Please. Thisby. Need. Help.* Thisby strained her eyes, trying her hardest to make heads or tails of the note, but it almost seemed as if it had been written by two people fighting over the same pen. The pain in her forehead was intensifying, so she shoved the parchment back into Jono's hands instead.

"I'm tired. Please just read it to me," groaned Thisby.

Jono took the parchment and began to read.

"It says, 'Jono, please tell Thisby we need her help. She must come to Three Fingers. The Drowned Frog. Can't say more now but all will be explained. The dungeon is counting on you. Sincerely, Grunda.'"

Jono flipped the parchment around and proudly pointed to the words he'd just read. Thisby waved it away, afraid that even looking at the writing again would cause her headache to return.

"That's not Grunda's handwriting," said Thisby, unwilling to let the excitement inside her show. "It's a fake. Somebody's trying to trick us."

"Just because someone else wrote it doesn't mean it's not from her! She said the dungeon is counting on you!"

"Jono, don't get excited. It could be a trap."

Jono studied the letter. If he'd had a brow, it probably would've been furrowed.

"Who do you think she meant by 'we'?" he asked.

Thisby's eyes lit up as she felt the exhaustion that had been weighing her down lift from her body.

"Iphigenia!" she yelled instinctively. She immediately blushed at her uncontrollable outburst.

The noise was enough to wake up Mingus. He rolled over once and then got right back to where he'd left off. Those nine hours weren't going to sleep themselves.

Thisby sat down at her desk, feeling dizzy. Her heart soared at the idea of seeing Iphigenia again, but it sank now just as quickly.

"Even if I believed this letter, there's no way I can go to Three Fingers. There's so much to do before the Wretched Scrattle."

"I can keep an eye on things when you're gone!" said Jono brightly.

"Getting out won't be easy," added Thisby.

She was beginning to wonder if she was looking for excuses not to go. If she allowed herself to get her hopes up about seeing Iphigenia and Grunda again, she'd be crushed if the letter turned out to be a fake.

"Nothing worth doing is ever easy," said Jono.

Thisby took a deep breath and tried to steady her mind. If the dungeon was really in enough trouble for Grunda to send this note, then she had no choice. Fake or not, she had to go to Three Fingers to check it out. She had to be sure.

"Are you sure you'll be all right watching the dungeon while I'm away?" she asked.

Jono tilted his head and shrugged.

"What's the worst that could happen?" he said.

# CHAPTER 9

The carriage rumbled and jolted along the dry dirt road, sending clouds of dust into the air, where they lingered in the breezeless afternoon. The result was a sort of spectral trail in the vehicle's wake, like a long-exposure photograph where the subject had refused to sit still.

Iphigenia leaned out of the open carriage window and breathed in the changing seasons. Winter was on its way out. Any day now, spring would be here, and there was an unmistakable sense of the world getting ready, of nature preparing for the arrival of an honored guest. Somewhere deep below the soil, the cicadas were tuning up their band, while in the forest the fireflies were practicing their dance moves.

"Would you care to go over it again?"

Iphigenia opened her eyes and snapped back to reality. She leaned back into the cab and became instantly aware of how stuffy it was inside, how absolutely suffocating.

Across from her in the pillow-laden carriage was a woman in neat military garb. Everything about her was fastened and buttoned and pulled tighter than could possibly be comfortable. Seeing her sitting among the piles of frilly pillows and the drippy floral embellishments of the carriage created such a stark contrast that it seemed a bit like a cruel joke at her expense.

"I think I know what I'm doing," said Iphigenia.

"You *think*?"

The woman tried to raise an eyebrow, but her face was too tight to allow it. It was more of an eyebrow shrug than anything.

"Yes. I *think*." After what she'd gone through to get here, Iphigenia wasn't about to be bossed around by anybody, general or not.

Her father, the King, had not been easy to convince. The last time she'd left the capital had been for the Royal Inspection last year, and after how that turned out, it was a hard sell to convince him to let her travel more than a hundred yards from the castle, let alone halfway back to the Black Mountain. On the surface, his resistance to the idea was based on his claim that Iphigenia wasn't "adequately prepared for the theater of war," but how such small skirmishes between a few farmers had suddenly garnered such a grandiose term was fairly suspect. Besides, everybody in the royal court knew that it was necessary for Iphigenia to learn "the trade," so to speak, in order to prepare for her inevitable ascension to Queen. Her father wasn't getting any younger, and he'd barely been taking care of himself since Ingo's death. There was no way to know when the day would come that Iphigenia would ascend to the throne, and to be ill-prepared for it could spell disaster for all of Nth. They eventually reached a compromise—the one that was currently sitting across from Iphigenia.

The general gave her a sour look. If the girl had been one of her soldiers, she'd have known exactly how to handle such blatant disrespect. But Iphigenia wasn't a soldier. She was the future Queen of Nth.

"I only want to make certain you are prepared."

"I appreciate your concern, Lillia. But I am prepared."

The use of the general's first name was another deliberate slight, an attempt to get her riled up, but she brushed it off. If there was one thing the general was good at, it was self-control. If there was another, it was exacting revenge. She was also skilled with a saber, a born leader, a decent cook, and pretty good at crocheting, but none of those talents were really pertinent to the current situation.

"Very well," said the general, and she left it at that.

Hours passed in silence. Evening fell. The sky went from pale blue to orange to purple to lavender, and just as it was about to settle into a nice proper veil of black, the carriage crested a hill and Iphigenia got her first look at Garun, a small town just a day's ride west from the Seam.[2]

Iphigenia had crossed the Seam farther to the north on her last trip back from the Black Mountain with Thisby, at the brilliant cosmopolitan city of Lode, famous for its fantastic stone-and-steel bridge, intricately paved streets, and fashionable stores. Lode was home to the greatest engineering minds in all the known world, a legacy that began with the construction of the stone-and-steel behemoth, the Bowing Bridge, almost two hundred years ago and continued today with the production of the latest technological marvels that were crafted in service of the King of Nth. Garun, on the other hand, was known for its suet—a sort of hard fat found around kidneys of beef or sheep. It wasn't even particularly good suet, they just had a lot of it.

---

2 When you look at a map, the white lines that divide continents into countries—and the countries into states or commonwealths or provinces or whatnot—are almost never neat, straight lines. Instead they look more like the kind of lines drawn by a toddler who has yet to master her fine motor skills. The reason for this, which you can see if you examine any map closely, is that most of these borders aren't created by human beings at all but by natural phenomena: mountain ranges, rivers, lakes, gorges, and so on. This, in turn, is because it can be quite difficult to march an army through and over and across mountain ranges, rivers, lakes, gorges, and so on. The Seam fell into the category of gorges—in sort of the same way a dragon fell into the category of lizards—and for thousands of years, the colossal rip in the land formed a barrier between the kingdom of Nth to the west and the kingdom of Umberfall to the east. Eventually, Nth took control of the gorge and all the land to the east of the Seam, all the way out to the marker that stands as the current border between the two countries . . . the Black Mountain.

Although it wasn't quite that simple. Nothing about history ever is. Even after Nth had successfully seized control of the land from the Seam to the Black Mountain from Umberfall, there were no records of settlers from either side occupying that territory for many centuries. This meant that all the vast stretch of land that sat between the Black Mountain and the Seam had been, for the vast majority of recorded history, unoccupied. Or at least that was what the history books said . . .

General Lillia Lutgard wasn't about to take the risk of moving the Princess through a city as public as Lode for the sake of a few creature comforts. They were a small convoy, only three carriages in all, and traveling with a company of just seventeen soldiers, including herself. The unit she'd arranged included some of the best soldiers in all of Nth, but even seventeen of the best soldiers could still fall at the hands of a hundred of the worst. It wasn't a risk the general intended to take.

Their mission was simple: negotiate a peace treaty between some small militias who'd been feuding over land just west of the Seam. It was really just a minor dispute between two noble houses, but after a few skirmishes had broken out, merchants had grown anxious about traveling through the territory, so it was brought to the attention of King Larkspur. As far as Lillia was concerned, local law enforcement should have handled it. Why the King had decided to send the Princess herself and one of his top generals was beyond her understanding. Still, it was never her style to ask questions. That wasn't how she'd become a top-ranking general in one of the largest standing armies in the world. But she couldn't help but feel a tinge of resentment for being placed on what was beginning to feel an awful lot like a babysitting mission for a bratty teenager who openly loathed her. She supposed that being a general wasn't all fun and wars.

They checked into their room. It was in a meager inn that they'd commandeered in its entirety for the sake of safety. The chubby, kindhearted mistress of the inn scrambled around like a madwoman, desperate to impress the royal family with her humble accommodations, while the soldiers laughed and drank and dined on everything her flustered husband could throw together on such short notice.

When at last Lillia had managed to calm her troops and send them staggering off to bed, she finished her meal alone and then headed up to her room. The mistress's husband was already snoring loudly on the bar, passed out from pure exhaustion and whatever drinks the soldiers had insisted he share with them "for the health of the crown," so she tried not to wake him as she slid an extra couple of gold coins beneath his arm. When she reached her room, she drew the key from her pocket and opened the door as quietly as she could, being careful not to wake the sleeping Princess. In a certain way, she was successful. The Princess definitely didn't wake up. The Princess definitely didn't wake up, however, because the Princess definitely wasn't there.

Thisby had been crouching for so long that both her knees ached. She first stretched one, then the other, out in front of her, grumbling as she did. There was no way to stand up straight or do both at once without banging her head on the rocks.

From a tiny, Thisby-size nook in the cave wall, she watched a procession of wagons enter the Black Mountain as they did every night. There was the familiar crackle of the blackdoor portal opening, followed by the sudden whoosh of fresh air being sucked into the cavern from outside. The guards would enter first, poking and prodding back the unruly adventurers who'd crowded near the portal in an attempt to get a look inside, and then came the wagons, rolling in slowly in a neat line. Thisby had been watching deliveries like these for days now, taking notes on when they arrived, how many guards were escorting them, and what sort of cargo they were carrying. From her notes, she knew the number of carts arriving daily was quickly diminishing, which made sense since the Wretched Scrattle would begin only a week from tomorrow.

Other than the slight variance in the amount of supplies the wagons were hauling in, it was the exact same routine she'd observed the night before, and the night before that, and the night before that. Only Thisby knew tonight was different. Tonight was the night she'd be leaving with them.

She wasn't stupid. She still suspected that the letter was some sort of trick, but none of the obvious leads had gone anywhere. Even though there was no reason to suspect that the Eyes in the Dark was involved, she knew that she could never be too sure, so she'd double-checked with Catface to make sure that nothing had passed through the Darkwell since they last spoke. Thankfully, that was a dead end. Thisby's more likely suspicion was that the letter could be some plot by Marl to get rid of her, but the timing didn't make any sense. If Marl wanted Thisby out of the picture, she'd most likely wait until the Wretched Scrattle was over and the after-the-games cleanup had been completed. Thisby's authority might've been diminished under Marl's rule as Overseer, but the gamekeeper would be a necessary tool in restoring order to the dungeon once the dust settled. Even someone as hardheaded as Marl had to know that. Getting rid of Thisby now would've made little sense. Not being able to come up with another reasonable explanation, Thisby started to entertain the possibility that Grunda might have sent the letter after all. Or maybe that was just what Thisby wanted to believe. Even a clever fish will take the bait if it's hungry enough.

Thisby felt sick at the thought of abandoning the dungeon when it needed her the most, but she knew that she had no choice. Not really. The well-being of the dungeon was heading in the wrong direction. She could feel it with every ounce of her being. If there was a chance to change its course, to save the only home she'd ever known, she had to take it.

Truth was, the dungeon had changed more in the last month than it had over the course of Thisby's entire life up to that point. In preparation for the Wretched Scrattle, monsters had been moved around the dungeon, new ones were introduced, new tunnels were dug, old passages were closed, there were more traps than she cared for—traps had never been Thisby's favorite feature of the dungeon, as they tended to injure the monsters more frequently than they punished careless adventurers—and the atmosphere had, in general, shifted away from the unity that followed in the wake of the Battle of Darkwell last year. The brief period of harmony had been replaced by a sort of seething anger, even among the monsters who normally had no quarrel with each other. In almost no time at all, the dungeon had shifted from feeling like the home Thisby wished it could be to feeling like the prison that everyone in the outside world already saw it as, and day by day the inmates were growing increasingly restless.

As the wagons were unloaded, Thisby began her descent down the cliff toward the wagons. Mingus swayed in his jar, looking nervous but staying absolutely silent. The wagon guards were new to the dungeon, hired on by Marl. They'd have no problem attacking Thisby, gamekeeper or not, if they caught her sneaking around. They had their orders. Thankfully, they also had their hands full at the moment. While they were unloading the wagons, an enormous birdcage full of howling disembodied heads had tipped over and broken open. The heads flew around the chamber, screaming obscenities and belching acid. The guards ran for cover, and Thisby used the distraction to slip beneath the canvas cover of a nearby wagon and lie down, as still as a corpse. After an hour or so, the last head was stuffed back into the cage, and with a jolt, the wagons began to move.

The wagons left the Black Mountain the way they came, back through a crackling blackdoor and out into the night. Even from her hiding spot buried beneath a cover of thick canvas, upon leaving the mountain it felt as if she'd emerged from somewhere deep underwater. The noise and motion of the world around her burst into being. Her old life vanished in an instant. A distant memory. The comfort of her home was ripped away and replaced by the cacophony of the crowded campsite.

Thisby risked a peek out from under the canvas as the wagon bounced its way down the long, dusty road through the camps. She'd seen them from above, but it was another thing entirely to be down there adrift in the sea of people. The endless rows of campfires and tents, of people young and old laughing, talking, eating. It was the most people she'd ever seen in one space, and she was suddenly aware that for all the time she'd spent around monsters, she'd spent precious little around actual human beings.

Last year, her visit to Lyra Castelis was the first time she'd spent a significant amount of time around people, but everyone in the castle seemed so alien to her, with all their makeup and perfume and strange manners. Down in the camps, however, the people were dirty and loud and wild. They were laughing and wrestling and bragging about their adventures. There was something enthralling about it, a certain wild energy that had been lacking from the noblemen and ladies in the capital. They reminded her a bit more of the monsters in the dungeon, only somehow she felt they were far more threatening. Thisby tried her best to regulate her breathing.

"HEY! What do you think you're doing?"

A guard's hand shot out mere inches from Thisby's face

and yanked away a young boy who'd wandered too close to the wagon, presumably trying to get a peek underneath the canvas. The boy's eyes widened in surprise when he caught sight of Thisby below the canvas, but he had no time to speak before the guard dragged him away by his shirt collar. The guard tossed the boy down into the grass as his father came over to check on him. Thisby slowly inched back from the gap between the canvas and sideboard and held her breath in the gloom.

"Hold," she heard the guard bellow.

The wagon stopped with a jerk. Thisby had to brace herself against an empty barrel to keep from rolling forward. Outside, she could hear the guard muttering to himself. He paced up and down the side of the wagon, just inches away. He was close enough that Thisby could smell his body odor and hear his nasally breathing. Her heart thudded in her chest as he rapped his fist against the side of the wagon. Then silence.

"Stupid kid," the guard muttered before shouting, "CARRY ON!"

The wagon jolted back to life, and Thisby finally exhaled.

She didn't dare peek out from beneath the canvas for the rest of the journey. It was only her second time outside the Black Mountain, and though she longed to see the stars, the swaying grass, and the rolling foothills, there was something more important waiting for her down the road.

★ ★ ★

*Snappity-clack! Snappity-clack! Snappity-clack!*

Jono's ankle bones popped and snapped as he sped through the darkened corridor.

The skeleton boy liked to run whenever possible. It was one of his greatest joys in life. He loved the feeling of the breeze on his bare bones as he darted through the dungeon passages, the sensation of his boots slapping the floor, the sense of freedom and exhilaration that it gave him . . . of course, it helped that he never felt tired, which, in his estimation, was the second best thing about being a skeleton. This first, of course, was the ability to make bone-related puns like, "I have a bone to pick with you," or, "See you to-marrow," but the opportunity to use them came up far less often than Jono would have liked.

Right now, however, the temporary gamekeeper wasn't particularly enjoying this run. It was hard to enjoy the running when he was running for his life.

Jono rounded the corner. Behind him, the gnolls barked and scrabbled at the marble floor of the corridor, running as hard as they could but struggling to find purchase on the slick surface. Thankfully, the tread of his boots—one of the few articles of clothing Jono would never head into the dungeon without—held fast against the wet floor. The end of the passage was only a hundred yards ahead of him now, his only way out. If he could make it to that door before the gnolls caught up, he'd be home free—gnolls didn't venture beyond that tunnel, not even in pursuit of a boy made entirely of the doglike creatures' favorite treat—bones.

It'd all started when Jono made the mistake of directly looking eye to eye at the gnolls—which, frankly, he thought was a bit of a stretch, because technically speaking, he didn't even have eyes—and now he was paying for his error. It was one of many mistakes he'd made over the last few days, but it was the one he was currently regretting the most.

Jono looked back and saw the four gnolls turn the corner. They were gaining on him. It was only about fifty yards to the end of the passage now. If he could only . . .

*Whump!*

He never saw the rock. There was just a sudden feeling of his toe striking something hard, followed by the sensation of falling, and then he was lying flat on his stomach. The gnolls were closing in.

Jono sighed. How disappointing.

He wasn't particularly worried about death. He'd been there and done that. He was mostly just upset about letting Thisby down. It was only his second day filling in for her as gamekeeper, and he'd already failed. She'd trusted him, and this was how he was going to repay her? By dying? At least he was going to see Ulia again. *Wait, who?* The name had come back to him for just an instant and then it was gone again, vanished in a flash of orange light that came streaking from the heavens.

The gnolls jumped back as another flaming arrow struck the ground. They squealed and split from their formation, ducking and running for cover as yet more flaming arrows twanged from somewhere on high. The gnolls scattered and ran back the way they'd come. Crunching bones and slurping marrow was great and all, but taking a flaming arrow in the neck was too steep a cost. As fast as the snarling gnolls had arrived, they were gone, shouting curses that faded into the darkness back down the corridor.

"Hello?" said Jono.

A young man emerged from the shadows, lowering his bow.

"Are you okay?" asked the young man, adjusting his glasses.

Jono nodded.

The young man's outfit was torn and ragged, patched with cave moss and odd scraps of hide.

"Thank you," said Jono, standing up.

The young man was tall, a bit gangly even, and had the look of a confused puppy dog, which clashed a bit with what he'd just done, bravely chasing off a pack of savage gnolls.

"I'm Gregory," the young man offered before Jono had the courtesy to ask.

"Jono. I'm the gamekeeper."

Gregory's face dropped.

"Oh, no! What happened to Thisby?"

"Don't worry! It's just temporary. I'm filling in for her while she's off competing in the Wretched Scrattle."

"The *what*?"

"The Wretched Scrattle," said Jono, picking up some things he'd dropped when he fell. "Big tournament to determine the new Master of the Black Mountain? The reason there are hundreds, maybe thousands of people gathered outside?"

Gregory stared blankly. The expression seemed well rehearsed.

"I figured that's why you were here," Jono continued. "Thought maybe you'd snuck in early to get a jump on the competition. Since you saved my life, I suppose I could let you go without reporting you to my superiors."

Jono hoped Gregory could read the playful tone of his voice but rightly suspected that picking up on subtle clues wasn't really Gregory's forte.

"Oh. Don't worry. I don't care about any Wrench and Scratchle. I can't think of anything I'd like *less* than to be Master of this place. Some treasure might be nice, though . . . See, I've got this girl back home, Becca . . . well, she's not really my girl, but . . ."

Jono tried to wrinkle his forehead to visually prepare Gregory for the bad news he had coming, but without a forehead, the task proved quite difficult.

"I'm sorry, but all the passages into and out of the Black Mountain are sealed until the end of the tournament. Well, except the blackdoor gate at the foot of the mountain. They're sealed to prevent cheating, you see. The tournament is sort of like a race from the bottom of the mountain to the top, so if people could just get in anywhere—"

"Darn it!" said Gregory. "Ain't that just the way!" He slung his bow over his shoulder and sighed. "At this rate, I'll never get home."

Jono studied Gregory's outfit and began to piece something together.

"Um, if you don't mind me asking, how long have you been down here?" he asked slowly as if he was afraid he might frighten the answer away.

Gregory began counting on his fingers, silently mouthing the numbers as he went. It went on for an uncomfortably long time.

"Forty . . . four? Yep! Forty-four weeks."

"Forty-four *weeks*?" screeched Jono.

"Yep. Give or take a day."

"B-but how? How have you survived this long?"

"The way I see it, the trick is to be afraid of everything. See, most people wanna fight, but not me. I don't fight, I run. And when I can't run, I hide. And when I can't hide, well, that's when I fight. But even then, it's really just to buy myself some time before I can run again."

"I suppose that's pretty sound logic."

"Oh! And I have this," said Gregory, pulling out a tattered, thin notebook that had been tucked into his belt. Jono recognized it at once.

"Thisby made this," he said.

"Yeah. It was a gift. She's a good friend," said Gregory. "It contains a lot of basic stuff that's helped me stay alive.

It's called *Thisby's Dungeon Survival Guide*. I call it TDSG for short. Don't think I could've made it more than a couple weeks without it."

Jono flipped through the notebook and realized that Thisby had left something similar for him. He handed it back to Gregory, who immediately tucked it away for safekeeping.

"Well, it looks like you're going to be stuck in here a few more weeks," said Jono. "But at least you seem to have the hang of it."

Gregory shrugged.

"I'm getting there," he said. "But you never know what's waiting around the next corner, right? Okay, well, it was nice meeting you! I'd better be going!" And with that Gregory waved goodbye and began to stroll down the corridor toward where the gnolls had retreated.

"Wait!" called Jono.

Gregory stopped and turned around.

"I don't suppose . . . you'd like some company?" asked Jono.

# CHAPTER 10

The Drowned Frog was the worst inn in all of Nth. This was not a matter of opinion but a simple statement of fact, like saying rain was wet or politicians cannot be trusted. It was also a fact that made its proprietor, Duggan McGuff, quite proud indeed.

For seven generations, the Drowned Frog had been handed down through the McGuff family from father to son like some sort of horrible genetic disease. With every passing of the torch, the elder McGuff had gone out of his way to make sure that the inn was in worse shape than when he'd inherited it—a tradition the McGuff family believed would "toughen up" their offspring to face the realities of a harsh and unforgiving world. By the time Duggan McGuff inherited the Drowned Frog from his father, it was essentially just a stinking hole in the ground surrounded by four crumbling walls, and in the past twenty years, he'd done as little as possible to improve it. After all, he had a son to think about.

Over the course of his tenure as proprietor of the Drowned Frog, Duggan McGuff had served almost every kind of customer the small village of Three Fingers had to offer: bandits, thieves, scallywags, scoundrels—he'd even served a rapscallion or two, but never any princesses. At least, not until that night.

"Here ya go, girlie," he growled as he slammed a pitcher full of yellow liquid in front of the second most powerful person in all of Nth.

Iphigenia studied the liquid sloshing in the filthy glass. It looked like it was supposed to be a beverage of some sort, but it was far too viscous, more like syrup.

"Water's fine, please," she said, practically already tasting the drink by smell alone.

"That *is* water."

"That can't be right," said Iphigenia.

Duggan scratched his many chins and considered offering up the water from the trough out back, where the pigs drank, but he didn't think the girl in front of him would be interested in that, either. She probably wanted that fancy clear stuff.

"You must be from the city," he said.

"Yes. That must be it," said Iphigenia, pushing the glass away as politely as she could manage. She looked around.

All of Three Fingers had been overrun by adventurers on their way to the Wretched Scrattle, and the Drowned Frog was no different. The usual clientele, which consisted of a few town drunks and a goat who'd once wandered in by accident and had since become a permanent fixture of the bar, had been supplemented by countless adventurers and bards from all walks of life. There was even a table of warlocks in the corner comparing spell books. It was for this reason that Iphigenia, despite the fact that on a usual night she might stick out like, well, like a princess in the Drowned Frog, tonight she was barely paid any mind. She was grateful for that. She'd left behind the safety of Lillia and the caravan to follow Grunda's plan, and now she was out in the world and completely alone . . . for the first time in her life.

Princesses weren't people insofar as the court of Nth was concerned. They, like all royals, were a commodity. Plain and simple. And it was in everybody's best interest to protect that commodity. If something happened to the next in line for the throne, the bloodline would be broken and everybody in power would be out of a job, so to speak. This was why when King Parlo Larkspur accidentally sent his son Ingo to his death in the Black Mountain last year, the court doubled down on its protection of Iphigenia. They barely let her use the bathroom by herself for the first couple of months. It wasn't until recently that they'd let up, and she suspected that it was very likely that they'd only done so because they were sick of her.

Even Iphigenia had to admit that was fair. Lately, she'd been a chore to be around, and furthermore, they definitely shouldn't have trusted her. The moment Lillia's back was turned, she betrayed her father's trust and ran away, hitching rides with traveling merchants from Garun to Three Fingers and recklessly endangering their entire bloodline. Without Ingo, she was the only one left. The last Larkspur. If she should perish, the fate of Nth itself would be in jeopardy.

This was one of the reasons that Iphigenia did not care for the way that the one-eyed man at the end of the bar was staring at her. She ducked away from the counter, trying to seem nonchalant about it, and began looking for another place to sit in the crowded room. She left behind her drink, which was beginning to attract flies.

"Aye! O'er here!" called a handsome boy. He waved to her with a hand still clutching a decorative silver butter knife and smiled.

The boy looked to be about her age and was far cleaner than any patron at the Drowned Frog had a right to be. At first glance, it seemed as if he was dining alone, but Iphigenia realized that the large man next to him in full plate armor was his bodyguard. The boy and his guard made no eye contact and pretended not to know each other. It was a game Iphigenia knew all too well. This boy was a noble.

"You can dine with me!" the boy said happily.

He motioned for her to sit down, and a second bodyguard who Iphigenia hadn't even noticed pulled out her chair for her. He'd done a much better job than the first guard with blending into the crowd. Iphigenia sat.

"Here, here. I insist, have some. You look hungry," he said, pushing a small plate over to her. "Don't worry, the food's not from"—he paused and drew a lazy circle in the air with his finger—"*here*. I brought it from home."

Iphigenia smiled politely back at him.

"Thank you," she said.

The bodyguard who'd pulled out her chair handed her silverware, and she thanked him as well. The boy sitting across from her studied her face for what felt like too long, and Iphigenia was suddenly aware of her mistake. She'd been so foolish.

"Don't I know you from somewhere?" he asked coyly.

Iphigenia might've been able to blend in with the rabble around Three Fingers, but nobles were typically taught to recognize the faces of those who served in the court of Nth. It was a matter of self-preservation and manners. The last thing you wanted to do was mistake a duke for a baron or some other unforgivable error.

"I don't believe we've ever met," said Iphigenia truthfully.

"Right," he said.

Iphigenia scanned his face to see if the glimmer of recognition had faded, but it was hard to tell. She supposed that the total absurdity of running into the Crown Princess of Nth in this dingy place acted as a sort of camouflage in its own way. Thankfully, regardless of what he suspected, he seemed to have lost interest in that line of questioning.

The boy pulled the napkin from his collar and handed it to the larger of his two guards, who immediately cleared his plate as well.

"Allow me to introduce myself . . . Vaswell Gandy, of the Flatbottom Gandys. But you can call me Vas."

"Okay, Vas."

There was a long pause.

"And you are?"

Iphigenia froze. "Thisby. Thisby, uh, Catface."

"Thisby . . . *Catface*?"

"Yes, of the, uh, Crampton Catfaces."

"The *Crampton Catfaces*?"

"Are you going to repeat everything I say? It's very annoying!" snapped Iphigenia.

"Oh! It's just an unusual name! I didn't mean . . ."

"No! I'm sure you didn't!" said Iphigenia in a huff.

"I'm sorry . . . Thisby." He lingered on her name a little more than she would have liked before continuing, "Are you entering the tournament? I've assembled a small team if you'd care to join us. Truthfully, I'm just in it for the sport. I'd be happy to cover your twenty-five gold entry fee."

"For the sport?"

Vas tipped his glass and idly rolled it around on its base, allowing himself to be momentarily hypnotized by the slow, swirling water. Iphigenia couldn't help but notice the noble boy's water was the proper color—which is, of course, *none*—unlike what the man at the bar had attempted to serve her.

"Well, that and to get away from my family, I suppose," he laughed. "We have a good team, I promise! Even if we don't make it to the top, with a team that good we're sure to come out with at least a few hundred gold apiece. It's sort of a no-lose scenario."

"Unless we die," said Iphigenia.

Vas let his water glass drop back to the table with a bang that drew the attention of the two bodyguards flanking the boy. They were trying their best to appear inconspicuous and sober, which was a tricky combination considering how large they were and how much they'd had to drink. For all their size, Iphigenia didn't think they looked much like skilled warriors. She'd seen the best soldiers in all of Nth firsthand, and she'd learned to pick up on the little details: the way they carried themselves, the sharpness of their gaze. These two looked like your average local toughs. Good in a scrap, enough to keep you safe in a seedy inn, but not exactly elite.

"Oh, don't worry! It's not them!" Vas laughed, discerning her gaze. "My real team gets here tomorrow. Trust me, they're very good. My father hired them special for the occasion. He wants to make sure I don't get myself killed. After all, if I died, who'd tend to the mines?"

Iphigenia supposed that he'd dropped that last bit to impress her. It was a challenge, to say the least, to impress the future Queen of Nth with boasts of your fabulous wealth. She was nine years old before she'd learned that not all toilets were made of solid gold. There was something else he'd said, however, that had piqued her interest.

"And what if you win?" she asked.

"If I win?" He laughed.

"Right. What happens if you win?"

Vas took a bite of a roll so he could quite literally chew over the question.

"If I was in charge of the Black Mountain? Honestly? I'm not sure. My father has suggested blasting a hole straight through it and building a proper gateway to Umberfall. I suppose that's an option."

Iphigenia tried to hide her shock and disgust. Some of it must have come through anyway, and Vas scrambled to apologize.

"Don't get me wrong! I hate Umberfall! But my father says there's money to be made in trade between us and them, and I happen to agree. I mean, I don't trust an Umberfallian as far as I can throw him, but money is . . . hey, where are you going?"

"Thank you for the food, but I must be going. I'm supposed to meet a friend," Iphigenia said, standing up.

"So soon?"

Vas shot to his feet as well, so quickly that it startled his guards, who drunkenly sprang from their seats and drew their swords. There was some commotion as people inched away from them, misreading the situation. Vas grew red in the face.

"Sit down!" he barked at his guards.

"I'm sorry, I really need to go," said Iphigenia.

"A-are you sure you won't join me in the Scrattle?"

"I really must be going!"

"Thisby! Wait!"

Vas tried to follow Iphigenia but she was too quick, weaving through the crowd and pushing her way out into the darkened streets of Three Fingers. The cool night air on her face was a relief after the warm, thick stench of the Drowned Frog. She moved briskly away from the inn, not daring to look back in case Vas had followed her. Unfortunately, she wasn't doing a great job of looking forward, either, and when she came around a corner, she ran face-first into something large and solid and stinking of sweat that sent her toppling backward.

Iphigenia looked up from her seat in the mud to see the toothless grin of the one-eyed man from the bar.

"In a hurry . . . *Princess*?" he chuckled.

Iphigenia tried to scramble away on all fours, but the man grabbed her ankle and yanked her back down to the ground. She spun and tried to claw at his one good eye, but he caught her by the wrist and dragged her to her feet.

"Yer a long way from the castle, darlin'! I'm guessin' they's a pretty reward fer yer return! Or mebbe . . . mebbe yer worth more ta Umberfall," he growled.

Iphigenia spit in his good eye, and his grip went slack just long enough for her to escape. She could hear him stomping and cursing behind her as she wove through the buildings and narrow alleys of downtown Three Fingers. It'd been raining only a few hours earlier, and the mud in the alleys was so thick that it yanked one of her boots clean off her foot. There was no time to stop so she ran on without it, ignoring the pain of the loose stones that suddenly seemed to be everywhere, jabbing at the sole of her foot with every step.

When she rounded the next corner, she found her path completely blocked by a hay cart. Behind her, the footsteps of the man were slapping closer in the wet mud, and she could hear his labored breathing. There was no way out.

The one-eyed man rounded the corner and paused. Then he laughed. It was a horrible, throaty kind of laugh. The kind that had never once known any real joy, only the celebratory mockery of other's misfortunes. The mud-soaked Princess had a grabbed a nearby pitchfork and aimed it directly at his face.

"You gonna run me through?" he laughed.

The man took a step forward.

"If I have to," she said.

A smarter man might have noticed that her voice did not waver. Not once. The one-eyed man was not very smart, however. He took another step forward so the tines of the pitchfork hovered mere inches from his face.

*"You gonna run me through?"* he laughed.

"Oh, yeah? You don't have the guts to—*AAAAH!*" he screamed as the pitchfork jabbed into his face, ruining his last good eye.

Shocked by what she'd done, Iphigenia dropped the pitchfork and tried to squeeze past the man, but even in inconceivable pain, he still had enough sense to wrap a meaty arm around her waist to prevent her from fleeing. She struck out at the wounded man, raining blows on his face and chest, but he was too furious to notice. With one powerful shove, he threw her backward into the hay cart. Her back struck hard against the sideboard, and she crumpled to the muddy earth.

The man was completely blinded but held his ground, blocking the only way out of the alley. He reached down, drew a long knife from his boot, and began to slash the air wildly, in wide arcs. There was no more concern with trading Iphigenia's life for money; that plan had gone out the window the moment he'd been blinded. His face was red with blood and fury, and spittle flew from his lips as he screamed in a fit of pure rage. They weren't even words, just howls of blind anger against a world that had finally punished him for his crimes. Iphigenia held her breath, trying not to give away her position.

He walked forward, slashing the air as he advanced methodically, until there was nowhere else for her to hide. In another step, he'd reach her. In a moment of desperation, Iphigenia began to crawl on her hands and knees toward the spot where a spoke had been broken off the hay cart's wheel. She wasn't sure it would be large enough to squeeze through but it was her only hope since everything else was blocked by bushels of hay. There was no other choice. She'd either fit through or . . . she refused to think about the alternative.

Iphigenia made herself as narrow as possible and began to squirm through the gap in the wheel. It was a tight fit, and the loose mud around the wheel made it nearly impossible to attain any leverage. Her hands clawed frantically at the wet mud, and her legs kicked feebly in the air behind her. She pulled her shoulders through as the man's dagger struck the side of the hay cart and he paused, realizing something was wrong. Iphigenia managed to wriggle through up to her waist by pulling on the axle, but her hips had become stuck. She pulled as hard as she could as the man dove for the ground.

Summoning every last ounce of strength available, Iphigenia gave one last pull on the axle. Her hips finally found the right angle and she was through, scrambling the rest of the way through the wheel, while behind her, the man's big hands pawed blindly around in the mud. She crawled through the slop beneath the wagon, and only once she was far enough away that she knew he couldn't reach, she looked back to see his angry, wounded face pressed against the wheel, screaming at her. She didn't linger. Before he could even stand up, Iphigenia was already clear through to the far side of the cart and on her feet, running as fast as she could, her chest heaving, her dress torn and completely covered in mud. This was how she looked when she rounded the corner and stopped dead in her tracks.

There, in the middle of the street, was a very large backpack with a very small girl attached to it.

"I think I'll sail across the Nameless Sea," said the Master. "I've always wanted to do that. Heck, maybe I'll even give it a name while I'm at it."

"But it has a name. It's called the Nameless Sea."

The Master quit folding his underwear and looked at his footman ghoul sourly.

"Do you even stop to think? Or do you just open your mouth and see what falls out?"

The Master pointed at his chamber door, and the ghoul excused himself. It wasn't the ghoul's fault that the Master was in a poor mood, but he knew somebody had to take the brunt of his frustration, and to the Master, any ghoul was as good as the next. All the ghoul knew for certain was that none of this was his fault, so anybody who wasn't him probably deserved their fair share of the blame.

Never before in the history of the dungeon had a Master of the Black Mountain abandoned their post. Once they'd taken their seat behind the Master's desk, they weren't allowed to set foot outside the castle—not even for a day trip down to Three Fingers or a quick visit to Schlumpy's Dairy for a vanilla hayseed milk shake.[3] After accepting the position, the next time that a Master typically left the castle was when their cold, dead body was inevitably flung down the slopes by their successor. Still, the current Master thought he was due a vacation and figured he probably wouldn't enjoy it very much if he were dead.

The arrival of Overseer Marl had been nice enough at first—there'd been less work than before, plus he'd gotten to tell that annoying old goblin to take a hike—but since the planning for the Wretched Scrattle had started, the Master couldn't help but feel as if he were living on borrowed time. Marl had assured him time and again that the Wretched Scrattle was foolproof. Even if an adventurer somehow made it all the way through the dungeon, there was no way they could pass the final test. He knew that from day one, and he wanted desperately to believe her. In the logical part of his brain, he was absolutely certain there was no way that he was going to be replaced as Master at the end of the Wretched Scrattle. It was impossible. They'd made sure of that . . . or so Marl said, at least. But he'd also read enough history books to know that these things somehow always had a way of ending with a dead dark wizard being thrown out of a tower by a heroic knight. Always. So now seemed like as good a time

---

3 Schlumpy's Dairy! Now with three convenient locations around the Greater West Black Mountain Valley area! Come try the new Strawberry Fig Cheese Delights or our world-famous vanilla hayseed milk shakes, only two copper apiece! Offer good for a limited time only. Present this book at participating locations!

as any to take a well-deserved vacation.

It would take several months, at least, for the Supplicants to find him. In the meantime, he'd either be replaced, in which case he'd never return, or the Wretched Scrattle would've failed to produce a winner, in which case Marl would probably be doing his job anyway. Either way his days were numbered.

"Going somewhere?" squeaked a horribly familiar voice.

The Master turned to find a familiar face sitting atop the largest of his many trunks that were scattered throughout the chamber.

"Grunda."

"Master."

"Didn't I fire you?"

Grunda crossed her arms tightly and grinned.

"Technically, I quit."

"As a matter of fact, I am going somewhere. I'm taking a little vacation."

"A vacation? It kinda seems like you're fleeing for your life," said Grunda.

"I don't see why they have to be mutually exclusive!" he snapped.

The Master turned his back on the goblin and returned to his folding, suddenly embarrassed to be holding his underwear in front of her. Goblin or not, she was still a lady.

"If you want an apology, you won't get one," he muttered.

"I don't want an apology."

"Then what do you want?" whined the Master, wadding up his underwear and stuffing it angrily into the trunk.

"Now that's a good question," said Grunda.

She snapped her fingers and suddenly appeared on the bed directly in front of the Master. For years, the Master had prided himself on instilling fear in all the denizens of the dungeon, but apparently she hadn't been paying attention. It was like staring failure in the face.

"I'm going to save the dungeon and I want your help."

The Master laughed. It was the fake kind of laugh that not even the person pretending to laugh enjoyed the sound of.

"I'm serious," said Grunda.

"I know," he said. "That's what makes it funny."

The Master sighed and his shoulders fell. He seemed relieved to be finished with the part of the conversation where he had to put on airs.

"Save the dungeon?" he laughed. "Save it from what? The Wretched Scrattle? It's too late for that."

"Thanks to you," said Grunda.

"If you think my opinion matters more than a flea fart in a hurricane when it comes to the whims of the royal family, you're kidding yourself," the Master sneered. "Maybe the King will do a better job listening to whoever takes my job when I'm dead."

"Now you're getting it," said Grunda.

"Is that so?" he asked, snatching back a blackdoor bead

that Grunda had picked out of his luggage. He returned it to the large assortment of them that was lining the bottom of his suitcase.

"Somebody is going to win the Wretched Scrattle," said Grunda.

"Is that so?" said the Master suspiciously. "I do hope you realize that it can't be you, right? You read the rules, I take it? No magic users allowed. Period. That includes wizards, mages, warlocks, witches, sorcerers, summoners, necromancers, geomancers, clerics, shamans, as well as creatures of the elemental, spectral, or otherwise innate supernatural origins? I'm afraid that means you're disqualified."

"That's why I had to speak with you now. Once the Wretched Scrattle starts, I won't be allowed back inside. But it doesn't matter anyway. I didn't mean me."

"Of course you didn't."

The Master gave up on his laundry and walked over to his personal bar, made from a hollowed-out giant's skull. He poured himself a glass of chartreuse liquid, added in three perfectly round spheres of ice, and slumped down into a large leather chair.

"This may come as somewhat of a shock to you, but I've never been much of a wizard," he said.

Grunda bit her tongue so hard it began to bleed.

"But what I lack in innate magical ability, I've always made up for in other ways. I've always been cleverer than the next wizard, or more devious, or more ambitious. I mastered the blackdoor machine. I did that by myself. I'm the only person who has been able to wield its power since it was first created by Elphond the Evil, the original Master of the Black Mountain and the greatest wizard who ever lived. Despite my magical deficiencies, I've destroyed wizards who were a hundred times more powerful than me. Do you want to know how?"

The Master took a long, slow drink of the chartreuse liquid and then set the glass down. When he did, several small sparks erupted from it.

"It's because I don't play their game. Most wizards want to play a game of wizard versus wizard, flinging silly spells at each other, but not me. Why play a game that I know I'm going to lose? I don't play the wizard, I play the person. I destroy my enemies by understanding them better than they understand themselves. I know what they're going to do next, and I anticipate their moves. Mostly, I just wait for them to make a mistake, and then I capitalize on it. This strategy served me well until it didn't—on the day I took over as Master of the Black Mountain. To be quite frank, it was the stupidest move I ever made."

The Master finished whatever liquid was in his glass.

"Being the Master is a losing game. It's rigged. Do you know why? It's because it's not our game. It belongs to the Eyes in the Dark. The longer I'm alive, the more I think we're all just playing his game, even beyond the Black Mountain, even past the Witchkünder Mountains, even across the

Nameless Sea. There's nowhere you can go where he can't whisper in your ear, where he doesn't watch you as you sleep. The Eyes in the Dark that Watch the World.

"I love the dungeon," he continued. "I've given everything I had to maintain the balance while being pulled in a thousand ways at once, and through it all I've kept it running. I've given my blood and sweat and tears to this place, and what has it given me in return? The chance to slink away in the night with my tail between my legs or face my inevitable demise. Some choice."

The Master walked back to his bed, shut the trunk he'd been packing with an emphatic *klatch!*, and looked at Grunda. For a moment, he thought that maybe he'd moved her to tears with his dramatic speech, but then he recalled that her dinner-plate eyes were always watery. He'd done his best yarn spinning in ages, and she didn't look the least bit moved by his performance. On cue, the goblin yawned.

"Are you done feeling sorry for yourself?" she asked casually.

The Master sighed.

"Okay. Fine. I'll bite. Let's say you're telling the truth. If it's not you, then who do you want to win the Wretched Scrattle?"

Grunda paused. It was her chance to really amp up the drama.

"Thisby Thestoop."

The Master blinked.

"Who?"

# CHAPTER 11

Thisby turned in time to see the girl in the muddy dress running for her full-steam but not in time to brace herself for impact. The two of them went toppling to the ground, Thisby landing on her backpack like a turtle.

"THISBY! THISBY! It's you!" her assailant screeched like a barn owl. She had Thisby by the shoulders and was shaking her rather violently. Her face was so mud-covered that it took Thisby longer than she'd like to admit to process what was happening. But when it hit, it hit all at once. It was as if their friendship had been locked inside a glass case in a museum—she could look in on it when she wanted, but she could never touch it, never be on the other side of the glass. The recognition of Iphigenia's face had been like a hammer, and once the glass had been shattered it was all suddenly real again. The little things like sneaking out barefoot to eat cake late at night in one of the castle's many kitchens; the big things like fending off wyverns or tumbling over waterfalls. There was so much crammed inside that one glass case that Thisby wondered how she'd managed to fit it all in.

Thisby's brain was so preoccupied with memories that her mouth forgot how to work.

"Iphigenia?" said Mingus.

"Mingus! Thisby!" yelled Iphigenia, completely unafraid of making a scene.

Thankfully, the people of Three Fingers weren't the kind to stop and stare. Stopping and staring led to knowledge, and as far as the villagers were concerned, knowledge led to nothing but trouble.

The girls stood up at last, Iphigenia helping Thisby up from the mud.

"H-how? How'd you . . . ," Thisby began, motioning at Iphigenia's dress.

"I was attacked. I got away. I pitchforked a guy in the face. It's all a blur. It's not important. But we should get inside before somebody else realizes who I am."

Mingus looked the Princess up and down and screwed up his face a little.

"Do you *really* think that's a problem?" he asked.

Iphigenia shot him a dirty look. Which, given the amount of mud on her face, seemed appropriate.

"We were supposed to meet at the Drowning Toad."

"The Drowned Frog," Iphigenia corrected.

"Should we go there?" asked Thisby.

"Not unless you like to eat your water with a knife and fork," said Iphigenia.

Instead they wandered through the city streets until they eventually settled on an establishment with the least disturbing sign they'd come across. It was a painting of a rather cheery-looking rat—seemingly snockered out of his gourd on whatever it was in the jug he was holding—riding a ferocious brindle tomcat as if it were a horse. The name of the inn was written above it in big red letters, The Rat-Upon-a-Cat, but, as they noticed on a chalkboard near the entrance, the proprietor had apparently been considering a name change in recent weeks, and The Ratastrophe seemed to be at the top of the list. It was likely that he was only trying to keep up with the times. Puns had recently arrived in Three Fingers, and although most people still considered them to be a passing fad, any leg up you could get in the overcrowded market that was the grimy, downtrodden, hole-in-the-wall inn game was well worth the effort.

The Rat-Upon-a-Cat was by no means fancy, but compared to the Drowned Frog, it was almost regal. The girls took a seat at the table farthest away from the inn's solitary patron, an old woman half-asleep at the bar, and looked at each other as if they weren't sure whether this was all some sort of strange dream.

It'd been months since Thisby's visit to Lyra Castelis. Iphigenia looked roughly the same—aside from the mud, of course—but in their time apart, Thisby had grown a few inches and couldn't help but wonder if it was obvious. She felt weirdly self-conscious about it, as if growing taller was some sort of slight to her former self, the one that Iphigenia had known and befriended. Last month, she'd actually had to add some fabric to the hem of her tunic, and if she grew any more, she was worried she wouldn't be able to fit through the narrow passages of the Floating River.

"So," said Thisby.

"So," said Iphigenia.

They both went silent.

"You're an absolute mess," said Thisby at last.

Iphigenia burst into laughter.

For the next few hours, the girls sat and chatted about everything and nothing in particular while the proprietor brought them tea and bread and an old quill and inkpot, which Iphigenia had specifically requested, much to Thisby's confusion. Thisby told Iphigenia all about what Marl had been doing to the dungeon, and Iphigenia told Thisby about what was happening in the castle, the looming threat of war between Nth and Umberfall, and how she'd managed to sneak away to Three Fingers. Eventually, the old woman at the end of the bar woke up enough to stumble out the

*"You're an absolute mess," said Thisby at last.*
*Iphigenia burst into laughter.*

door, and the proprietor politely let the girls know that he'd made up a room for them whenever they were ready. And finally, they found themselves alone in the main room with the dying embers of the fire.

"What happened to Grunda?" asked Thisby.

The question had been chewing at her guts for some time, but she was too afraid to risk ruining a nice evening to ask.

"I don't know," said Iphigenia. "The last time I saw her, she was at the foot of my bed, telling me that I needed to come here to Three Fingers to find you. You haven't seen her?"

Thisby just sort of shook her head and stared at her empty teacup, saying nothing. Iphigenia didn't ask for further explanation.

"She gave me this," said Iphigenia, pulling out a piece of paper.

She handed it to Thisby, who flipped it over twice just to be certain of what she was seeing. It was an entry form for the Wretched Scrattle.

It looked just like the ones Thisby had seen the men in black, the "buzzards," carrying into the Black Mountain weeks ago. She'd escorted a large group of them to Castle Grimstone, where they'd had the forms notarized by Marl. Knowing the kind of security the buzzards had been traveling with and the caution they were taking in protecting the forms, Thisby was surprised to see one now.

"How'd she get that?" asked Thisby.

"You know Grunda."

"I thought I did," said Thisby.

Iphigenia felt strangely guilty that she'd seen Grunda last. Somehow it felt like a betrayal, even though she was certain that she hadn't done anything wrong.

"Look, Thisby. I'm not sure what's going on exactly, but Grunda told me she wants you to enter the Wretched Scrattle," said Iphigenia. "She wants you to win. To become the new Master of the Black Mountain. It's why I came all the way here. It's why I escaped from my caravan and risked my life to bring you that entry form."

Thisby set the form down on the table and slid it away from her as if it was a plate of food she wanted to send back.

"I'm sorry but I can't," she said.

"Why not?" asked Iphigenia.

"Because I'm not cut out to be Master," said Thisby.

"And the current Master is?" asked Iphigenia, the pitch of her voice rising. "Come on, Thisby, that little old blowhard can barely lace his own boots!"

Thisby thought that was a fair point, but there was a difference: the Master was a wizard. Sure, wizards were untrustworthy and clandestine and backward, but in a way that was kind of what made them perfectly suited for the position of Master of the Black Mountain. Thisby was no wizard.

"I'm not saying he's perfect, but . . ." Thisby trailed off as she tried to get her head around what she really wanted to say. "I'd be no good as a Master. For starters, I'm only twelve, well, thirteen soon enough, but still. I'm good at being game-keeper. I like caring for the monsters of the dungeon. That's what I know."

"Couldn't you care for them better as Master?" asked Iphigenia.

"I'm not so sure. Masters have to make horrible decisions. They have to do things that I could never do," said Thisby.

"Or do you just not want to do them?" asked Iphigenia.

Thisby was beginning to feel as if this conversation was slipping away from her. It felt like Iphigenia wasn't listening to her. She didn't want to be Master. Why wasn't that enough?

"When I become Queen, I'm going to have to make hard decisions. That's what happens when you have power," said Iphigenia.

"But maybe I don't want power," said Thisby. "I'm not you."

The words felt a bit harsh, but Iphigenia didn't seem particularly wounded. Instead she sat still and quiet, studying her friend.

"It was important to Grunda," said Iphigenia calmly.

"Then she should be here!" snapped Thisby.

Her words seemed to reverberate in the silence that followed until they were interrupted by the sound of the inn-keeper shuffling through the back kitchen, carrying a tray of clinking glasses.

"I-I'm sorry," mumbled Thisby, but Iphigenia waved her off.

"No, it's my fault," said Iphigenia. "I know you don't want to think about Grunda right now. It's just . . . I don't know why she's not here, but she clearly thinks this is important. She thinks that you need to become the new Master. She believes that if the wrong person takes control of the Black Mountain, it could mean the end of the dungeon altogether. I'm not going to tell you what to do. It's your life. You can do whatever you want. In fact, Thisby, listen . . ."

Iphigenia leaned her elbows on the table and grasped Thisby's hands in a reassuring way.

"I want you to listen to me now, okay? And don't get upset, and please don't say anything until I've finished what I need to say. Okay?"

She waited for Thisby to nod in agreement to her conditions before she continued.

"I want you to know that you have a choice. I believe in you, Thisby. If you enter the Wretched Scrattle, you will win. You'll become the next Master of the Black Mountain. And I know for a fact that you'd be a good Master. Thisby, you have all the talent in the world, you can do anything you set your mind to, but just because you can do something doesn't mean you must. This is a hard choice, but it needs to be *your* choice.

"There's another way out of this that I don't think you've considered. You could leave the Black Mountain and never come back. I'd find a position for you in the castle. You could be the gamekeeper there—sure, horses and peacocks aren't as exciting as nightmares and cockatrices, but I'd make sure you had everything you ever wanted. Before you make your decision, I want you to really, truly think about your options. I know it doesn't feel like it sometimes, but you do have them. You have a choice."

Thisby sat quietly, her head buzzing with everything Iphigenia had said. She loved the dungeon. It was her home. But images of her living in the castle, of an endless slumber party with her best friend, of the rich food and lush lawns and cozy beds bullied their way into her mind. Did she actually want to be Master? No. Not necessarily. But if Grunda was right and being the Master meant saving the dungeon, was it really a choice at all? If it meant giving the monsters who lived there a better life than they had now, that was all she really wanted.

"Iphi," said Thisby, squeezing her hands. "I don't want to be Master. But I can't just walk away. I'll do it. I'll enter the Wretched Scrattle."

"You're sure?" asked Iphigenia softly.

"It's my home," said Thisby.

Iphigenia smiled at her and released her right hand. Thisby lifted the quill from the inkpot, and without any further hesitation, she signed the form.

Marl took the last sip of sweet red tea and scowled at her empty cup. The Wretched Scrattle was set to begin soon, and she needed tea to think.

"You," she called to the ghoul who she'd worked with every day for the past week but couldn't remember the number of. "More! Tea! *MORE. TEA.* Are you stupid or something? Go!"

She snapped her fingers repeatedly at the ghoul until he slunk out of her chamber dejectedly, mumbling something vulgar under his rancid, undead breath. Marl pretended not to notice. There was no use in chastising him now. He was the last ghoul in the entire castle who knew how to get from her office to the kitchen and back again without getting lost, and she depended on him far more than he depended on her.

Before coming to the castle, Marl had never been so . . . uncomposed. For twelve years, she'd studied psychometry at the Grand College of Arcanology—*go, Werewolves!*—the best magic school in all of Nth, perhaps the entire world. She'd been near the top of her graduating class and had even been voted "Most Skulky" by her classmates. After graduation, she'd spent six years as a spy for the court of Nth, installed deep undercover in the kingdom of Umberfall, and in all that time she'd never missed a beat, never lost a moment of sleep. She'd sacrificed everything for her career, for Nth, and this was her reward. Finally she was in a position to make herself insanely wealthy and leave it all behind like a thief in the night, but something was nagging at her, some awful little voice in the back of her mind.

It wasn't her conscience. At least she was sure of that. In all her years as a spy, doing dirty work for the Nthian crown, she'd realized that she must've been born without one of those and was thankful for it. They seemed like awful little nuisances. No, this voice was definitely something else, something coming from outside like the voice that had pointed her to the book about the Wretched Scrattle in the first place, but whatever it was, it did seem rather insistent on unnerving her.

*You're never going to make it out alive,* it said. *That money doesn't belong to you. It belongs to the dungeon. Leave.* That kind of thing. It was all very annoying. Especially because the voice that seemed so intent on driving her away didn't seem to realize that she was just as eager for her departure as it was, probably more. Marl hated it here. It was the worst place she'd ever lived—and that was saying something.

Umberfall had been a miserable place. A totalitarian nightmare where every person was born into slavery and had to work to earn their freedom . . . which, naturally, no one ever did. Each day she witnessed the horrors of starvation and pestilence and hatred and war. And yet, she'd begun to miss her life there. She'd had friends at least. Being at the top of the Black Mountain was the loneliest place in the world. She rarely even dressed for work anymore, and she hadn't skulked through the shadows in weeks. What was the point in skulking without a proper skulkee to skulk around with?

At least it would be over soon. Her office was already littered with bags of gold, the entry fees collected from the gullible adventurers who waited outside the Black Mountain even now, eager to rush headlong to their doom. It would be easy for her to steal away now with enough money to sustain herself for years. All she'd have to do was grab a wheelbarrow full of gold and slip out the front door, but she wasn't trying to just steal enough gold to live like some lazy merchant. Not with all the hard work she'd put in to get herself to where she was now.

Right under the Master's nose, she'd turned the dungeon into a machine designed to funnel money directly into her own pockets. One of her first scams was the "passage tokens," which she'd insisted be printed on gold coins. She'd pocketed over half of them herself immediately, squirreling them away into her secret stash and elevating the value of the remainder, which she traded to the dungeon's more industrious monsters for armfuls of treasure worth a hundred times the value of the small gold tokens.

Then there was the Wretched Scrattle. The greatest money-making scam of all. Twenty-five gold a head—well, minus the five that went to the king—and almost all the so-called "treasure" she was bringing in to entice entrants was fake; wooden coins painted gold, glass gems, and other cheap trinkets. She'd had to hire on extra security to ensure that nobody at the base of the mountain got too good of a look in the wagons on the off chance somebody would recognize the fakes, but that was a small cost, all things considered. And that wasn't even the best part of it.

At first she'd planned to simply sneak away during

the commotion of the Wretched Scrattle, but lately she'd begun to have bigger ideas. When the time was right, she could displace the Master and start a bidding war between Nth and Umberfall for the dungeon's allegiance. She'd play both sides against each other and make herself infinitely wealthy in the process. It would be risky, but if she pulled it off . . .

*You're never going to pull it off,* said the voice.

"Oh, shut up," said Marl aloud.

There was a knock on her chamber door.

"Did you honestly forget? Four doors down! Make a left! The kitchen is on the right! The tea is in the lower cabinet! Next to the stove!" bellowed Marl impatiently.

"I'll keep that in mind," said a very human voice.

Her door swung open and in walked an unhappy and alarmingly fastidious woman.

"General Lutgard!" squeaked Marl, rushing to put herself back together.

She shuffled some papers on her desk, ran her fingers through her messy, mossy-green hair, and tightened the belt on her robe, which was perhaps a bit more open than was respectable for entertaining company.

"Overseer," said General Lillia Lutgard with a lack of inflection so pronounced that its deficit was noticeable in and of itself.

"W-what are you doing here?"

Marl tried to stop herself from glancing around nervously

at the bags of gold coins in overflowing sacks scattered around the office. The General walked in and folded her hands behind her back dramatically. It was the pose of a high-ranking officer, and it struck fear into Marl's sleep-deprived mind.

"I see you've made yourself comfortable," said Lillia, looking around.

Marl's underarms suddenly felt very damp.

"Yes, well, I . . . the Wretched Scrattle has been a big success!"

"I'd like to speak with the Master," said Lillia. It wasn't a question.

"Y-yes. Right. He's very busy. But I could, um, I could . . ."

Before the Overseer could finish her thought, a black-door opened in the center of the room and out popped the Master with a wide grin on his face. He spread his arms in a warm, welcoming gesture.

"General Lutgard, so good to see you!" he said cheerily. "Welcome to the Black Mountain!"

"Master," the General said formally. "I'm here to discuss—"

"The Princess, I know, I know," interrupted the Master. "The moment I received word that she was seen heading this way, I sent my best scouts to search for her, my dear General. It's a real shame. She's such a powerful, strongheaded young woman. Qualities that will make a great Queen, no doubt, but in youth they can prove quite troublesome."

Marl cringed. It wasn't surprising that the Master had

hidden this from her—the Master loved to keep secrets—but she hadn't been told a thing about the Princess going missing near the Black Mountain. This was a power move, plain and simple. Marl gave her most withering glare to the little man, but he didn't notice. In fact, neither the Master nor the General seemed to acknowledge her presence.

"I appreciate your assistance," said Lillia.

The Master nodded graciously.

"One more thing," Lillia continued. "The Princess formed a very strong connection with a young girl who works here in the dungeon. Thisby Thestoop, I believe. Your gamekeeper."

"Hm. The name does sound familiar," said the Master.

"I'd like to speak with Ms. Thestoop as soon as possible."

"Ah, but that's not so easy, unfortunately," said the Master. "You see, our gamekeeper has temporarily relinquished her post in order to enter the Wretched Scrattle. I received her entry form days ago. Notarized it myself. She's not here at the moment—tournament rules and all that. I suspect she's somewhere down among the throngs of people eagerly waiting for the doors to open tomorrow morning."

Marl's jaw dropped. She didn't bother to pick it up.

"She *what?*" Marl demanded.

*I told you you'd never pull it off,* said the voice.

"Shut up!" snapped Marl.

The Master and Lillia both turned slowly to face Marl, staring at her as if she were a complete stranger who'd just wandered into the room and interrupted their conversation.

"Excuse me?" said the Master.

"But! I mean, that's impossible! I didn't give her permission to take time off to go gallivanting around in the Wretched Scrattle! I never saw her entry form! I demand to see her entry form!"

"It should be in your pile. See for yourself," said the Master casually before turning back to General Lutgard.

Marl went over to the stack of last week's entries and began furiously digging through them. There was no way the gamekeeper had entered the Wretched Scrattle. Hadn't she been working in the dungeon this whole time? How could she not have noticed Thisby was gone? She continued to dig. And then . . . there it was. As plain as day. Thisby's entry form, which had all the official stamps and stickers and seals and marks.

"There must be some mistake. The documents are magically protected. She cannot enter unless an official member of the royal family approves!"

The Master scratched his chin. "Ah, well, I think that likely explains our current predicament, doesn't it? Check the bottom. Who signed off on her entry?"

Marl scrolled quickly to the bottom of the form, and her heart sank when she saw the big, unmistakable loopy swirls.

"Iphigenia Larkspur," she whispered automatically.

"For not reporting that right away, I beg your forgiveness, General," said the Master. "I was under the impression that this had been done through the proper channels."

"It's not your fault," said Lillia. "You're not the one tasked with serving as a line of communication between the King and the dungeon."

Lillia shot Marl a pointed look, and the Master stepped forward to bow in a show of humility.

"General. Please forgive her incompetence. Overseer Marl has been overworked on account of the Wretched Scrattle. I'm sure if she'd known Princess Iphigenia was missing, she would have reported it right away. Come. We can use the blackdoor machine to take a quick look around the dungeon. Perhaps we'll get lucky and spot something helpful."

With that, he threw a blackdoor bead at the ground and a glowing portal opened before them. The General stepped through without a second look back at Marl and vanished. The Master hung back a moment and turned to the frazzled Overseer.

"I wouldn't get too comfortable here if I were you," he said.

The Master stepped through the blackdoor before Marl could respond, and as suddenly as he'd arrived, he was gone. The portal snapped shut behind him.

Marl sat down at the Master's desk and sighed.

*Well, that could've gone better,* said the voice.

Marl sighed.

"Where's my stupid tea?" she grumbled.

★ ★ ★

The morning the Wretched Scrattle began, Thisby dressed, shouldered her backpack, set Mingus's lantern on its usual hook, and waddled down the creaky stairs of the Rat-Upon-a-Cat, where she found Iphigenia up bright and early, eating breakfast.

"Took you long enough!" said the Princess, setting down her toast. "Come on. We have a lot to do and very little time!"

Thisby was far too tired to argue but managed to stall long enough to snag the as yet unbitten piece of toast from Iphigenia's plate, so at least she didn't have to leave on an empty stomach. Outside, the town was deserted. Most of the crowd had already begun the trek to the base of the Black Mountain, and Thisby was finally able to see the sheer destruction that the hordes of adventurers had wrought upon the poor village.

Three Fingers had never been designed to accommodate the mass of people that the Wretched Scrattle drew. The dirt streets had been pitted and ravaged by wagon wheels, and the little bits of vegetation that once grew on the small farms had either been trampled flat or eaten by horses. Litter was everywhere. Fences were smashed, gates broken, windows shattered. It reminded Thisby of the City of Night after the tarasque had gone on its rampage.

For the shopkeepers, though, it had been a period of unparalleled success. Most of them were already looking for ways to use their newfound wealth to uproot their businesses and move to nicer locales, while the few that were determined to stay behind were busy buying up whatever was left. Salty Sam's, a general store located on the least desirable corner of the town square—downwind of the pig farm—was one of the businesses that had elected to stay.

As the girls approached the store, an old man with the same number of eyes and teeth (one) was standing out front with his arms akimbo, examining the empty store next door, which had just been put up for sale. The paint on the For Sale sign was still wet, and he squinted at the building as if he expected something to change at any second.

"Whaddya think?" he asked the girls as they approached. "I'm thinkin' o' expandin'. Knock down this wall right here, have a li'l breezeway connect the two buildings. Whaddya think? Come on, out with it! Tell me the truth!"

Thisby, who'd never met this man before in her life, was a bit concerned that he seemed so eager to trust a complete stranger with such a major life decision.

"I'm not sure," she said honestly.

"Hmm. Me neither. Yer right. When yer right, yer right. I could never fill that space with goods. In a month, it'd be just another warehouse. Convenient, sure, but that's a storefront property right there. Be a total waste."

The man rubbed his bald head, thinking it through.

"'Course I could buy it an' jus' rent it out," he continued. "Don't s'pose you know anybody lookin' to rent a storefront." He chuckled.

"Not off the top of my head."

He paused and looked at the girls as if he'd just now thought to check and see who it was giving him business advice.

"Ah! Prin—" he started, but immediately cut himself off.

"Hello, Sam," said Iphigenia.

"I s'pose yer here for yer package! Right this way! Jus' come in this mornin'."

Salty Sam walked them over to his shop, which hadn't yet opened for the day. He unlocked the door with one of the many seemingly identical keys on a large brass ring and led them inside the dark store, which smelled of stale pipe tobacco and incense. Sam reached out a gnarled tree root of a hand and turned a knob affixed to an iron pipe. A row of small gaslight lanterns tinkled to life overhead, casting a warm glow that revealed countless rows of shelves so jam-packed with odds and ends that it felt like they were walking into an oversize version of Thisby's backpack.

"A friend of yours?" whispered Thisby.

Iphigenia lifted a brass oil lamp off a shelf and studied it. It was intricately patterned and quite pretty.

"Sam's an old friend of the family," she said, setting the lamp back down. "Used to be one of the biggest importers of goods from across the Nameless Sea back in the day. There's not a town in the entire kingdom where the Larkspurs don't have connections."

Thisby watched Sam walk on ahead, seemingly paying no attention to them. When he reached the door behind the counter, his gigantic key ring came out again, and he began to search through it. It was amazing he was able to tell the keys apart.

"And you trust him?" asked Thisby, not taking her eyes off the man. "Not to tell anyone who you are?"

"He's loyal to the Larkspur family. Not to mention that he's a businessman and naturally, I'm paying him well for his discretion. Besides, I needed somewhere to ship it, and the inn where I'm staying would've been *much* more suspicious."

"Somewhere to ship what?" asked Thisby, but it was too late. Sam had the door open and was waving them back behind the counter.

Thisby followed them into a small back room, where Sam removed the lid from a crate and presented Iphigenia with a brown paper package from inside.

"Hope it fits, 'cause I'm no tailor!" he laughed.

"What is it?" asked Thisby.

Sam nodded politely and excused himself from the room.

"If you need anythin', I'll be up front."

When Sam had closed the door, Iphigenia presented the brown paper package to Thisby.

"Here," she said. "I got you something. For your birthday."

Thisby hadn't wanted to say anything and was touched that Iphigenia remembered. In light of everything else, turning thirteen had seemed so unimportant, almost selfish to even think about, but that was the thing about best friends: they did all the being selfish for you.

"You didn't have to," said Thisby.

"Nonsense. Just open it," she said.

Thisby pulled the string and unwrapped the package. Inside was a tunic, a shade of blue so dark that it was nearly black, with delicate silver embroidery around the neckline, cuffs, and hem. The craftsmanship was remarkable.

"It's beautiful. I don't know what to say," said Thisby.

It wasn't entirely a figure of speech. Over the course of her life, the only gifts Thisby had ever received had been from Grunda, and she wasn't sure if there was a proper response that polite society used other than the obvious "thank you," which felt woefully inadequate.

"Here. Look," said Iphigenia, taking the tunic from Thisby's hands.

Without another word, she grasped the collar of the tunic with both hands and tugged as hard as she could. The seams gave way, and a nice split ripped the neckline.

Thisby gasped.

"Just wait," said Iphigenia with a grin.

From the spot where the tunic had ripped, little blue threads had sprouted to life and begun weaving around each other in an intricate dance. In almost no time at all, the tunic had mended itself completely. It looked as pristine as when Thisby had taken it out of the package.

"It mends itself!" exclaimed Iphigenia. "Dries and cleans itself, too, if you give it enough time. Knowing what you put your clothes through on a daily basis, I figured you'd get your money's worth more than anybody."

"Iphi, I . . ." Thisby trailed off as Iphigenia handed her back the tunic.

"It's nothing," said Iphigenia casually. "Besides, we couldn't have you winning the Wretched Scrattle smelling like you'd just crawled out of the Deep Down, right?"

"Iphi," said Thisby. She'd wanted to say more, but it was the only word that didn't seem completely jammed in her throat at the moment.

Thisby stared at the tunic and then at her friend, who was positively beaming. How she, an orphan from the Black Mountain, had gotten so lucky as to become best friends with Iphigenia, the Princess of Nth, was something she could not comprehend. It was beyond her wildest imagination.

"Thank you," said Thisby.

"Don't mention it. There are perks to being friends with the heir to the throne," laughed Iphigenia.

"Not just for the clothes," said Thisby. "For everything."

She hugged her best friend.

Iphigenia flushed with embarrassment. Her family wasn't exactly the hugging kind, and the gesture still felt a bit strange to her.

"I–it's nothing," she stammered. "Just be safe in there, okay?"

Thisby withdrew from the hug, brought back down to reality by the mention of what she was about to do.

"You should really get going," said Iphigenia.

Thisby nodded. It was a long hike to the mountain

entrance, and the road would be crowded. She picked up her backpack and noticed that Mingus had fallen asleep in his lantern again.

When they made their way back through the shop, Sam was nowhere to be seen, but Thisby could hear someone moving boxes around upstairs and knew that had to be him. Lazy dust motes lingered in the still shop air, lit by the gaslight lanterns, and they danced and swirled around the girls as they made their way toward the door. It reminded Thisby of a clockwork snow globe that she'd found once, a sentimental treasure that had been left behind in the dungeon by an explorer who hadn't made it back. When you wound it up, a pair of ice skaters would spin on a glass pond amidst the drifting fake snow to a tinkling song. Only now she and Iphigenia were the ice skaters, twirling in an endless circle.

She pushed the door open, and the spell was broken by the heat and light of the morning. A cart of cabbages rattled past, and Thisby could smell that they were already well past their prime. This was the real world. She took a few steps away from the door and into the dusty street before she turned.

The Princess stood tall in the doorway with a strange smile on her face. It was both playful and dead serious at the same time, the smile of a master sword fighter heading into a duel.

"Now there's just one thing left for you to do," said Iphigenia.

"What's that?"

"Win."

# CHAPTER 12

Waves of people undulated and churned outside the archway at the foot of the Black Mountain. Thisby was afloat in a sea of bodies, jostled around, drowning in the odors of nervous sweat and freshly sharpened steel, of extinguished campfires and the desperate, last-minute meals that had been hastily prepared over them this morning.

She was closer to the back of the crowd than the front. The colorful tents that had covered the ground only last night had been folded and tucked away by morning. The stakes had been pulled from the earth, and the wagons had all but vanished, leaving behind only tracks and donkey droppings. The party was over now. The Wretched Scrattle was beginning.

Thisby pulled out a small notebook and flipped through it, not really reading the pages. It was mostly sketches of dungeon plants. Next to her, a boy only a few years older than herself kept bumping into her backpack as he shifted his weight from side to side, humming nervously. His sword was really more of an over-polished pigsticker, and with a cursory glance, Thisby could tell that he'd buckled his hand-me-down armor incorrectly. He'd obviously tried to don it himself and hadn't done a very good job.

"Excuse me?" she said.

The boy stared straight ahead.

"Excuse me, but you've put your armor on all wrong. I could help you with it, if you'd like," she offered.

"Maybe he's hard of hearing?" offered Mingus.

He'd been quiet up until now, and it was pretty clear that he wasn't comfortable with the crowd, either. His muddy ochre color—one that Thisby jokingly called "wet snot"—was a dead giveaway.

"Excuse me, would you like some help?" Thisby asked louder.

When there was still no response, she reached out to tap the boy on the arm to get his attention, but an older woman smacked her hand away.

"What are you doing?" she hissed. "Worry about yourself!"

"I was just trying to—"

"Don't touch him!" she spat, clawing again at Thisby's outstretched hand.

Thisby withdrew her hand and locked eyes with the older woman but immediately regretted her decision. The woman's eyes were sunken and wild. She looked dangerous. It was a look that Thisby had seen before in cornered gnolls and sickly fire bats.

"If he's too stupid to buckle his armor properly, that's his own problem!"

Her words dripped with venom. Thisby took a step back and bumped into someone behind her, who gave her a shove. The crowd was restless.

"I was just trying to help . . . ," began Thisby, but she was having a hard time finding her words in the face of such nastiness.

"Are you stupid?" she rasped. "The more treasure he gets, the less there is for us!"

"Come on," said Mingus. "We should go."

"Not yet!" said Thisby, finding her voice.

She shoved her way over to the boy and tugged on the misplaced strap.

"This one goes underneath," she said. "Are you listening?"

At last, the boy shook himself awake and stared at Thisby as if he'd just woken up from a dream. He began to fumble nervously with the strap on his breastplate.

"Oh. Th-th-thank you," he mumbled.

The woman hocked a loogie on the ground and glowered at Thisby. It was obvious she was saying something quite nasty under her breath, but Thisby couldn't make it out. She was already wading through the crowd to distance herself from the awful woman.

Thisby couldn't help but think of the crowd of Deep Dwellers she'd encountered last year. These people didn't have the same level of desperation or sadness, but she could still sense their fear, and it was powerful. But there was something else there as well. Another sensation mixed in with the fear. It was one that the Deep Dwellers hadn't possessed. A kind of hunger or excitement. Greed. She could practically taste it, and it made her ashamed to be a part of it all.

The sound of a booming horn silenced both her thoughts and the crowd.

Everyone froze.

The Wretched Scrattle had begun.

Thisby dodged through the throng of people, trying her best not to be crushed in the stampede. She'd never seen so many people so eager to rush headlong to their likely deaths.

Up ahead, as the crowd funneled in through the enormous blackdoor at the base of the mountain, she could hear an occasional zapping sound followed by intense wails of pain. It didn't take long for Thisby to connect the dots. In Three Fingers, she'd overheard some adventurers claim they'd witnessed a warlock trying to sneak through the blackdoor, only to get zapped so hard with a bolt of green lightning that all that was left behind was a pair of smoking old boots. It was undoubtedly one of the many fail-safes Marl had designed to ensure that no magic users entered the Wretched Scrattle.

When Thisby heard this, she'd gotten a little worried about Mingus's slime healing magic, but Grunda had explained to her last year that there was a difference between what Mingus was able to do and the sort of magic practiced by wizards and their ilk. The metaphor she'd used was that Mingus's healing was more like rubbing baking soda on a splinter to draw it out and that "proper" wizard magic was more like growing a new finger that didn't have a splinter in it to begin with. Thisby wasn't really sure she understood what Grunda had meant by that, but she'd also never claimed to understand magic, nor did she want to. What Thisby did know, however, was that a smoking pair of boots was something to be cautious about. Actually, there was a lot to be cautious about, and exploding warlocks were probably the least of her worries.

Thisby had made up her mind early that the best way to survive the Wretched Scrattle was to think like Marl. Cold, analytical, uncompromising. And if Marl's strategy involved stopping adventurers as soon as they entered the mountain, the first thing she would do would undoubtedly be placing a series of simple traps on the other side of the blackdoor. Probably something as straightforward as a pit full of spikes. It was a crude trap, but it would serve to weed out the weaker adventurers who were never going to make it very far anyway. It made sense in an awful way. The overeager people would be near the front of the pack, and they would also be the types to not look before they leapt.

It bothered Thisby to think like this. She hated the idea of treating people as if they were disposable, even if they were desperate jerks eager to slaughter monsters in exchange for gold. Most of them weren't evil. They were just greedy and hoping to make off with an armful of treasure before they met their untimely demise. Still, whether it bothered her or not, Thisby had no choice but to think like the Overseer if she was going to make it to the top of the dungeon.

Thisby worked her way toward the blackdoor portal but stayed near the corner. She was banged around by the tidal wave of adventurers, most of them more than twice her size, but when she finally managed to reach the entrance and peeked her head in, she realized that her caution had been well advised.

Just as she'd suspected, immediately on the other side of the entrance into the Black Mountain was a pit—or rather, what used to be a pit and was currently a pile of unhappy adventurers stacked atop each other in a very deep hole. The pit had been successful. So successful that it was now was overflowing with people who were trying to crawl out while some less considerate adventurers used them as a human bridge. The people on the top of the pit seemed to be doing okay—aside from the light trampling, of course—but Thisby shuddered to think about what it must be like for the people trapped at the bottom.

She inched her way around the edge of the pit, trying not

to look down. She wished that there was some way to help the poor people who'd fallen in but knew there was nothing she could do now. She was going to have to get used to the feeling. There'd be a lot more fallen adventurers along the way, and she couldn't save them all. Not if she wanted to win the Scrattle and save the dungeon. Thisby took a deep breath and hurried on toward the commotion ahead.

In all her years as gamekeeper, Thisby had never heard such a racket. Screaming and cursing and the clanging of swords roared down the hall, echoing through the smoky torchlight haze. As she walked on, several adventurers came bursting through the fog. They were headed in the opposite direction, back toward the blackdoor through which they'd entered only moments ago, realizing that maybe adventuring wasn't really for them after all.

Up ahead, the tunnel widened into a chamber Thisby recognized at once as what the denizens of the dungeon called "the basilica." The basilica was a long hallway, a hundred feet wide, with ceilings even taller than that. The length of it was lined with crumbling stone arches and pockmarked walls that provided plenty of nooks and crannies for monsters to hide. From the Overseer's point of view, it made perfect sense to funnel people through here to thin the crowd a bit.

Thisby emerged into a scene that was deafening and frantic. The action of the crowd was so chaotic that she had to duck behind a fallen column to gather her wits and plan her next move. Peeking out, she saw more or less what she'd expected: the army of the dungeon was composed mostly of rock imps and skeletons with a few dire rats here and there. The skeletons were doing the majority of the fighting with their scimitars and shields, while the rock imps pounced on those who attempted to flee from the scene. It took several rock imps to bring down a full-grown man, but they were quick, and most of the adventurers didn't see them coming until it was too late. Their camouflage was that flawless. The dire rats were mostly just there for show, but a few of them had managed to corner some of the adventurers who'd tried to flee from the imps.

All in all, for the amount of commotion it was creating, it was a fairly unimpressive battle, and Thisby wanted nothing to do with it. This, she realized, was part of the genius of Marl's second trap. She knew that most adventurers rushing into the dungeon would be eager for some action, and the Overseer was happy to oblige. There were plenty of young men and women who'd only entered the tournament as an excuse to cross swords with a skeleton, so they could scamper back to Three Fingers to sit at the bar later and brag to their friends about the time they competed in the Wretched Scrattle. If those people wanted action, you might as well give it to them here, while they were still in reach of the exit.

Thisby skirted around the outside of the basilica, ducking from hiding spot to hiding spot. The fray had kicked up enough dust that it helped to conceal her movements so long as she avoided wandering too close to the fallen torches and lanterns that now littered the ground. More than once a group of rock imps passed within a stone's throw of her position, but she always froze when they did, careful not to alert them with the slightest movement, as rock imps could sense their prey by feeling its vibrations through the stone. She made her way through the chamber until she'd found a good, secluded spot behind a pile of rubble that used to be a Dünkeldwarven statue, and she stopped and pulled out a notebook, which she read by Mingus's dull glow.

The exit she was looking for was an almost undetectable passage in the northwest corner of the chamber. According to her notes, the passage would lead her past the rock golem's cave, and since Thisby knew the poor rock golem had met its untimely end a few weeks earlier, it seemed like the safest path. She tucked the notebook away and looked at Mingus.

"How are you doing so far?" she whispered to him.

"So far, so good," he chirped.

Thisby knew it was a lie. His wavering faint light gave away his discomfort at being so close to battle, but it'd be pointless to call him out on it now.

With the fighting mostly confined to the center of the room, Thisby moved with relative ease around the perimeter. A nervous-looking dire rat stalked a bit close to her, but all it took was her tossing him a raw onion from her backpack—one of the few nonessential food items she'd brought with her, thankfully—and the dire rat happily scampered off after the much easier and tastier meal. It was a rule of the dungeon that Thisby had internalized at a young age; there are two ways to satisfy a hungry monster: it can eat you or it can eat something else. Always present it with another option whenever possible.

Once inside the narrow passage, she paused and let out a long sigh of relief. The sound of battle grew muffled and distant only a few steps into the wall. As far as she was concerned, the adventurers were the most dangerous part of the Wretched Scrattle, and she was glad to be rid of them for the time being.

Thisby moved with caution through the passage, keeping an eye out for trip wires and foot plates. If Marl had gained access to the Master's blackdoor machine, there was no corner of the dungeon she wouldn't have been able to find and booby-trap. If the Master had kept his machine from her, though, then Thisby was going to have a much easier time making her way to the top of the Black Mountain. The problem was that there was no way to know. Around every corner, a gruesome death could be waiting.

There was a tapping noise up ahead that made Thisby's heart leap in her chest.

"Mingus . . . go dark," she whispered, and he complied.

Thisby crept down the passage as silently as she could until she heard voices speaking softly up ahead and stopped to listen.

"Now what?" said a gruff voice.

"This way," said another. This one was soft and lilting. It

had an almost musical quality.

Thisby inched forward to get a look.

"That sounds like a guess," sighed a young boy.

Thisby got close enough to peek out from the shadows of the passage. If someone with keen eyes had glanced over, she knew that she likely would've been spotted, but at the moment the trio was preoccupied.

The young boy was dressed in finery and was clearly some kind of noble. Thisby was immediately reminded of Ingo, considering how harshly this handsome and clean young man contrasted with his surroundings. Only where Ingo was dark, this boy was light. While Ingo's features were sharp, this boy's were soft. He was somehow both Ingo's counterpart and opposite simultaneously. The thought troubled Thisby after what had happened last year.

Across from him stood a rakish man with an eye patch who was scanning the doorway—thankfully not the one in which Thisby was hidden—and next to him was a heavyset, bearded man in some of the most colorful robes Thisby had ever seen. The boy brushed a lock of blond hair out of his face and smiled at the heavyset man.

"Bero," he said with an almost mocking politeness, "you're not getting paid to guess."

"I—I know," stuttered Bero.

Bero was easily a foot taller than the boy and outweighed him by a hundred pounds, but Thisby got the impression that he wasn't the kind of man who could even comprehend that

*Thisby was far too preoccupied by the glowing red eyes of the creature slinking down the wall behind them.*

that was the sort of thing that could be used to one's advantage.

"Vas," rumbled the one-eyed man.

"What is it?" snapped the boy, who Thisby was quickly beginning to dislike.

"Trust him. He's got good"—the one-eyed man paused to consider his wording carefully—"intuition."

Vas placed his hands on his hips.

Bero's cheeks turned pink at the compliment.

They continued to talk among themselves, but by that point, Thisby had lost track of their conversation. She was far too preoccupied by the glowing red eyes of the creature slinking down the wall behind them.

Before she had a chance to consider whether it was really a good idea, Thisby burst forth from the tunnel, waving her arms over her head and shouting like a madwoman. The one-eyed man spun on his heels and drew his longsword, as the larger man ducked and covered. Vas shot Thisby a look that moved imperceptibly between being startled and angry before returning to startled when the beast lunged at the group. It landed inches away from where Vas stood.

The monster wasn't one that Thisby had ever seen before in the dungeon. It stood taller than her at the shoulder and resembled something like a bull crossed with a lizard, yet for how clumsy it looked, it moved like a ballet dancer. The one-eyed soldier ran at it, putting his body between Vas and the monster. He slashed it with his longsword but only managed to catch one of the many rigid spines protruding from its back. The beast responded with a tail whip that caught the man square in the chest and sent him flying across the room.

"Donato!" yelled Bero.

Vas took off running, but before Thisby even had time to properly curse him for being a coward, she realized he was running toward the monster. The blond boy grabbed a bow, which had been left propped against an unlit brazier, and nocked an arrow. Thisby watched the shot sail wide, and the monster turn its attention toward Bero.

Bero, for all his size, looked about as tough as a bag of overripe bananas. He threw his hands up in what Thisby could only think of as a "not in the face" pose and turned away from the monster as if that might make it disappear. The monster charged.

Mingus squealed helplessly in Thisby's ear as her mind raced. "Do something!"

"Like what?" snapped Thisby.

"I don't know! Something!"

So she did. Something.

Thisby dropped her shoulder and ran, slamming her entire body as hard as she could into the side of the beast, T-boning it midstride. It wasn't much of an impact, and it definitely hurt her more than the monster, but it was enough to ever so slightly alter its course. The beast missed Bero by mere inches and skidded to a halt. The monster looked nonplussed by the maneuver and cocked its head curiously at Thisby, like a confused puppy. Bero slowly withdrew his hands from his face to find himself miraculously undevoured.

"Why'd you do that?" screamed Mingus.

"You said, 'Do something!'"

"I didn't mean do that!"

The monster dug its claws into the hard earth of the cavern floor, ready to charge. There was no way to outrun it now; the monster was too quick and Thisby was too slow.

The beast growled. Thisby closed her eyes tight and prepared for the worst when she heard a tremendous crack. Through her eyelids, she saw a flash of purple light, and by the time she opened them, the beast was tumbling sideways, where it stopped only once it collided hard with the wall of the cave. Thisby was still rubbing the spots out of her eyes when a second bolt of lightning exploded from across the room and struck the rocks just inches above the creature's head. Crumbled stone showered down on it, and with a pathetic whine, the beast was gone as quickly as it had arrived, scrambling back into the shadows from which it had emerged.

When her eyes finally returned to normal, Thisby looked across the room and saw Bero lowering his spell book, the residual magic still crackling in the air around him, creating trails of blue and purple sparks. The one-eyed man stirred in the corner of the room as Bero tucked his spell book back into his satchel, and slowly but surely everyone's pulses returned to normal.

"What was that thing?" Vas asked with an air of forced

casualness. His hands were still trembling as he lowered the bow.

"Hodag," mumbled Donato as Bero helped him to his feet. "Haven't seen one o' them in years. Sorry, it caught me off guard, boss."

"Just don't let it happen again," said Vas.

Thisby couldn't tell if he was joking.

"Um," said Thisby without a follow-up thought.

Vas brushed himself off and stood up straighter.

"Oh! My manners! Excuse me!" he said, practically bouncing over toward Thisby. Apparently his nerves had settled quite quickly. "Vaswell Gandy of the Flatbottom Gandys, but you may call me Vas. Pleased to make your acquaintance. This is Donato Wince, of course, the best hunter in all of Nth!"

Donato nodded curtly and took his bow back from Vas.

"Pleased to meet you, milady," Donato said with a wink at Thisby. At least she assumed it was a wink. There was an equally good chance it was just a blink. With an eye patch, there's no discernible difference.

"And this, our savior, the man of the hour, is Bero Lor. On the off chance the lightning bolts didn't tip you off, he's a sorcerer."

"Conjurer, actually," said Bero humbly. "It's not me, it's the spell books. I just read them. Technically, magic users aren't allowed to compete in the Wretched Scrattle."

"Just reads them? He writes them! He's too humble," said Vas.

"Wait! Yeah! That's right! No magic users were allowed to enter the tournament! How'd you get in?" asked Thisby.

Bero blushed. "Small loophole in the fine print. I don't technically possess any magic, not myself. The books do, and magical implements and tools *are* allowed. The catch is that like Mr. Gandy was saying, I also happen to write the books. That makes me a bit more, uh, versatile."

"Versatile. Good word for it," said Donato.

"My father paid top dollar for that versatility," said Vas with a grin. The statement was followed by an awkward pause that showed up a bit too late and hung around a bit too long.

"Soooo . . ." Vas trailed off, looking expectantly at Thisby.

"Oh, right! I'm Thisby. And this is Mingus."

"Thisby? Must be a popular name around here," mumbled Vas.

"I guess," said Thisby.

Somewhere in the distance a dire cricket chirruped.

"That's it? Just Thisby then?" coaxed Vas.

"Oh. Thisby Thestoop. I'm the, uh, gamekeeper here."

Vas, Bero, and Donato looked at Thisby, absolutely dumbstruck. She might as well have told them that she was the future Queen of Nth—who, coincidentally enough, was the other "Thisby" who Vas had met just the other day.

"Are you sure?" asked Vas.

"Yes, I'm sure!" said Thisby. His incredulity irritated her. Just because she didn't think it was worth boasting about didn't mean she didn't want to be taken seriously.

"The gamekeeper of *this* dungeon?" asked Vas.

Thisby's face felt hot.

"Yes, of course of this dungeon!" she snapped.

A big, goofy smile spread across Vas's face.

"I'm sorry! It's just . . . this is incredible! I can't believe our luck!" He beamed.

"What do you mean?" she asked, hesitant to warm up to him despite his brilliant smile and straight white teeth—or perhaps it was because of them.

There was something about apparent perfection that made it hard to trust somebody. Nobody's perfect. Thisby knew that. So when she saw something that *seemed* that way on the surface, it was easy for her to imagine all the lies that so-called perfection must be concealing.

Vas laughed. "I mean you can help us! Be our guide! We'll pay you, of course! Handsomely! Anything you want! Name your price! What better advantage is there than having the Black Mountain's own gamekeeper along?"

"I-I'm sorry. I don't think I can help you."

Vas's face fell. "What? Why?"

"First of all, I'm a little at a loss myself. Overseer Marl has changed so much. That beast that just attacked us . . . I've never see it before in my life."

"Don't worry about that! You can tell us what you do know! Show us the shortcuts! Give us some tips! We'll handle the rest. Donato has an extensive knowledge of beasts from all over Nth. I'm sure he'd be happy to share some of that with you, too, if you were interested."

"I would love to hear it," Thisby admitted. "But there's another problem."

"Which is?"

Thisby paused. She didn't think Vas and the others seemed the type, but there were plenty of high-level adventurers who'd eagerly slit your throat if you were foolish enough to out yourself as their competition. She dismissed the thought as paranoid. They might be strangers, but so far, they'd shown her nothing but kindness. That the idea had even crossed her mind was enough to remind her there was more than one way to get lost down in the dungeon.

"I'm actually competing in the Wretched Scrattle," she said.

Vas went silent, pursed his lips, and put his hands on his hips. After a moment, he freed his right hand so it could rub his chin thoughtfully. He made a motion like he was stroking a beard, but his face was as clean as Thisby's. Technically speaking, it was much cleaner. Vas sighed, tapped his foot, and furrowed his brow. He was making a real show of how deeply he was contemplating this unforeseen turn of events.

"And you plan to win and become Master?" asked Vas.

Thisby nodded. She couldn't bring herself to say it out loud. It still didn't feel right to think of herself as going after the job. Part of her was still hoping for a way out.

"Not a problem," he said at last.

"What do you mean?" asked Thisby. She was genuinely curious.

"I mean, I don't care if you want to be Master. I'm just here for the sport of it. Maybe grab a little treasure along the way, sure, but it's fine if you want to be the new Master. When we win—and we will win, with you on our side—we'll win as a team. And in the end, if you decide that you'd like to be the Master of the Black Mountain, you can go right ahead. I don't really want all that responsibility, anyway. Besides, you already work here, so it'll be a much easier transition for you, right? Done and done. I'm glad that's settled."

Bero made stunned noises, opening and closing his mouth like a fish out of water. He obviously had something he desperately wanted to say, but wherever the words were lodged, they weren't coming up anytime soon. Donato just laughed.

"Why would I trust you to just hand the position over to me?" asked Thisby.

"Fair question, but I have one for you. If it wasn't for Bero's well-timed lightning bolt, do you think you would've made it out of this room? It seems like maybe sticking together could be beneficial for all of us."

Thisby paused. She wanted to be angry. She wanted to tell the arrogant noble boy that he had no idea what he was talking about, that she knew the dungeon better than anyone and that she'd be just fine on her own, better even. But she couldn't. He had a point. She did know the dungeon better than anyone . . . at least, she used to. But that dungeon was gone now. The new one would be full of surprises, and without some help, what really were her odds of winning?

"I'll take you as far as Castle Grimstone," Thisby announced. "Once we're there, we can part ways at the gates and then it's everyone for themselves."

Vas removed his right glove and extended a well-manicured hand. Thisby shook it. It would be cliché to say that his hand was as soft as a baby's bottom, and worse than that, it would also be untrue, because it was far softer. Compared to Vas's hand, a baby's bottom was like a troll's neck stubble.

"You've got yourself a deal," he said, looking around. "Now, which way to the castle?"


The arms of the blackdoor machine danced around the room, loading and unloading scrying spheres—crystal balls showing different locations inside the dungeon—at a record pace. On the walkway below, the Master stood with his hands folded neatly behind his back, bathed in the cold glow of the machine's viewing screens as they changed rapidly, flicking between events in the dungeon.

From where he stood, he was quite comfortable. The air was nice and cool on his freshly bathed skin, his robes had been recently laundered and smelled of lavender, and his personal servant would be back any moment with a warm beverage. His current comfort level clashed dramatically with what he was watching unfold in the Black Mountain, far below his slippered feet.

The violence was incredible. Monsters and adventurers battled at every turn. He watched a pack of wolf moths carry off a pitchfork-wielding farmer. He saw a slughemoth swallow three adventurers whole. On one screen, he watched a minotaur who had seized control of a bridge in Giant's Crossing swatting off anyone who attempted to cross, and on another, he spied a quartet of unwary adventurers as they walked brazenly into a room full of creeping death vines, mistaking them for normal plants. They didn't walk out again. He almost threw up when he saw what the acidic oozes had done. Worst of all, he was beginning to think that maybe Overseer Marl had been right all along: nobody was going to win this thing—and it wasn't just because of her "foolproof" plan, but because nobody would even make it to the castle gates alive.

There was a knock on the door, and the Master eagerly turned away from the screens, happy to be done with them for a moment. He was less happy when he heard Marl's voice mewling from the other side.

"Open the door, this instant!" demanded Marl.

The Master paused for a deliberately long time.

"No," he said at last.

"You open this door, right now!"

The Master paused again, relishing every sweet second.

"We had an agreement. You have complete access to every room in the dungeon, except the blackdoor room. I need someplace for peace and quiet."

"Open the door right now, you little worm! I—" Marl cut herself off.

The Master listened to Marl's huffing and puffing from the other side of the thick metal door until her breath slowed and became inaudible.

"I completely understand your need for solitude," said Marl, who'd clearly decided to try honey where vinegar had failed. "But in light of recent circumstances, I'm afraid I require access to the blackdoor machine."

"And what might those circumstances be?" said the Master. Every question he asked from his side of the door was like a tiny gift for himself.

On the other side of the door, Marl gritted her teeth. The Master could almost hear it through six solid inches of metal.

"You know very well what those circumstances are! Your gamekeeper has entered the Wretched Scrattle, and in doing so, she's endangered the whole operation. Now let me in!"

The Master waited as long as it took to quit grinning before he finally relented and opened the door. As the door slowly opened, he found himself face-to-face with a version of the Overseer that he wasn't prepared for. His grin returned in spite of himself.

Her tangled green hair was like an overgrown weedy garden, and it was obvious from both the look and smell of her that she hadn't changed her robes in days. Her lapels were spotted with stains from the strange red tea she always drank, and it'd left quite an unpleasant crimson residue on her teeth as well. The Master had expected her to burst into the room like a wailing banshee the moment he opened the door, but she clearly didn't have the energy for that. If he'd had to pick a verb, he would've probably said that she "slouched" into the room more than anything. The Master almost felt bad for her . . . almost.

"My, my, my—" he began, but Marl interrupted him with a wave of her hand.

"Save it," she said.

Marl walked in and slumped down in the only seat in the house, the lowered bucket seat that attached to an arm that could be raised to access any portion of the blackdoor machine.

"This is bad. This is really, really bad," she groaned.

The Master leaned against a railing and studied her.

"Why?" he prodded. He wasn't ready to play his hand, but she seemed more than eager to play hers, so for now, simple questions were best.

"Why?" she mocked, lifting her face from where she'd buried it in her long, elegant fingers. "Frankly, I don't know why you're not worried. Don't you understand what happens if that gamekeeper wins the Wretched Scrattle? You can have your fun at my expense, but if that gamekeeper wins, you're out of a job, too!"

"Aren't you the one who wanted to entice people with the promise of them taking my job if they won? You'll have to excuse me for not being too sympathetic," said the Master.

"You know that nobody was ever supposed to actually win," she said. "You knew the plan."

"Oh, I knew the plan," he said.

And he did. Better than she thought he did. He'd seen the bags of gold littering her office through the scrying spheres. He'd known that the minute she'd made enough money, she'd disappear into the night. Only, she hadn't. The money had piled up but she'd stuck around. The Master knew there was only one reason a thief sticks around after they should've cut and run and that was because there was a bigger score coming just around the corner.

Odds were, Marl had decided she wanted the Black Mountain for herself. If that was true, the Master knew she'd just be waiting for the chance to off him or whoever won the Wretched Scrattle the second their back was turned. He'd be the easier target, he supposed, since she already had access to him and Castle Grimstone. If somebody else won, it presented too many unknown variables. And if the gamekeeper won, that would be the worst possible situation. Marl might have been going a little crazy as of late, but she wasn't blind. She knew that many of the monsters in the dungeon loved the gamekeeper. Thisby would be much harder to get rid of without risking a full-on monster revolt.

"You worry too much. Look at me. Do I look worried?" said the Master.

Marl's eyes darted over to him, a new alertness appearing behind her heavy purple lids.

"You have a point. Why aren't you worried?" she asked.

The Master rubbed his chin. "You just said it yourself. Nobody will win the Wretched Scrattle. Do you doubt your own plans?"

"Of course not!" barked the Overseer, standing up. Her ire was rising again. It seemed to be her last source of strength. She pointed an angry finger at the Master's face.

"But let's say the gamekeeper does win . . . or someone does! You've said yourself that these things have a way of blowing up in your face!"

"Oh, and now you listen to me!" laughed the Master.

"You think this is funny? What do you think will happen to you if somebody wins the Wretched Scrattle? You think you'll just walk away? Live out your days on a farm somewhere? Nobody has ever retired from being Master of the Black Mountain. The job is a death sentence. You know that. The old Master dies. That's the way it is."

"I'm not one for tradition," said the Master.

"You think you have a choice?" Her words were more threat than question.

"There's always a choice. You just have to be smart enough to see it."

Something changed in the room. An obvious thing to say would be, "the room grew colder," only that wasn't exactly it. It was more like the room had always been cold and the people inside it had finally just given up on pretending that it wasn't.

"You want her to win," snarled Marl.

The Master frowned at her disingenuously. "Now why would I *possibly* want that?"

"You've struck some sort of deal with the gamekeeper. Is that it? You help her win the Wretched Scrattle and she spares your life? You coward! You'll ruin everything!"

With that, the Overseer, who'd seemed so frail only a moment ago, stood up tall and straight like a cobra ready to strike. The Master took a step back.

"The Wretched Scrattle was your idea!" exclaimed the Master, suddenly realizing he was quite sweaty.

"No, no, no, no, no, no, no. You're wrong. You're wrong. You're wrong. It was never my idea, but I took it anyway. I was so stupid. I should've taken the money and run when I had the chance, but the opportunity was too good. I got greedy. I could've had it all if you'd just played your part. I should have just left. I should have just left."

With a flick of her wrist, Marl withdrew an alchemist's bottle from the sleeve of her robe and dangled it between her thumb and forefinger.

"Marl, stop! You can still leave! You've got your money! You don't need to do this! Just take the money and go!"

"It's too late now."

Marl flung the bottle at the Master's feet. The bottle shattered upon impact, and within seconds the purple goo that had spilled out had multiplied in size and was constraining his ankles. In another few seconds, it had grown up past his waist and was squeezing his legs so tightly he could no longer feel his feet.

"You can't do this!" he shouted. "I'm the Master!"

"You're nobody," Marl cooed, an awful smile curling the corner of her mouth.

The purple ooze had climbed up to his neck and was beginning to constrict his throat, making it hard to breathe.

"You don't understand! The girl needs to win! You'll start a war! You idiot! You—"

His screams were choked off as the goo entered his mouth and nose. Moments later, it covered his entire body, leaving him fighting for breath on the floor, entombed in a cocoon of vile purple mucus. The Master writhed and struggled until he no longer could, and then everything went dark.


"Not that way," said Thisby.

Donato sighed, backtracked to the fork in the tunnel, and took the left path instead.

"Not that way, either," said Thisby.

The hunter stopped and leaned against the crumbling stone wall with one outstretched hand, hanging his head as he did.

"There's only two ways," he said.

Thisby stepped forward and began feeling around the wall, knocking on seemingly random stone blocks and putting her ear up against them.

"I swear there used to be a secret passage here. I wonder

if the Overseer had it filled in."

Donato waved his arm down the left passage. "We could spend another hour looking . . . like we did at the last fork . . . or we could keep going this way."

Thisby ignored him and continued her search.

"That way leads to death bears," said Mingus, swaying gently in his lantern.

Everybody froze.

"It talks?" said Vas as a huge, doofy grin rapidly consumed his face.

Mingus turned bright pink with embarrassment.

"Yes, I talk! And I'd appreciate not being called 'it,' thank you very much!"

Vas was unconcerned with his faux pas and had already swooped in and pressed his face against Mingus's lantern, causing the poor slime to recoil in horror. This also put Vas much closer to Thisby than she felt comfortable with. She was about to suggest he back off, but something about the fading pine-needle scent of his soap was actually quite nice and made the words get lost somewhere between her brain and mouth.

"What's his name?" he asked Thisby—who was suddenly acutely aware that she might not smell as pleasant as he did.

"My name is Mingus," said Mingus. "We just covered that I can talk, so why are you asking her?"

It took Vas reaching up a curious finger to tap on Mingus's jar for Thisby to realize that things had gone too far. She grabbed Vas by the shoulders and guided him away.

"He doesn't like that," she said.

"Oh," said Vas.

"Fascinating," said Bero, who'd been fairly quiet up until this point, walking at the back of the group and reading his spell books.

"Yeah, that's all very interesting," said Donato. "But can we pick a way and just go? We've only got a few more hours left until nightfall."

Thisby knew he was right and understood his urgency. To the untrained adventurer, day and night made no difference inside a mountain, but just as it was outside, everything in here had its own natural rhythm. And even inside the Black Mountain, just like the rest of the world, the most dangerous things always came out at night. The trick now was figuring out which way to go. Mingus was right that they shouldn't go anywhere near the death bears, but the opposite way led them below Hangman's Falls, and Thisby was almost certain, based on what she'd seen so far, that that way would be full of traps. Still, when faced with a probable trap or imminent doom, there was really only one choice to make.

"We go right," she said. "Away from the death bears."

"Fantastic," said Donato, who'd already begun walking that way, grumbling to himself the entire time.

Thisby could only catch bits and pieces of what he was saying, but she could've sworn there was an air of disappointment that he wasn't getting a chance to square off against death bears. It hadn't taken her long upon meeting him to realize that Donato wasn't like the run-of-the-mill adventurers competing in the Wretched Scrattle. She briefly considered taking him up on the earlier offer of picking his brain about monsters, but it seemed like, at least for now, he was in no mood to talk shop. It was a shame. Thisby had always been curious about monsters that lived outside the dungeon.

The dungeon had far and away the widest selection of monsters anywhere in the world, but that didn't mean there weren't places where monsters still roamed free; they were just increasingly rare. Most monsters had been driven out of their natural habitats by the rapid advancement of humans, but there were still pockets of them here and there. Some of them were even quite famous, such as the troll communities along the Hyrion River or the imps who lived on the edge of the Yule Woods.

The latter had even given rise to a story that was frequently repeated among monsters of the dungeon: the story about a city of monsters located deep in the heart of the Yule Woods that dwarfed—no pun intended—the capital city of Nth. The city, as the story went depending on who was telling it, was governed completely by monsters, and their only irrevocable law was that no human was ever permitted inside the city walls. It was a tall tale, of course, and nobody with any sense truly believed it, but it was a nice story that made the monsters who heard it feel better about their lot in life, and as Thisby knew well, those were the kinds of stories that tended to stick around.

Thisby hung near the back of the group, distancing herself from the irritable hunter. As they walked, she noticed that Bero had closed his spell book and was gazing at Mingus. When Mingus noticed, he turned away and proceeded to glow a deep, angry red.

"I'm sorry for staring, Mingus," muttered Bero. "But you really *are* quite fascinating."

Mingus made a disinterested *hmpf* noise, but Bero sped up his pace anyway. With his big frame, it proved impossible for him to fit side by side next to Thisby in the narrow hallways, so he stayed one step behind, speaking directly into the lantern as if Thisby wasn't there.

"It's just . . . I thought your kind were only a legend," said Bero enthusiastically.

This was enough to get Mingus's attention. He turned around and his hue changed to a curious mauve.

"Huh? What do you mean, 'my kind'? Thisby, slow down."

Bero smiled at Mingus, showcasing his bright red cheeks, which were getting deeper red by the second as he struggled to keep up with Thisby's brisk pace. Thankfully, Thisby slowed down as per Mingus's request, and Bero nodded appreciatively.

"You know what you are, don't you?" said Bero gently. "You're not an ordinary slime. You have to know that much."

"I know I came from the Deep Down," said Mingus.

"The Deep Down?" snorted Bero before bursting into full-blown laughter.

It was a pleasant laugh, one without an ounce of cruelty or spite, but Mingus was growing impatient regardless. Donato, far ahead at the front of the line, turned his head to shush the conjurer but quickly abandoned the cause.

"What's so funny?" asked Mingus.

"I just can't think of anything further from the truth! The Deep Down!" laughed Bero. "You're a *pewder sér*. Or, as they're more commonly known . . . a star jelly."

Mingus turned white.

"Although there's nothing 'common' about you, and you're not from 'down' anywhere. You, my rare friend, come from as far 'up' as it goes! Beyond the stars."

Thisby looked back at Mingus to make sure her friend was okay. He was almost translucent.

"A . . . star jelly? How?" asked Mingus, struggling to find the words.

"That part you'd have to tell me! How a star jelly ended up in the deepest, darkest part of the Black Mountain . . . well, that's a total mystery, isn't it? Before we met, I thought star jellies were just a myth. But you're real enough! You probably have some questions for me, and I'd be happy to answer them to the best of my ability, but I have some questions I'd love to ask you as well! Once you've had time to, um, digest this, of course."

"Right. Sure," said Mingus.

Thisby was about to say something comforting but instead began to scream. The ground had given out from under her and she began to plummet.

Thisby hated traps. Nine out of ten times they were just as likely to hurt a monster as they were to stop an adventurer, although seeing as how she was now technically an adventurer herself, it seemed as if she'd stumbled upon the elusive one out of ten times when it'd worked exactly as intended. Despite this success, or perhaps in spite of it, her opinion of traps wasn't set to change anytime soon.

It was a small comfort, but when she hit her head during the fall, she'd been so momentarily stunned that she didn't even feel her arm break when she hit the ground. The instant she'd gathered her wits, however, she absolutely felt it . . . hence it being only a small comfort.

Lying on the ground, in hysterical pain, her right forearm visibly broken, Thisby scanned her immediate surroundings and tried her best to focus. The room she'd landed in was big, much more so than the hallway they'd just been in, and above her she could see light spilling down through the hole. It was the lone source of light in the room, a single beam cutting down into the darkened chamber as dust motes danced in the shaft. Her eyes began to adjust.

Everybody else had fallen as well, and they lay sprawled out around her, with the exception of Donato, who'd already pulled himself up to his feet and was leaning against a piece of a metal gate that had nearly impaled him moments ago. He made eye contact—singular—with Thisby and winced, apparently pretty banged up himself. Vas lay unmoving, and Thisby could hear Bero groaning behind her. But there was another noise. One that she couldn't place.

It sounded like drops of water on a hot pan. Or maybe it sounded more like a wet log thrown into a hot fire? Thisby listened closer. Hissing. It was definitely hissing. Hissing was never a good sign.

She clambered to her feet using only her left arm, as even the slightest pressure on the right sent shooting pain all the way up into her neck. Donato, who must've heard the hissing as well, drew his sword and stood protectively over Vas's unconscious body.

"What is that? Basilisk?" he whispered to Thisby.

She listened carefully. The hissing grew louder.

"I don't know," she said. "It's no basilisk. Could be new."

"Great," said Donato.

Thisby genuinely couldn't tell if he was being sarcastic.

The sound had begun to wrap around them like a slowly tightening noose, causing them to inch closer and closer together, huddled for safety beneath the lonely pillar of light. Thisby stared so hard into the pitch-black room beyond that her eyes began to play tricks on her. It was a phenomenon with which she was all too familiar. She knew that if you stared too long and hard at the dark, it began to move of its own accord, strange shapes would emerge, things that weren't really there would reveal themselves. Usually, it was only an illusion. But now, it was impossible to tell what was real and what wasn't.

There was definitely something out there. That much she knew. It was what she didn't know that frustrated her. If she only knew where she was, if she only knew what they were dealing with, she might be able to formulate some sort of plan.

"Mingus, glow!" Thisby whispered, but the only response she got in return was a pained little squeak. "Mingus! Come on!"

"I—I can't!"

"What do you mean, you can't?" rasped Thisby.

"I don't know! I just . . . I can't! I'm really freaking out right now, okay? I'm dealing with some pretty heavy stuff! Just this morning I thought I was a regular old slime. Now everything's so confusing. What am I? Why am I here?"

"Seriously? You've gotta deal with this right now?"

"It's like, you think you know who you are . . ." He trailed off.

"Ugh! Never mind!" said Thisby.

She unshouldered her backpack, threw open the flap, and began to dig around the inside with her one good arm. Every time her broken arm moved, she winced with pain and she had to fight back the urge to scream, but at last Thisby found what she was looking for. Donato looked over his shoulder just in time to see the gamekeeper flipping through a note-book.

"Some light reading?" he scoffed as the hissing sound grew louder and more irritable.

Thisby ignored him. She propped the book open on top of her backpack and turned the pages with her left hand until she found what she was looking for . . . a map.

"If I can figure out *where* we are, I might be able to get us out of here," she said.

"Wait. I can help, too," groaned Bero.

He stood up groggily and opened the small spell book he kept tucked into his belt. Using the lone beam for light, he read aloud from its pages. Within seconds, the room in which they stood was flooded with an incredible white light that settled down into a soft fireplace glow, which seemed to emanate from both everywhere and nowhere at once.

It took Thisby's eyes several seconds to adjust, and when they did, she realized the room in which they'd landed was a grand old dining hall of sorts, frozen in time mid-banquet. Long tables were set with plates of fossilized food, while fully clothed skeletal guests sat behind them, still clutching their goblets in eternal reverie. Nearby, a grand hearth was littered with the embers of a fire that hadn't burned in centuries, and at the front of the hall, upon a small stage, sat a quartet of the dead, holding musical instruments whose notes had been lost to the crescendo of time. There was one other feature of the room that caught her attention—and

perhaps it was the first thing that should have been mentioned—a colossal snake whose body was easily thicker than
the trunk of a large oak tree had completely encircled the
hall, blocking every exit.

# CHAPTER 13

"Lindorm!" bellowed Donato.

The serpent's head rose slowly from between two tables that were closer to the center of the room—and thus herself—than Thisby had hoped. The lindorm was nearly identical to a black snake, with the exception of the two long, curved horns that protruded from its massive head. Hissing angrily, the lindorm reared up so high that its horns scraped against the vaulted ceiling, knocking loose centuries-old mosaic tiles that fell like glittering rain. The monster's jaws split open both up and down and left and right, revealing fangs dripping with bright green saliva.

Unlike the hodag, Thisby had heard of lindorms,

although she'd never encountered one in person. Up until a moment ago, she hadn't even been completely convinced they were real. Lindorms were something of an urban legend down in the dungeon. Once in a while, a ghoul would wander too deep into the mountain and boast about running into one, but Thisby never put much stock in that kind of gossip. The two-hundred-foot snake towering over her was a sort of indisputable truth, however.

"Run!" yelled Donato.

Ignoring his own advice, the hunter hopped up onto a nearby table and charged directly at the nearest part of the thing, his sword in hand. The lindorm responded with a lightning-quick strike, smashing the table clean in half. Donato leapt to an adjacent one just in time and continued his sprint toward the creature, finally reaching it and managing to sink his sword deep through the lindorm's scales. Thisby expected to hear it to cry out in pain, but shockingly, it barely seemed to notice. The lindorm reared back for a second strike. By sheer luck, Donato avoided the creature's fangs but was knocked prone as the side of the snake's boulder-size head collided with his left shoulder. Donato's sword remained where it was, jutting out of the monster's side.

A flurry of glowing blue darts sailed over Thisby's head, and she turned to see Bero, spell book open, chanting and pointing dramatically. The blue darts shot from his hand and collided with the lindorm, exploding into little puffs of glittery sparkles that were more decorative than effective.

"I said, 'RUN!'" shouted Donato from the ground.

He hopped up to his feet, wrenched his blade free from the lindorm's side, and began to slash wildly, putting as many nicks into the monster's scaly hide as he could manage.

"Take Vas! Go! I'll hold it off!"

Vas had finally begun to wake up on his own due to the commotion, and Bero helped him the rest of the way to his feet. Vas threw his arm around the bigger man's shoulder, and together the two of them began limping toward the far end of the room, as far away from the head of the creature as they could get. Thisby was watching them climb over the lindorm's tail and wondering how she could do the same with her broken arm, when she heard a scream from behind and turned.

The lindorm had Donato in its jaws.

His sword had clattered to the floor beneath where he'd been lifted into the lindorm's jaws, and Thisby darted forward and picked it up.

"What are you doing?" shouted Mingus in her ear, but he was drowned out by the pounding of her own pulse. His voice sounded far away. Underwater.

Using her one good arm, Thisby drew the sword back like an ax and swung it as hard as she could into the lindorm. It was no use. The blade rebounded like she'd struck a steel beam, and the vibration shocked her hand so badly that she immediately dropped the sword. For the next few seconds,

*Thisby stood in the center of an endless whirlpool of scales.*

the hunter continued to struggle hopelessly against the monster's jaws, but the fight was over. The lindorm's fangs sank into him again, and there was one last, horrible scream before Donato vanished for good, down the creature's throat.

Mingus's voice faded in from somewhere very far off until Thisby could just barely make out what he was screaming. It was the word *run* over and over again. The moment the word finished its long journey from her ears to her brain, her legs kicked into gear without waiting for a second opinion.

The lindorm hissed at her and struck. Thisby slid beneath a nearby table and moments later the table was gone, exploding into a shower of wooden shards and plates of petrified food that rained down over her as she crawled back to her feet and continued to run. She wove in between tables and chairs as the lindorm gave chase. Somewhere up ahead, she could hear Bero and Vas yelling, but it was impossible to make out what they were saying.

Thisby skidded to a dead stop, her path blocked by a tree-trunk-size section of the lindorm's body. There was no way over it, at least none that would be quick enough for her escape, so she turned, half expecting to see the lindorm's open jaws coming for her, but instead she was greeted by an uncomfortable silence. The head of the beast was nowhere to be found. Black coils wrapped around her like rope on a large spool, where she was the axle. The lindorm's body completely encircled her.

She stood in the center of an endless whirlpool of scales.

She could see its ribs rising and falling with each breath. Feel the waves of its movement. It was hypnotic. From where she stood, there was no way of telling which end was the front and which end was the back, so there was no way of knowing where its head might emerge. Thisby spun around at each slight variation of sound: every clattering of a plate or fork, every loose mosaic tile finally breaking free and dropping to the floor. She turned so quickly that she began to feel dizzy.

"What do we do?" begged Mingus.

The question was largely rhetorical, which was one of the reasons why Thisby was so shocked to hear what came next. It wasn't the main reason.

"Yoooooou diiiiiiiiieeee," hissed the lindorm in a voice that seemed to come from everywhere all at once.

Thisby was so simultaneously startled and relieved to hear the lindorm speak that she almost laughed. If it wasn't for poor Donato, she very well might have. There was still a good chance that she wouldn't make it out of this alive, but at least now there was hope. There was always hope when you had a chance to talk things over.

The coils continued to swirl around her as she struggled to find the right words.

"Lindorm," she said. It was as good an opening as any. "We're not your enemy."

The lindorm contemplated this.

"You're in my nessssssssst."

"It was a mistake! We fell through the ceiling!"

"Yesssssss, the Oversssssseeeer," hissed the lindorm with contempt. "Shhhe put the hole. Shhhe is to blame. But no matter. You came through. You mussssssssst die."

Thisby felt dizzy again as she turned around and around in order to discern where the voice was coming from.

"Can we talk face-to-face? If you're going to kill me, it only seems fair."

Thisby felt the most delicate change behind her, almost like the most delicate breeze. She wouldn't have even noticed except that it caused the tiny hairs on the back of her neck to stand up. She turned to see the lindorm reared up so high that its horns almost touched the ceiling again. It stared at her intently. Its body had stopped moving.

"Faaaaaaaaair," it said.

Thisby tried to stop her mind from racing. She'd been in worse situations before, and she knew that panicking never helped anything. All she needed to do was come up with some sort of bargain. Something to which the lindorm couldn't say no. Something clever. Something cunning. Something brilliant.

"Please don't kill me," said Thisby.

"Whhhhaaaat?"

"Please don't kill me."

The lindorm paused. Perhaps it was considering her plea or perhaps it was simply stunned by the frankness of it.

"Whhhhhhy not?"

Thisby had to admit it was a fair follow-up question,

despite not having an answer ready. She didn't know anything about lindorms in particular, but she mulled over what she'd gathered so far. She knew that the lindorm didn't like the Overseer. That was obvious. Also, Thisby had lived her whole life in the dungeon and she'd never seen a lindorm. Not once. That was no easy task for a monster its size. That meant it valued its privacy.

"Because," she said, "if you let me go, I'll win the Wretched Scrattle and become the Master of the Black Mountain. And when I do, I'll make sure this room is sealed off and you never have to see me or anybody else ever again."

"Annnnd ifffff yooooou looooosssssssse?"

"If I lose, then you let one free meal get away. But you already ate my friend, so I don't think you're hungry. You only want to kill me so I don't come back. But the only way you're going to make sure that neither I nor anybody else ever comes back is to give me a chance to win. So let me go. You have nothing to lose and everything to gain."

There was a long silence as the lindorm considered the bargain.

"Whhhhhhy shhhhhould I trusssst yoooooou?" it hissed.

"Because I've been playing nice up until now."

The lindorm swooped down until it was directly in front of Thisby, daring her to make her next move.

"I haven't said anything about the fact that you called this your nest."

The lindorm opened its jaws and hissed angrily. Flecks of

bright green spittle flew at Thisby, and she held up her good arm to shield her face.

"It's not a threat!" she yelled. "But the only way you're gonna keep your babies safe is if I win and become the Master of the Black Mountain! I'll make sure nobody ever bothers you or them ever again! I promise!"

The lindorm closed its jaws, and its body began to move again, this time sliding out of Thisby's way and revealing an exit on the far side of the chamber.

"Doooooon't coooooome baaaaaaaack," said the lindorm.

Thisby wasted no time hurrying toward the exit to join up with Vas and Bero, the excruciating pain of her broken arm returning now that the adrenaline was wearing off. The lindorm watched her go, its eyes transfixed on the small girl and her backpack until the lantern glow disappeared into the darkness of the tunnel.

Iphigenia sat on a hill and watched as big, fluffy clouds drifted over the Black Mountain, casting purple, bruise-like shadows on its deeply pockmarked skin. Nothing grew on the Black Mountain, but it still had a sort of primitive, naturalistic beauty, like the skeleton of some long-dead thing. It would've been a perfect opportunity to practice plein air painting but Iphigenia was well aware of her limitations as a painter and doubted she'd be able to do the scene justice. Besides, even if she'd wanted to try, she'd left all her paints back in the capital. So instead she sat very still and tried to imagine what was happening inside the mountain.

She tried to convince herself that Thisby wasn't somewhere in mortal danger, but her imagination simply wasn't that good. If there was a person who'd put herself in mortal danger more frequently, Iphigenia had yet to meet them and was certain she didn't want to. She pictured Thisby hanging from a cliff, running from an angry troll, and being swallowed alive by a wyvern before she stumbled, at last, onto a mental image of Thisby playing piano alongside a long-fingernailed vampire, and the thought made Iphigenia laugh until she forgot the whole pointless exercise. And it really was pointless, which was exactly how the Princess had felt ever since Thisby left for the Wretched Scrattle. As long as Thisby was in there and she was out here, there was nothing she could do.

If Iphigenia was being perfectly honest, she thought that General Lutgard would've tracked her down by now. Perhaps Lillia's mind was so well-honed for strategy that she didn't have any room left for investigative work. Iphigenia had been staying at the Rat-Upon-a-Cat in Three Fingers under the pseudonym "Thisby Catface" since the Wretched Scrattle began, and she—in case that name wasn't enough of a clue—hadn't been trying too hard to remain inconspicuous. She was frankly shocked that outside of the incident that first night, nobody had recognized her since. She figured it probably had something to do with how she was dressed—she'd switched over to a rather drab outfit she picked up at Salty

Sam's—and how long she'd been going in between baths. The lack of a private tub in her quarters, not to mention the lack of handmaidens present to fill it with hot water, cover the surface with rose hips, brush her hair, and present her with pillowy-soft towels the moment she was done had proved to be a fairly effective counterargument to her initial disgust at going more than twenty-four hours without bathing.

Although there'd been some initial excitement at being completely independent in a brand-new place, by the end of Iphigenia's first full day alone in town, Three Fingers had already exhausted its appeal. That morning, after she'd wished Thisby luck and sent her off to the Wretched Scrattle, Iphigenia had strolled the city, visited the shops, had dinner at the nicest restaurant in town—which was roughly equivalent to the worst restaurant in the capital—and finished her evening with a walk through the meadow to watch the sunset, when at last she'd lain down to sleep in her scratchy straw bed and the foolishness of her plan finally dawned on her. What was she going to do now?

As soon as the next morning, she found herself missing the hustle and bustle of the castle. She missed having work to do. She missed having people to talk to. She missed the feeling of an existence with consequence. Yesterday, Iphigenia snatched up every book in Three Fingers that she could get her hands on, but she didn't feel like reading. She needed action. She needed excitement. She needed a bath.

The little hill on which she sat watching the Black

Mountain had quickly become her favorite respite from the village. The only downside was that it was far enough away from Three Fingers that when you went back, you had to reacclimate to the stink. After twenty minutes or so inside the village, though, you hardly noticed the smell, but those first few were absolutely torturous. It wasn't uncommon for lifelong residents to go "nose blind," a rare condition in which prolonged exposure to the town's intense stench actually caused their sense of smell to disappear. Iphigenia was optimistic that she hadn't lived in Three Fingers long enough to suffer irreversible nose damage but had been disturbed the other day when she realized she couldn't smell a lilac bush.

Iphigenia reopened her book, a rather boring history text, and nodded off within minutes. When she awoke, it was to the sound of trumpets—which was every bit as unpleasant as you'd imagine. She jerked awake and looked out to see a royal carriage, the same one she'd traveled in all the way from Lyra Castelis, rumbling up over the horizon in a cloud of dust.

It was about time.

Iphigenia brushed the dry grass from her dress and headed down to the road, prepared to face what was likely a screaming, red-faced Lillia. She was so certain it'd be quite the scene that she was nonplussed to see only the well-manicured hand of the General appear to wave her aboard. Iphigenia exhaled. She couldn't help but feel a bit disappointed. Still, there was nothing else to do now but hike up her dress and climb the small ladder that the footmen had laid out for her.

Everything inside the royal carriage was exactly the way it'd been when she'd seen it last, including the stony-faced General Lillia Lutgard, who, if she was disturbed by the Princess's disappearing act, was adamantly refusing to show it.

"Are you about done?" asked General Lutgard.

Iphigenia plopped down on the cushions and stared at the General, who was pouring a cup of coffee from a silver carafe. Lillia rapped twice on the driver's-side wall of the carriage, and they began to move with a bit of jolt.

"Excuse me?" said Iphigenia, hating that she'd somehow lost the upper hand.

"Are you about done?" repeated the General with a sigh before she continued, "With whatever it was you thought you were doing."

Iphigenia felt a little relieved that the General was at least showing some signs of annoyance.

"Yes, I suppose I am."

"Good," said General Lutgard.

Iphigenia waited, hoping for more.

"Is that it?" she asked.

"You tell me," said the General. "I'm happy to let you spend a few more days in Three Fingers if you're not satisfied with your little vacation."

"You knew where I was?"

"Of course. I spoke with the Master of the Black Mountain. I know where you've been and I know why you came.

To help your little friend enter the Wretched Scrattle."

"You're angry," said Iphigenia, barely suppressing a smirk.

"You won't get a rise out of me like your father, dear. Frankly, I don't care what you were doing here. That's no business but your own. You are the future Queen. What I don't care for is how you did it. By risking your own life, you also put mine at risk. You're trying to make me into an enemy when I am, in fact, one of the greatest allies you could possibly have. I serve the crown and I serve you, lest you forget. You could have ordered me to bring you here after we finished the mission we were on, the one your father entrusted you to see through. That is well within your authority, and I would've been in no position to deny you. You could have acted like a Queen, but instead you ran away like a child. No, I'm not angry with you. I am, however, disappointed at your stupidity and shortsightedness."

Iphigenia's face turned bright red.

"How—how . . . who do you think you are! I'm going to be your Queen!" she screamed.

"If you behave like a child, I will treat you like one. If you behave like a Queen, I will treat you like one."

"Stop this carriage!" screeched Iphigenia.

With a lurch, the carriage came to a complete stop.

"See how easy that was?" said Lillia.

Iphigenia was so angry that she missed the handle several times before she managed to finally grab it and fling the carriage door open. With a loud smack, the door banged into the side of the carriage, and the noise spooked the horses, who jerked the whole thing forward, throwing Iphigenia clean from the coach. She stood up and spun to see Lillia standing in the door to the carriage, looking smug. It was too much to bear.

"I'll have you demoted! You'll be mopping floors in the dungeon by the time I'm done with you!" yelled Iphigenia.

"You sound just like your brother."

Iphigenia's heart stopped, and she felt tears begin to well up in her eyes. If it wasn't for the sound of a second carriage coming down the road, she was sure she would've burst into tears. They both turned to watch.

It wasn't a carriage but a proper war wagon, the kind meant for hauling supplies around a battlefield. It was heavily reinforced, and the armored plates that surrounded it were dented, having seen more than their fair share of combat. Iphigenia would've been intimidated by the approach of such a vehicle except it was flying the flag of Nth. Below that was a second, smaller flag, emblazoned with a crest that looked vaguely familiar, but Iphigenia couldn't quite push through her anger to remember. When it came to a stop no more than twenty yards away, a handsome young soldier hopped off and approached them, holding his helmet tucked beneath his arm. His outfit was standard issue for the Nth military, but like the wagon, his gear had seen better days.

"General Lutgard! I'm so glad we found you! Urgent news!"

It took Lillia directing several expressive nods toward the Princess for the soldier to realize who he was in the presence of, and once it dawned on him, he practically did a double take before dropping down to one knee and apologizing. Iphigenia waved him to his feet. It wasn't his fault he didn't recognize her. She had caught her reflection in one of the mirrors inside the carriage, and she'd barely recognized herself.

"What news?" Iphigenia asked, mostly so he would stop apologizing.

"Can we speak in private?" he asked.

When Lillia hesitated, Iphigenia chimed in, "I have a place. We'll take you there."

The carriage led them back into town, where they convened in Iphigenia's room at the Rat-Upon-a-Cat, which she'd called home for the past few days.

The handsome soldier, who'd introduced himself as Oren, was the commander of the men stationed at Hagstooth Pass, the northeasternmost post of the Nthian army. The Hagstooth Pass station was home to a small company of soldiers tasked with an extremely important job: serving as the dividing line between Nth and Umberfall in the Witchkünder Mountains.

Oren politely refused the seat he was offered, as it was the only chair in the room and he was a gentleman. Yet decorum dictated that if one member of the party was not seated, then everybody else should stand as well, as an act of solidarity, so the three of them stood around Iphigenia's small room while a perfectly good chair remained unoccupied. To make matters worse, the soldier could not stop shifting his weight from foot to foot as if he desperately wanted to pace or had to use the bathroom, and either way it was putting Iphigenia on edge. When she tried to make eye contact with him, he seemed intent on looking anywhere else.

"You've probably already guessed why I'm here," said Oren, staring at his feet and then glancing toward Lillia, whom he seemed less hesitant to address.

"You tell me," said Lillia sternly. She was clearly tired of his hemming and hawing.

"Agents from Umberfall have slipped across the border."

While this wasn't exactly good news, it wasn't particularly shocking, either. Nth and Umberfall had a long history of spying on each other. It was what Marl, the current Overseer of the Black Mountain, had been doing right up until her recent appointment.

"And?" asked Lillia.

The agent hesitated only briefly, remembering that Lillia's patience was rapidly dwindling.

"And they have entered the Wretched Scrattle."

Lillia crossed her arms.

"There's more," added Oren before she had a chance to ask. "We captured one of their spies. He told us that when they win, it's only the beginning. We think this means full-on war. General, if the Umberfallians take over the

Black Mountain, they're going to weaponize the dungeon."

Iphigenia had heard this all before. Marl had used the same argument as a reason why she should be placed in the dungeon as Overseer in the first place. It was a frightening thought, to be sure. There were some in the capital who believed that the only sure way to prevent such a thing from happening was for Nth to do it first, but thankfully, cooler heads had always prevailed. And when Iphigenia took power, she was ready to ensure the tradition of Nth remaining hands-off with the Black Mountain. But the fear was there. The fear of the dungeon somehow turning against the people of Nth was real, and it would never go away.

"The Master himself told me there were protections in place to ensure that nobody from outside Nth could enter the tournament," said General Lutgard, intentionally trailing off to imply that she wanted an answer without having to ask a question.

Oren obliged. "We know that they're working with somebody from inside Nth. A traitor. What we don't know is the specifics of their agreement."

General Lutgard grew indignant. "I was told that the magical barrier that allowed physical entry into the mountain was designed in a way that it would prevent—physically prevent—certain types of people from entering the mountain . . . not just wizards and sorcerers but also Umberfallians or anybody without the proper paperwork—"

"Magic is only a riddle, designed to be solved," interrupted

Iphigenia. "The same way that rules are made to be broken. All the Umberfallians had to do was find somebody inside Nth, somebody who could freely enter the tournament."

Lillia frowned and shook her head, "This is why I don't trust magic."

Iphigenia smiled at her and immediately regretted the implied forgiveness, still feeling the sting of the General's words from earlier.

"So, who is this traitor, exactly?" asked Lillia.

"All we have is a name. We've already deployed a unit to the suspect's father's mining operation in the southern reaches for further questioning."

"And what is his name?" sighed Lillia, clearly annoyed that she had to ask.

"Vaswell Gandy," said Oren.

Iphigenia's jaw dropped. "Of the Flatbottom Gandys?"

# CHAPTER 14

Thisby sat with her back against the mossy cave wall and flipped through her notebooks by the soft glow of Mingus's blue-green light. She was hoping to find a map that might show where they'd ended up. The detour through the dining hall had sent them into a previously undiscovered section of the dungeon, something that up until that point she'd assumed wasn't possible.

For hours after the encounter, they'd wandered around a series of perfectly round narrow tunnels that seemed as if they'd been made intentionally for the lindorm to travel through. Thisby couldn't help but think that if Donato were still with them, he'd have been able to help verify that idea.

She also suspected that they wouldn't have passed through the same tunnels so many times before she'd finally come up with the idea to leave a trail to mark where they'd already been. It was the kind of idea that would've been second nature to a hunter.

There was a shuffling noise near the rounded entrance to the cave, and Mingus dimmed his light.

"Hello?" whispered Thisby.

"Hello," replied Bero, emerging from the dark and entering their makeshift camp. "Vas still asleep?"

Thisby glanced toward the back of the cave at Vas, who was, in fact, still fast asleep and snoring in a way that was somehow more charming than annoying.

"Yeah," said Thisby.

"How's your arm?" he asked, crawling awkwardly into the small cave.

It was cramped inside, a bit more of a nook than a proper cave, but Thisby thought it was comfy enough. She'd definitely slept in worse.

"Better," she said, waving it as evidence.

When Mingus's healing magic wasn't quite getting the job done, Bero had managed to mend her arm with a spell from one of the many books he carried with him in his satchel. The book this particular spell had come from was white and bore a crest of a leech wrapped around a dagger. He told her it was all healing spells. Thisby thought that it might have been an exaggeration to say that her arm was "healed," but at the very least it was usable. It was still hard to make a tight fist.

"You find anything?" he asked.

"Not yet."

"Mind if I look?"

Thisby shook her head, and Bero grabbed a notebook from the small pile of them she'd pulled out of her backpack. He turned the pages quickly, barely looking at them, like a child pretending to read.

"Are you okay?" Thisby asked.

Bero set down the notebook slowly.

"We grew up together," he said. "Donato and I."

Thisby set her notebook down as well.

"Actually, we served in the army together, believe it or not."

Thisby went to ask the inevitable question, but Bero answered it first.

"I know. I don't look like much of a soldier, do I? But in the army, everyone has their part. Magic users especially. We do things, we see things, things that nobody else gets to see . . . not that they'd want to. Donato was, for lack of a better term, my bodyguard. That's what they do—pair a soft-bodied wizard type like me with somebody more capable in battle and send us into the field together. He saved my life. More than once. And what did I do to repay him? I ran away. Ran like the coward I am. And now he's dead."

Thisby said nothing.

"Well, that's how these missions go, I suppose. I knew that in the army and I know that now. And my mission is to make sure he lives," he said, gesturing at the soundly sleeping Vas. "That's my mission."

Thisby opened her mouth to say something, but no words came out.

"You don't need to say anything," said Bero with a sad smile. "I saw what you did back there. You ran in to help Donato without a second thought. You risked your life for someone you barely knew. That's the difference between us. One of many, I hope."

Bero reached into his satchel and withdrew a small water-skin that Thisby suspected wasn't full of water and took a long drink from it. He offered a drink to Thisby but she politely declined. He laughed a bit too loudly, and Vas stirred in his sleep.

"Why did you take this job?" asked Thisby. It seemed rude, but she couldn't help herself. Bero just didn't seem the type.

"The world is always changing," said Bero. "That's the first thing they teach you at the Grand College of Arcanology—*go, Werewolves!*—and it's as immutable a law of nature as any that I've ever learned. The balance shifts constantly. Good to evil, evil to good. You know this mountain is important, I assume?"

Thisby nodded but wasn't quite sure she was defining "important" the same way as he'd meant it. Bero nodded back in agreement anyway.

"Outside these walls, people think that the Black Mountain is pure evil. After all, it is the thing that grew over where the Eyes in the Dark fell—if you believe the legend."

She hoped Bero didn't see her shiver when the chill ran up her spine at the mention of the Eyes in the Dark.

"But that's too easy an answer. The Black Mountain isn't evil. Nor is it good. It's the needle upon which those scales rest, forever swaying in the breeze. It's the dividing line between order and chaos. If those scales were to ever tip too far, if one side were to upset that balance . . ." Bero trailed off.

"That's what wizards do. Magic folks, like me. We maintain the balance."

"And shoot sparkles out of your hands," Thisby said automatically.

Bero paused and then burst out laughing. Vas sat up half-awake, mumbled something incoherent, and then fell immediately back asleep.

"Yes, and shoot sparkles out of our hands," admitted Bero.

There wasn't much conversation after that. Thisby made her way to bed and left Bero to flip through her notebooks. She awoke several times in the middle of the night to find him still awake, still reading through her notebooks with bleary eyes, taking long pulls from his seemingly bottomless waterskin. He barely seemed to notice her at all.

When Thisby crawled out of her sleeping bag the next morning, Bero and Vas were already up and standing outside their small cave, examining their surroundings. Bero had one of Thisby's notebooks open and was pointing out something to Vas, who had his face scrunched up as if he was trying very hard to understand. When Bero saw Thisby, he waved her over excitedly.

"I think I found a way out of here!" he said, pointing to the notebook.

Bero had gotten up early to scout ahead—if he'd slept at all—and had found a path that potentially led out of their current uncharted area. He'd even been so bold as to add his own notes to a previously unfinished map Thisby had drawn several years ago.

"Where does it lead?" she asked, trying her best to hide how upset she was that a stranger had written in one of her precious notebooks.

"There are actually several paths from here, but they all funnel into an area you've labeled with a horned skull and crossbones," Bero remarked.

"Giant's Crossing," said Thisby.

She'd been hoping to avoid Giant's Crossing, since it had seemed to her like an obvious spot for the Overseer to place a trap. It was a choke point that separated what was generally considered the top third of the dungeon from the bottom two-thirds. If you were making your way from the bottom of the mountain to the top, as everybody in the Wretched Scrattle was, it was almost inevitable that you'd pass through the crossing at some point, and that was what frightened her.

It was a perfect spot to eliminate careless competitors.

Giant's Crossing was a series of narrow bridges stretched like crisscrossing guitar strings over the mouth of a yawning abyss three hundred yards wide. On every side were thundering waterfalls, which fed down into the widest part of the Floating River, known as Long Lost Lake—at least that was what Grunda had called it. Thisby had never fully understood how such a huge lake could be lost for very long. If you had the misfortune of falling into Giant's Crossing and the thousand-foot drop didn't kill you—which it most definitely would—the horrors waiting below the surface of Long Lost Lake would be waiting to finish the job.

Thisby studied the map again. Assuming that Bero's additions were correct, there didn't seem to be any way to avoid the crossing.

"Is something wrong?" asked Bero.

"Not yet," said Thisby gravely.

The Master awoke, or perhaps it's better to say "hatched," from a shell of crusted purple goo. He spent several minutes choking and gasping for air on his filthy cell floor before finally getting his wits about him and considering how he'd ended up in such a predicament.

"This is what I get for helping a goblin," he muttered to himself.

Leaning against the only piece of furniture in the room—a foul-smelling straw mattress—he picked out bits of slime that were painfully caked in the horseshoe of hair that encircled his thankfully mostly bald head as he took inventory of his situation. The outlook wasn't great.

The Master, in his many years as such, had never left Castle Grimstone. He'd never set foot in the dungeon, and that included the room he was currently in, called, confusingly enough, "the dungeon." While it may seem obvious that *the* dungeon would have *a* dungeon, it was, oddly enough, perhaps its least utilized room.[4]

He was only a few floors below Thisby's bedroom, really just a stone's throw from the castle gates, and yet he might as well have been in the Deep Down for as much good as it did him. He checked his pockets and was surprised to discover that in her haste to capture him, Marl hadn't taken his things. He still had a few gold coins, a bottle of facial moisturizer—which he desperately needed at the moment—and his scrobble. It was the last of these that gave him any hope at all. If he was lucky, the gamekeeper was still alive and possibly willing to free him.

---

4 It's not particularly shocking, but the reason "the dungeon" was called "the dungeon" was because it'd begun as one. There were several iterations of the dungeon's origin story, but the most popular one was that during the construction of Castle Grimstone, Elphond the Evil had dug down into the Black Mountain in order to build a dungeon—the traditional kind of dungeon with big iron-barred cells and shackles affixed to the walls, maybe some skeletons here and a torture rack there, that kind of place—but when he was digging down into the mountain to make room for it, he'd accidentally discovered the massive structures the Dünkeldwarves had built thousands of years earlier. When Elphond found these, he decided to claim it all as his own, as a natural extension of his "dungeon," and the name just sort of stuck. So, technically, there was still "a dungeon" in "the dungeon," although, for the sake of clarity, the dungeon within the dungeon was commonly referred to as "the hold."

There was a chance that she wouldn't. The Master and Grunda had struck a deal: he'd give Thisby's entry form the official stamp without Marl finding out, and if Thisby won the Wretched Scrattle and became the Master, he'd get to leave the Black Mountain in one piece, never to return. The way he saw it, if somebody aside from Thisby won, they'd take him to the hangman as soon as they'd settled into his chair. If nobody won and Marl stuck around, it'd only be a matter of time before a blade found its way to his neck as he slept. And getting rid of Marl himself was too risky as long as she had the backing of the King. He was doomed any way he sliced it; the only option was to take Grunda's deal and hope the gamekeeper would be true to her word.

Still, he wasn't eager to call her and ask for help. It was hard to imagine what she would get out of freeing him from prison, and the Master had a hard time understanding why anybody would ever do anything unless they stood to gain from it in some way. Ultimately, however, he had no choice but to try.

The Master was fishing around in his pocket for the scrobble when he heard voices coming down the hall and saw the first flicker of torchlight. He removed his hand from his pocket and waited as the voices grew near.

"These things happen," said one of the voices. "It's not worth worrying about."

"I know, it's just . . . poor kid," said the other voice. "You know I used to babysit her sometimes during goblin holidays."

Their footsteps grew closer, and the Master considered pretending to be asleep. It seemed like a pretty classic eavesdropping ruse, but he was still the Master and refused to lower himself to such infantile tricks.

"Let me go. Now," he boomed when the voices reached his cell.

The two ghouls who appeared were shocked to see the Master awake and mostly uncrusted. The taller of the two ghouls he recognized as one of his gate guards, and the smaller one looked familiar, but he couldn't place where he'd seen her around the castle. The bigger one was carrying the torch, while the smaller one carried a bag filled with scrolls and a hammer. They both instinctively bowed.

"Master!" said the smaller ghoul. "So good to see you awake!"

"Let me out of here right now or I will fry what is left of your desecrated husks in molten lead and use your parts as paperweights for all eternity!"

It was a pretty good threat as far as threats go.

"I-I'm sorry, but we can't," said the bigger ghoul.

"What do you mean, you can't?" snarled the Master.

"Overseer's orders," said the small one. "Said you were a traitor to the crown. Anybody who helps you has to answer to the King of Nth."

The Master's face turned bright red.

"And that's worse than answering to me?" he yelled.

Truthfully, as long as he was behind bars, he knew that it

was. All this time cultivating an aura of fear in the dungeon and it'd been undone by that conniving bureaucratic wizard.

"Fine," said the Master, realizing his threats would be idle so long as he was the one locked up. "Be that way."

The ghouls muttered some sort of awkward farewell and attempted to hurry on, but the Master stopped them as he approached the cell bars.

"What's in that bag?" he demanded. "You can surely at least tell me that."

The ghouls hesitated, because it was likely that they weren't supposed to tell him that, but the smaller one relented. She pulled a scroll out of her bag and handed it to the Master through the bars. He unrolled it.

The scroll contained a crude portrait of the game-keeper beneath big red letters proclaiming, *10,000 GOLD REWARD*. Smaller print at the bottom read, *Dead or Alive*, only the word "Alive" was in much smaller print. Below that, even smaller yet, were the words *See Overseer for details. Must provide proof.*

"She's put a bounty on her," said the Master.

"We've been putting them up all over the dungeon," said the smaller ghoul.

"Marl's orders," added the big one. He seemed quick to point out that he had no say in the matter.

"Right. Of course," said the Master, handing the scroll back.

The two ghouls hurried out of the hold as quickly as

possible, and when the Master was sure they were gone, he pulled out his scrobble, tapped the crystal three times, and waited for Thisby to pick up.

The trip to Giant's Crossing was mercifully uneventful. Thisby moved slowly and kept an eye out for secret passages, while Vas and Bero trudged along behind her, chatting about nothing and everything at the same time. Through her unintentional eavesdropping, Thisby learned that Vas's father had been sick and, according to Vas, was beginning to think about retiring from the "mining game." They talked about Donato as well, but in much lighter tones than Thisby had heard from Bero last night.

She wondered if Bero was trying to remain upbeat for Vas's sake, and Thisby found herself extremely upset by the notion. Bero had just lost what might have been his closest friend in the entire world, but instead of consoling him, the poor little noble boy just "wanted to keep things light." Why put any worry lines on his precious little forehead? He was still treating this whole thing like some sort of game. It was disgusting.

"What do you think, Thisby?" asked Vas.

She grimaced. "What do I think about what?"

He laughed. "About my plan? Weren't you listening?"

Vas bounded over to Thisby and got uncomfortably close to her.

"Well, you're the one I should be selling the idea to!

You're going to be the next Master of the Black Mountain!"
He beamed.

Thisby said nothing, but Vas continued undeterred.

"Picture this! A cart that runs on rails! A whole mess of
them, actually! No horses needed! My father has been working on a prototype for some time now. What I'm proposing is
that we bore a hole straight through the mountain and open
up trade between Nth and Umberfall! What do you think?
It's a win-win! Nth makes money, the Black Mountain makes
money, you make money, I make money, naturally, since I'd
own the rails—"

"I think it's disgusting," she cut him off.

He looked genuinely wounded.

"What? Why? We don't have to be friends with Umberfall to trade with them. I know, it's complicated. But Father
always said—"

"I don't care what your father said, and I don't care about
Umberfall! What I care about are the creatures that live in
this mountain. Why don't you get that? Why does nobody
get that?" shouted Thisby.

"But—"

"Why can't everyone just leave us alone!"

Thisby stomped off ahead, leaving a bewildered-looking
Vas and Bero behind.

She was rounding a corner when a buzzing from her
pocket made her jump. Her heart was still racing when
she realized that the noise was coming from her scrobble.

Glancing back over her shoulder, Thisby made sure that Vas and Bero weren't close enough to hear her and opened it carefully.

Sure enough, the Master was on the screen, though looking much the worse for wear.

"Gamekeeper!" he shouted. "It's you!"

Thisby wasn't sure who else it could have been, but she could tell he wasn't looking like his normal self, so she forgave the weirdness of the introduction.

"What's going on?" she whispered. "Where are you?"

She wasn't sure why she didn't want Bero or Vas to see that she had a direct line to the Master, but she knew that she didn't. At least not yet.

"I'm in the dungeon."

"You're in the dungeon?" asked Thisby. "Where?"

"In the dungeon!" he repeated impatiently.

"The dungeon's very big. You're going to have to be more specific," she said.

The Master sighed.

"I mean the *hold*," he said.

"Oh, well, you should really just say that next time. It's very confusing."

She wasn't wrong.

"Never mind! I need to warn you, Marl's gone off the deep end. She's thrown me in the dun—the hold, and she's put out a bounty for—"

"Wait! Shhh!" whispered Thisby.

Vas and Bero's footsteps were coming closer.

"I've got to go!" said Thisby. "I'll be in touch soon!"

She snapped the scrobble closed and crammed it back into her pocket just as Vas and Bero rounded the corner. They looked just as uncomfortable to see her as she did to see them.

"Thisby, I'm sorry. I didn't mean to upset you," said Vas.

"Never mind," said Thisby. Thanks to the Master's call, she'd momentarily forgotten what she was angry about, but now it all came flooding back. "Come on. We're almost there."

It was easy for Thisby to tell when they were close to Giant's Crossing. She'd felt the rumbling through the soles of her boots for some time already, and when they'd gotten close enough to smell the wet, fishy air, the roar of the water-falls made conversation hopeless.

As they emerged into Giant's Crossing, Thisby heard Vas squeak and turned in time to see him nearly lose his balance. He took a step back and pressed himself against the wall, his legs as wobbly as a day-old fawn. Thisby would've laughed if she hadn't felt the sharp snap of vertigo herself.

She took a few steps out onto the large, arching stone bridge. The perpetual motion of the waterfalls, combined with the constant rumbling vibration of the chamber, made her feel as if she was sitting inside a bass drum rolling down a hill. It was enough to cause even a fleet-footed person such as herself to lose her balance if she wasn't careful, and in that way, Giant's Crossing itself was already a sort of trap.

Unfortunately, being that this was the Wretched Scrattle, it wasn't the only trap. Thisby spotted the other one standing on one of the many bridges that crisscrossed below theirs, in the form of a twelve-foot-tall minotaur carrying a war hammer in one hand as if it were a child's toy.

Thisby stopped and tapped Bero on the shoulder, and pointed down at the minotaur. He nodded and then showed Vas, who nearly had a heart attack. Thisby held a finger up to her lips to indicate they should be quiet, and then she proceeded to lead the way, stepping carefully across the stone bridge.

Everything in Giant's Crossing was wet and covered with a fine layer of slime, including the annoyingly railing-free bridges. Years of spray from the waterfalls—not to mention an unsettling amount of pterodactyl droppings—had done their best to make everything as slippery as possible. Thisby had good boots and was accustomed to being careful, but she quickly realized she was the exception. Glancing over her shoulder, she watched Vas and Bero flail their arms in an attempt to keep their balance.

She looked again down over the side of the bridge they were on. The minotaur was still there but had stopped moving. He cocked his head and appeared to be listening. Thisby turned back to the others and waved for them to stop moving, but Vas had his eyes fixed firmly on the path in front of him, preoccupied with keeping his footing; a task that was immeasurably difficult in his fancy leather dress boots.

*"I know who you are," laughed the minotaur.*

In *Thisby's Dungeon Survival Guide*—which she'd hastily written for Jono when she realized that he'd be filling in for her as gamekeeper—she'd included a list of items that anybody who wanted to survive in the dungeon more than a couple of hours must bring with them. At the very top of that list, above swords and daggers, above a waterskin and rations, above even the ubiquitously helpful "ten-foot pole," was, in all caps, "A GOOD PAIR OF BOOTS." It was astounding to her that so many adventurers arrived in fancy, slick-soled dress boots or riding boots or something else entirely impractical for traversing a dungeon.

Thisby looked over at their destination across the bridge and back again at Vas just in time to see him slip and fall face-first onto the bridge with a loud, wet smack. When she looked down toward the minotaur, he was gone.

Thisby pushed past Bero and dragged Vas to his feet.

"Run!" she commanded, pulling at him.

He shrugged helplessly and pointed to his ear. It was very loud in here.

Thisby took a deep breath.

"RUN!" she screamed at the top of her lungs, inches from his ear.

Vas recoiled but only for a second, and then Thisby saw something terrible that made her heart freeze. The minotaur had reappeared, leaping from bridge to bridge as casually as a child jumping on rocks to cross a shallow stream. On his second jump, he almost missed and was barely able to pull himself up. When he did, Thisby noticed that he was laughing. This was all a game to him.

Thisby tugged at Vas's collar, but he refused to run.

"I'LL FALL!" he screamed in her ear. "I WON'T MAKE IT!"

The minotaur was closer now. Only a few jumps away.

"COME ON!" yelled Thisby.

"I CAN'T!"

"YES, YOU CAN!"

The minotaur was just about to jump again when they caught their first break. A pair of adventurers appeared at the end of the bridge just below the one on which the minotaur stood. For a moment, the minotaur remained in a state of limbo, stuck between his two quarries, but in the end, he chose the new arrivals.

Unleashing a bellow loud enough to be heard over the roar of the waterfalls, the minotaur jumped down and charged them. The first one held his ground, drawing a short sword out of a scabbard. The other, however, realized the foolishness of this endeavor and decided to jump for it. She launched herself at the closest bridge but didn't make it. It struck Thisby as odd that the woman didn't scream on her way down until it dawned on her that she probably did, only to have her last scream swallowed up by the thunder of the falls. As foolish as her leap of faith had been, however, she was correct in the assumption that the man would suffer a worse fate. The minotaur swung his war hammer like a flyswatter and sent the man sailing into the abyss.

Thisby pulled at Vas again, but when he refused to budge, she let go and ran. Bero watched her run, unsure if he should stay or go as the minotaur turned his attention back to them and began his ascension. Thisby was at the end of the bridge before she looked back and realized Bero had stayed behind as well, bound by duty. He'd pulled out a spell book and was looking frantically for something that might save them from the doom that was coming for them all.

With a tremendous bellow, the minotaur burst forth as if he'd risen up out of the abyss itself. He landed on the bridge, soaked in mist and thrilled by the hunt. The impact of his landing shook the thin walkway to the point where Thisby winced as she waited for it to collapse. The bridge remained. Unfortunately, so did the minotaur.

Her view was blocked by the minotaur's massive form, so she saw only the flashes of Bero's spells as they burst around him like fireworks. The monster slowed and shielded his eyes from the lights, but didn't stop walking forward.

"Cheater!" the minotaur bellowed.

Still shielding his eyes from the flashes, the minotaur drew back his war hammer and swung wildly, missing both Vas and Bero. He howled, stepped closer, and drew back for another swing.

"WAIT!" shouted Thisby, running back toward the minotaur. "PLEASE, WAIT!"

The beast turned in her direction, as if noticing her for

the first time. He snarled.

When Thisby had first been brought into the dungeon as a baby, she was carried in by a minotaur. True, he was planning to eat her, but he didn't, and that was what was important. Last year, when she'd summoned all the creatures of the dungeon to battle against the Deep Dwellers, minotaurs had fought alongside her and the rest of the monsters. These were not mindless creatures. They could be reasoned with.

"STOP! I'm Thisby, the gamekeeper! I'm on your side!"

"I know who you are," laughed the minotaur. "And I'd like my ten thousand gold."

"Your what?" asked Thisby.

The minotaur's war hammer whooshed by so close that it brushed her hair on the way down. The shock wave as it struck the stone bridge knocked Thisby off her feet and sent her sprawling. She looked up in time to see the minotaur lifting the hammer again with both hands. This was it.

Thisby closed her eyes tight and thought of the gardens of Lyra Castelis. She pictured the rows of perfect flowers. When she'd first seen them, she'd thought they were so unnecessary. But now, the moment before she'd die, they were all she could think about.

"COME ON! GET UP! GET UP!"

Thisby opened her eyes to find that the minotaur was still there, his war hammer still drawn back, ready to turn her into paste. But he wasn't moving. She stood up.

From between the minotaur's legs she could see that Bero was frantically waving her over.

"WE'VE ONLY GOT A FEW SECONDS! HURRY!" he shouted at the top of his voice.

Thisby scrambled forward on all fours, ducking between the minotaur's wet, hairy legs, trying her best to hold her breath as she did. When she came through the other side, Bero was chanting something from a page in his spell book and holding Vas's hand. Vas reached out his other one for Thisby.

"TAKE IT!" he shouted.

"I'M SORRY! I'M SORRY I LEFT YOU BEHIND!"

"JUST TAKE IT!" yelled Vas.

"IT WAS A REALLY BAD THING TO DO! AREN'T YOU MAD?"

"JUST TAKE MY HAND!"

Time snapped back into place all at once like a snapped rubber band, and the minotaur released his swing. All his pent-up momentum that had been intended to turn Thisby into a rather unsightly stain was released into the bridge itself. It broke clean in half.

They began to fall. Instantly. There's a tendency to believe that if someone was standing on a bridge when it began to fall, they might be able to do something like scramble up the sides as it collapses and dive to safety, but that's not how physics works. When things fall, they fall instantly. Thisby fell instantly.

The next sensation she noticed was someone grabbing

her hand, and then her falling began to slow, causing her stomach to lurch. She threw up. For some reason that her panicked brain couldn't quite comprehend, she knew that something was wrong when her puke began to fall faster than she did. Actually, everything was falling faster than she was. The bridge that had collapsed had collided with other bridges, shattering huge chunks off them, and the pieces of those old stone bridges whizzed by as she drifted slowly down into the void.

When her wits returned for long enough to realize what was happening, Thisby looked over to see that Vas was holding her hand and Bero's in his other, while Bero continued to chant a spell from his book.

"This-Thisby . . . are we . . . ," said a terrified Mingus.

"Flying," said Thisby.

But she knew that wasn't exactly true. It was more like falling in slow motion. Like sinking through an invisible jelly.

Thisby's pulse began to gradually return to normal, and she looked up to see the cloud of dust left behind by the fallen bridges parting overhead. It sparkled where it caught the light and was actually quite pretty in a way. The waterfalls, too. She felt their cool mist on her face and almost felt like laughing. It reminded her of a dream. A dream she used to have every night but hadn't had in at least a year. A dream of falling. Of floating down the ladder that led up to her bedroom at the top of the mountain. All three hundred and four steps. Thisby closed her eyes.

When she opened them again, Vas squeezed her hand to get her attention.

"It's kind of pretty, isn't it?" he asked as if reading her mind.

Thisby's guts twisted up, and she thought she might vomit again.

"Do I have to keep holding your hand?" she asked. "For the spell to work?"

"I'm afraid so. Unless you want to risk the fall," he said, laughing.

Thisby weighed her options.

Her next realization came all at once. It was a bit like catching on fire and then jumping into a river only to remember that you can't swim. And the river was full of piranhas.

"Long Lost Lake!" she shouted.

"Hmm?" said Vas. He sounded as casual as someone lazily daydreaming at a picnic, trying to make sense of the shapes of clouds in the sky.

"That's where we're landing! Long Lost Lake!"

"So?" he asked.

Thisby shuddered and strained her eyes against the oncoming darkness below them.

"We'll be fine!" said Vas. "You worry too much!"

And that was the last thing Thisby heard before the spell wore off and she plummeted though pitch blackness, crashed into the freezing-cold water, and saw stars.

★ ★ ★

When Thisby Thestoop was four years old, Grunda took her to meet with the goblin elders. It was the last night of a sacred goblin holiday known as New Blood Howling, and the elders of Grunda's tribe had all gathered in the Black Mountain to perform the traditional rites.

The old goblin nudged and prodded Thisby awake in the middle of the night and told her to get up, there was something important they had to do. A proper human mother would've carried the sleepy four-year-old to where they were going, but as a rule, goblins never carried their young, not to mention Grunda was not her mother. So the two of them walked side by side from the bedroom Thisby had only recently moved into—four being the age where goblins earned their independence and were expected to be completely self-sufficient—across the wooden gangways and down all three hundred and four rungs of the ladder on their descent into the dungeon.

Her mind still hazy with sleep, Thisby shuffled dreamily into a large room filled with thick smoke streaming from braziers of blue fire. Grunda guided her gently forward, since she couldn't see more than a foot in front of her face. From somewhere lost within the veil of smoke, she could hear softly beating drums, strange chanting, and the bleating of goats, which—she didn't realize until she was much older—had likely been brought there for sacrifice. Grunda tugged sharply on the collar of Thisby's nightgown when she'd walked far enough. Thisby stood there for some time rubbing her smoke-irritated eyes until the curtains of smoke withdrew and the four biggest goblins she'd ever seen emerged before her.

A normal child would have been inconsolable. Most adults, too. But Thisby stood still, only moving to rub her eyes, as the four goblin elders encircled her, examining her as if she were a prize pig up for auction. They bent in and sniffed her with their upturned noses, prodded her with their long, knotty fingers, and mumbled things in their strange, grunting language. When at last they seemed to reach a consensus, they stepped back in a straight line and waited for Grunda to speak. Grunda grunted something at them in Goblin, and they responded in kind before retreating back into the smoke as silently as they'd come.

Without another word, Grunda led Thisby back to her room, tucked her into bed, and left her alone in the dark, wondering if what she'd just experienced was all some sort of strange dream. Thisby was still questioning the reality of the night's events when Grunda came knocking on her door the next morning.

"I suppose you have questions about what happened last night," said Grunda.

Thisby nodded and sat up.

Grunda pulled out a chair for herself, the same chair that Thisby still owned, and sat down across from the young girl sitting on her bed.

"Last night, I took you before the goblin elders because

I had questions about your future. Their magic is strong. Ancient. Older and more powerful than any magic in all of Nth. You came to this dungeon in a very unusual way, and I wanted to know what fate has in store for you. Do you understand?"

Thisby nodded, although she felt less than confident that she did.

"Now this next question I want you to think very hard about before you answer." Grunda took a deep breath. "Do you want to know what they saw? Do you want to know your destiny?"

Thisby nodded again.

Grunda exhaled. "I assumed as much."

The goblin pulled her chair closer to Thisby, sliding it across the floor so it made an incredibly annoying squealing noise, and looked straight into the four-year-old's eyes, addressing her like she was an adult and an equal. Grunda cleared her throat.

"You are not remarkable," she said flatly. "You have no great destiny. There is no hand of fate guiding you on your path to do great things. If you do something great, it will likely be purely by accident."

Grunda took Thisby's tiny hand in her own, which wasn't much bigger.

"But it's okay, because you're going to try. Sometimes you're going to succeed and sometimes you're going to fail. Your success will be somewhat random and not entirely dependent on your effort, although it couldn't hurt to try, I suppose. I hope this gives you some peace of mind."

She patted Thisby's hand in a way that indicated it was more of a thing she thought she was supposed to do than something she would do naturally. The goblin stood up and slid her chair back to its original spot, repeating the same awful squealing noise.

"Come on," said Grunda. "Get dressed. There's work to do."

The water was so black that there was no way to tell if her eyes were open. She assumed they were, if for no other reason than as a reaction to the terror and shock of being dropped into Long Lost Lake.

Thisby began to swim in a direction she hoped was up. Her chest was hurting from the pressure of holding her breath.

She swam as hard as she could but something was hanging on her, pulling her down. Something was trying to drag her to the depths, grabbing her around the shoulders. She reached a hand back to pry the creature free and realized it was no creature at all but the weight of her backpack. There was no choice but to wriggle free.

Thisby had one arm free of a shoulder strap when the thought pierced her brain like a banshee's wail . . . Mingus! He was still attached!

She groped blindly until she felt Mingus's jar. Her hand slid upward, looking for the hook. When she found the clasp, the same easy clasp she'd operated millions of times without thinking or looking, she fumbled with it. Desperate, Thisby tapped on the glass of Mingus's jar, pleading with him wordlessly as she thrashed her legs to prevent herself from sinking lower. The tapping must have shaken him back from wherever he was because within seconds, Mingus burst with bright blue light and finally she could see him, looking at her. With the help of Mingus's light, she opened the clasp.

She unhooked Mingus's jar, shrugged her way out of the final backpack strap, and swam for the surface. Despite the searing pain in her chest, she couldn't help but take one last look back at her backpack as it drifted down into the depths of Long Lost Lake, finally vanishing beyond the bubble of Mingus's light. Moments later, Thisby burst through the surface of the water and swallowed big gasps of air that hurt her chest as much as holding her breath had. She'd never been so hungry for air in her life.

Several yards away, Vas was pulling Bero by his collar toward a dark spot afloat on the surface of the water. He dragged Bero's limp body unceremoniously onto the small island of rocks, which was barely large enough to fit them both, and then helped Thisby out of the water as she came paddling over. Thisby flopped down onto the edge of the island and set Mingus's lantern down beside her, every muscle in her body straining and sore. She was relieved to hear Bero mumble something, cough, and roll over onto his side. She was less relieved when reality sank in.

"My backpack."

"What?" said Vas.

"My backpack . . . I lost it . . . ," she said, trailing off.

It felt as if she'd lost an arm. On her very first day as gamekeeper, Grunda had given her that backpack. Over the years, she'd added pockets and compartments to it, put in so much work to get it exactly the way she liked. In some ways, it was her oldest friend, even older than Mingus. Her backpack had bailed her out of countless jams, had been her home away from home as she'd traveled the dungeon. She knew its every proclivity, the way certain pockets didn't like to stay closed. She knew its every smell and stain, each one containing a small history of their time together.

Now it was gone. Just gone. Not to mention the number of irreplaceable notebooks and all the other meager treasures she'd acquired while working in the dungeon that were contained within it. There was nothing she could do, as her backpack was likely already at the bottom of Long Lost Lake—the name of which now felt like salt in a fresh wound.

"We'll get you a new one," said Vas dismissively.

Thisby didn't even have the energy to be angry.

"I'm sorry," said Mingus quietly.

He understood the importance of her backpack at least. She gave her friend a sad little smile and stood up. Things were bad now, but they were about to get much worse if she just lay there. There was work to do.

Thisby lifted Mingus's lantern high above her head, and

the cold black mirror of Long Lost Lake reflected his blue light back at her. The lake stretched as far as she could see, an expanse of merciless water spreading out in every direction until it acquiesced to the darkness, where the fingers of Mingus's light could no longer touch. She tortured herself momentarily with the thought that there could very well be solid land just beyond the edge of his light, but she didn't let the feeling consume her. Aside from a few rocky islands like the one they were on, there was no sign of shore.

"There's nothing," she said.

Vas helped Bero sit upright and made sure he was okay. It seemed as if the fall had taken a lot out of him or perhaps, more accurately, the spell casting had. Thisby had heard stories of wizards and sorcerers falling into comas or even dying from overexerting themselves magically, but she'd always kind of assumed those were just tall tales.

"What do we do?" asked Vas.

Thisby realized that, when it came right down to it, Vas was as helpless as all nobles were—with the exception of Iphigenia, of course, although she had to admit the Princess had rubbed her the wrong way initially as well.

Bero spoke up, his voice hoarse, and choked, "My books. Where are my books?"

Vas looked ashamed.

"I don't know. I didn't see them. The water was so dark. I'm so sorry," he apologized.

Seeing Vas prostrate himself caught Thisby off guard. Just

when she thought she had the noble boy pegged, he always found a way to surprise her. It was like he was doing it on purpose.

"There!" shouted Mingus.

It was the first break they'd had all day. In a nearly impossible coincidence, Bero's satchel of books had landed on one of the few other rocky islands in the otherwise empty lake. Considering the surface area of the lake compared to the surface area of dry land, the odds that the books would land where they did were infinitesimally small. It also wasn't a coincidence at all, although nobody besides Bero suspected as much. Magic books had a tendency to survive catastrophic events. It was one of the benefits of containing so much raw magical energy. Regardless, the fact that the books had survived the fall was still good news. There was however, also bad news.

"How do we get them?" asked Vas, knowing full well there was only one possible answer to the question.

Thisby thought of the monsters that she knew inhabited Long Lost Lake: mermaids, kelpies, nixies, water horses (which were far more dangerous than they sounded), catoblepas, vodynoy, sea slimes, water elementals . . . the list went on and on. But there was one monster that she was more worried about than all the others combined, one lone creature that lived near the dead center of Long Lost Lake, one creature that was the reason that Thisby took a step back from the edge of the island. The ammit.

As a rule, Thisby wasn't afraid of monsters in the dungeon. She respected them, she showed them deference when necessary, but it wasn't fear. Not exactly. With the ammit, it was different. It was fear, pure and simple. Spine-tingly, goose-bumpy, pit-of-your-stomach, lump-in-your-throat fear. The mere thought of the creature turned her legs to jelly and not even stiff jelly . . . runny jelly. Which was sort of ironic in a way, since running was the last thing she could imagine doing with legs made of jelly.

She'd seen the ammit only once, a long time ago when one of her trips around the Floating River inevitably passed through Long Lost Lake. After that, she learned better than to attempt to cross through the center of the lake, but when she was younger and less experienced, she'd made the mistake more than once, until she came face-to-face with the ammit.

There was an island somewhere near the center of the lake, a lonely flat plateau that rose just above the surface of the water, barely breaking its plane. So low that you'd barely notice it from a distance if it weren't for the ring of tall reeds that surrounded it. Nowhere else in Long Lost Lake did reeds like these grow, except the one tall circle around this particular island, which formed a blind. Years ago, on that fateful trip, when she saw the island surrounded by reeds, Thisby's curiosity got the best of her, and she wandered too close. That was when she saw it, crouching and peeking out from behind the tall grass.

The ammit's body was shaped like a hippopotamus, only

twice as large, and was covered in bony bumps and scales. It had a ring of bushy reddish hair, like a lion's mane, that encircled a crocodile's face out from which shone two gleaming yellow eyes. There was something particularly awful about its construction. Something ancient and primal and cruel. It emanated the dreadful feeling that it was designed for one purpose and one purpose only . . . to devour.

By the time she saw it, it'd already spotted her. It stared at her. Almost through her. She felt time stop. She'd never before, and thankfully never after, experienced such a sense of immense dread. The feeling of wanting to run, wanting to scream, but only being able to watch. And that was what she did. She watched. It was all she could do. It could have walked over and swallowed her whole and she would've just kept watching. Never moving. She locked eyes with the ammit, and it just stared back, unblinking, as still as a statue yet horrendously alive. Her boat drifted past. It didn't try to eat her. It didn't even attack. It just stared. And that stare alone was enough to ensure that Thisby never ventured anywhere near the center of Long Lost Lake again.

Now, however, there was a problem. Several of them, actually. One of them being that there was no way of knowing how far out toward the center of the lake they were. Another being that they had no boat. The thought of swimming out to that dark and distant rock only to look up and see those big yellow eyes staring back at her was more than Thisby could bear.

"I can get them," said Vas, already removing his boots. "It's not far."

Thisby wondered if he'd read something in her expression that'd made him offer to go himself. It seemed too kind a gesture for her to believe it.

"It's not safe," said Thisby bluntly. It was a serious understatement.

"I didn't come to the Black Mountain for 'safe'! I came for danger! Adventure! You know, that whole deal!" said Vas as he dropped his second boot onto the rocky island.

Thisby knew she should say something more. That she should explain what kinds of horrors were waiting out there in the dark. But somebody needed to retrieve the books, and she knew it couldn't be her. So instead she did something that made her thoroughly ashamed of herself . . . she did nothing.

With a splash, Vas hopped down into the freezing inky water.

"Woo! That's brisk!" he said, laughing. "Okay, give me the light."

He stuck out his hand, and it dawned on Thisby what he meant.

"What? No! Are you crazy?" said Mingus.

"Well, I can't see in the dark!" said Vas.

"Thisby . . . ," pleaded Mingus, but Vas was right. There really wasn't another way.

"He can't see in the dark," Thisby repeated unhelpfully.

"You can't be serious!" blurted Mingus.

If she hadn't lost her bag, she could've given him one of dozens of waterproof candles she'd lugged around with her for just such an occasion, but as it stood now, Mingus was the only source of light in a very dark place. There wasn't another option. Thisby wasn't thrilled with the idea of sending her best friend off with a relative stranger, but what choice was there? Even if she went herself, Mingus would still have to go.

"Please, Mingus. It's the only way," she said, ignoring the other way she'd just considered.

Mingus said nothing, and that was good enough for Thisby to pick up his jar by the handle and pass it to a shivering Vas.

"Just be brave," said Thisby, crouching down to be near his level. "You'll be okay. It's a short trip. We survived the Deep Down, remember? This is nothing."

"We'll be fine," said Vas.

"Please be careful," she said to Vas.

He nodded.

Thisby wondered if he mistook her concern for Mingus as concern for himself. It seemed likely, and she didn't care for the implication, but she didn't bother clarifying. He was risking his life, after all, and she didn't want to seem ungrateful. Mingus gave Thisby one last look that was either disapproving or pathetic, it was hard to tell, and then they were off.

Thisby watched Vas swim away as Mingus's sad blue light

faded into the distance. Soon, his light was nothing more than a lonely, distant star in a black blanket of sky, and Thisby became suddenly acutely aware that she herself had been swallowed by absolute darkness. She waved vigorously, but she could no longer see her own hand in front of her face. So she listened instead. There was the rhythmic splashing of Vas's swimming, and then somewhere, far beyond Bero's nervous breathing, she heard a noise like grass parting, followed by something very big slipping into the water.

After her run-in with the ammit years ago, Thisby had done some research. What she learned didn't do much to assuage her fears. Her instinct had been correct: ammits ate people. But so did a lot of monsters; trolls, ogres, wyverns, minotaurs, vampires in their own way, even water horses (to reiterate . . . much more dangerous than the name implies). Actually, most of the monsters in the dungeon would eat people if they were hungry enough. But the information she'd found contained one crucial difference: ammits ate *only* people.

Thisby found it hard to imagine there were enough adventurers to feed a creature this size, but she certainly didn't feed it, so the food must be coming from somewhere. She'd never dared ask Grunda. She did her best not to think about the ammit at all. Which had been a fairly successful strategy up until now.

The splashing of Vas's stroke stopped.

Thisby didn't want to think that the ammit had already

gotten Mingus and Vas, but the thought was unavoidable. She heard Bero's breathing getting shallower. He must've heard it as well.

"Did you hear that?" His voice was shaking.

Thisby groped in the dark and found his arm.

"Quiet. Stay still," she whispered.

It was the most rational plan she could come up with. Thisby listened to the silence, straining her ears to separate the sound of Bero's breathing, the occasional dripping of stalactites, and anything else. There was something else, but she couldn't be sure what it was. Water moving.

A scream tore through the cavern. It was Vas.

A light blazed to life, bright red, like a hot coal in the darkness, and what Thisby saw made her heart drop. Vas was swimming for his life toward her, holding Mingus aloft with one hand, and behind him, standing on the island where he'd just been, was the ammit.

Everything went dark again, but she heard Vas's frantic splashing and cursing as well as the sound of the ammit diving back into the water. It wasn't being careful to conceal its location now. When the light came back, Mingus and Vas were closer to her and the ammit was gone. Vanished below the water. She saw ripples. The light went out again.

The next thing Thisby heard was Vas swearing and splashing near the edge of their small island. She fell to her knees and felt around frantically in the darkness, cutting her fingers on sharp rocks as she followed the noise. In the darkness, she found Vas's arms and pulled to help him out of the water. Mingus's light came back on, and Thisby realized what'd happened: Vas had dropped him. Twenty yards back out into the water, Mingus bobbed like a buoy, and in the glow of his red light, Thisby saw the water around him begin to swirl.

Without thinking, she dove into the water to be engulfed by the most complete darkness she'd ever known. The shock of the cold hit her hard enough to take her breath away. By the time she found it again and began swimming, Mingus's light had come back on and the crown of the ammit's head had breached the black water behind him. Thisby swam with everything she had, every ounce of her fighting with absolute clarity of purpose to go just a little faster, to swim just a little harder. There was no runny jelly in her arms and legs now. There was no time for it.

Mingus blinked his light on and off. Red. Black. Red. Black. Red. Black. With every flash, Thisby watched the ammit emerge more from the water. It felt as if time had slowed down.

She was finally there and grabbed ahold of Mingus's cold, wet jar, pressing it to her cheek so she could feel him sliding around through the glass.

"I'm sorry. I'm sorry. I'm sorry," she said.

"Thisby. It's okay. It's okay."

This time Mingus stayed lit. He needed to see his friend. For as long as possible. He needed to focus on her face so that she would know that it was all right.

The ammit loomed over them. The monster opened its colossal jaws, and Thisby could see the rows of jagged teeth and smell the ancient decay. For a reason she didn't understand, she didn't close her eyes or look away. The world slowed down and then . . . something incredible happened. The ammit continued past them. Thisby felt the pull of the tide as the enormous beast dropped back beneath the water. She felt her thrashing feet tangle in its mane and kick the bumps on its leathery back as it brushed past.

The taste of relief turned sour in her mouth when she realized where it was headed.

"No!" she cried.

There was no reply.

With Mingus in hand, Thisby began to swim back toward the island, following the wake of the ammit. She begged her tired muscles not to quit on her. Not now.

Mingus lit brighter than ever, and in his light she could see the island where Bero was desperately digging through his spell books as Vas lay exhausted and shaking on the ground, too tired to move.

"Bero!" she yelled. "It's coming!"

It wasn't much help, but it was all she could do.

Bero finally decided on a book. He was busy peeling apart the waterlogged pages when the ammit resurfaced only a few feet from where he stood. Thisby splashed closer, her arms screaming at her, aching with cold and fatigue. She was close enough now to see Bero's face and the surprising look

*A scream tore through the cavern. It was Vas.*

of calm that had come over him. The conjurer looked down through half-lidded eyes and began to recite words from the spell book. A glow began to emanate from his body, shining out through his skin as if he were a sheet of parchment held in front of a lantern.

The ammit came to a stop at the edge of the island, the tip of its long snout no more than a few feet from Bero, whose glow grew stronger and brighter, until Thisby saw him take one hand, reach it into his chest, and bloodlessly withdraw his own heart. Bero held it out in front of himself as if it were any other mundane object—a rubber ball, a muffin, a teacup—and the ammit sniffed it with its massive nostrils for several seconds before it opened up its mouth and gently took it from the conjurer's outstretched hand as if it were a loyal dog receiving a treat from its master. Thisby thrashed and kicked as hard as she could, but by the time she'd reached the island, the ammit was gone, sunken below the water, and Bero had fallen to his knees.

Thisby was too winded, to stunned, to speak for some time. She simply lay there, panting, waiting for her breath to return and staring at the conjurer, who refused to return her gaze. Instead Bero's eyes remained fixed on a single spot on the unremarkable ground.

"What . . . ," she gasped.

"I . . . did . . . what I did," he said, bereft of emotion.

"But how?"

The conjurer stood up and sighed, shifting his focus to

something unseeable in the darkness out over the water.

"I never used the thing anyway," he said. And with that he seemed to snap awake, turning to Thisby for the first time and offering her a sad smile that seemed oddly lacking in any actual sadness.

Vas had been unconscious throughout the whole affair, exhausted from his swim, and only now did Thisby think to check to make sure he was breathing, which, thankfully, he was. She relaxed her shoulders as she laid her hand across Vas's chest, feeling it rise and fall.

She patted her pocket and was relieved to find that her scrobble had survived her dip in the lake. Sticking her hand into her pocket, she was also surprised to find that her tunic was completely dry to the touch. She'd almost forgotten it was magic and smiled at the memory of receiving her birthday gift from Iphigenia.

Everything else might be terrible, but at least she was dry. It was good to be thankful for the little things.

# CHAPTER 15

The first person to reach the door of Castle Grimstone was a thirty-four-year-old farmer from the river town of Ranth by the name of Auggie Mudd. When he'd reached the impassable steel door, inlaid with thousands of skulls and covered in a tangle of jagged spikes, he found a bare spot on it and knocked. Because it was only polite.

Auggie's success had been the result of pure dumb luck. Or, perhaps more accurately, pure dumb probability. If you put enough rats in a maze, eventually one of them will make it to the end. That's just how probability works. And in the Wretched Scrattle, probability had worked in favor of Auggie Mudd.

The usual way someone entered the Black Mountain was to take the long, winding path up through Feldspar's Folly—the mountain pass created by one of Castle Grimstone's chief architects, Matthias Feldspar, whose ghost still haunts it to this day—all the way up to the large front gates. Once inside the gates there were two paths, one that led down into the Black Mountain and the other that led up into the courtyard of Castle Grimstone. What this meant was that your typical adventurer began their exploration of the dungeon at what was essentially the very top of the mountain, just below the castle, and worked their way down. For this reason, the weakest monsters were at the top of the dungeon and the more dangerous ones were at the bottom. This might seem obvious. Dungeons 101 stuff. However, the polar opposite was true during the Wretched Scrattle.

The reason for this was, quite obviously, because the goal of the Wretched Scrattle was to reach the top of the dungeon and Castle Grimstone. If the adventurers had gotten their start at the usual entrance, the tournament would have been over in a matter of hours. So Auggie Mudd and the rest of the participants in the Wretched Scrattle had begun their journey at the base of the mountain, where the black-door gate opened.[5] Starting a trip at the ground level of the

***

5 The dungeon, of course, continued on down below ground level, down quite impossibly deep past the City of Night and beyond that even into the Deep Down, but only the most foolhardy adventurers in the Wretched Scrattle went down instead of up. Though more did than you might think.

dungeon and traveling all the way up to the gates of Castle Grimstone—assuming you didn't encounter a single monster and made every correct turn—took an absolute minimum of a day and a half. Which was exactly how long it took Auggie.

Auggie Mudd knocked even louder, but there was still no response. He looked around to see if there was some kind of lever or switch, possibly a door chime, and when he couldn't find one, he grew frustrated. Auggie couldn't help but think that maybe this dungeon *was* sort of tricky after all. Up to this point, he'd been pleasantly surprised by how easy everything had been.

After searching for a few minutes, and considering giving up all the while, Auggie found a button to the right of the door that was shaped like a little silver skull. That was probably why he'd overlooked it, as the whole skull motif of the door made it blend right in. Very tricky indeed.

He pushed it.

There was a loud buzzing noise followed by a voice he didn't recognize. It sounded tinny and distant.

"What is the secret of magic?" asked the voice.

Auggie scratched his chin.

"I don't know," he said honestly.

There was a brief silence followed by mechanical whirring and clicking noises, and in a flash, hundreds of tiny balls of light streamed into the chamber through the eyeholes of different skulls. Auggie screamed as the balls of light began to sting him, swarming and darting faster than any physical creature had a right to move. He threw his hands up over his head and crouched down on the floor as the stinging grew more intense. It was no use. Auggie Mudd was dead. It wasn't fair or deserved or justified. He was not a particularly bad man nor was he a good one, and his death was not an act of divine retribution, nor was it a punishment for his hubris. His luck had just finally run out.

Thisby turned to the two boats behind her and signaled to Vas and Bero that they needed to crouch. The path ahead was low, and they needed to keep their hands on the oars to steer around the rocks. They'd been at this for hours now, and every muscle in Thisby's body ached from the stress of it. The good news was that she'd already bounced the magical glass boat off several rocks and had yet to see any chipping or cracking on the hull, so it seemed as if Bero had been correct about the durability of his spell. Unfortunately, there were still plenty of other issues to contend with.

Navigating the Floating River with a map was difficult enough. Doing it by instinct and memory was next to impossible. Still, the river was undoubtedly the quickest way back to the top of the mountain and therefore their best chance of winning the Wretched Scrattle. Thisby had done her best to push thinking about what she'd do if she won out of her mind, but the thoughts kept creeping back in. First things first, she'd have to undo all the changes that Marl had implemented as Overseer. She'd bring back Grunda, of course.

Better yet, she'd offer to make Grunda the new Master of the Black Mountain, and then Thisby could go back to her job as gamekeeper, only this time with somebody competent as her boss.

She wondered how Jono was handling her responsibilities while she was off running around the dungeon. She'd quickly come to think of the skeleton boy as a friend, and she was worried about him. She'd had her whole life to prepare for her tenure as gamekeeper, but Jono had only trained under her for a few weeks. It was a lot of responsibility for one person to take on. Too much.

Her boat passed over a rock as her thoughts wandered, and the jolt of it nearly threw her overboard. Thisby grabbed the sides of the boat and tried to steady it, calling back a warning to the others. She couldn't help but think about how much easier this all would've been if she hadn't lost her backpack and notebooks. Thinking about her poor backpack sitting forever on the bottom of Long Lost Lake was heartbreaking. At least she still had a heart to break. Unlike Bero.

She'd wanted to know more about the spell he'd performed to appease the ammit, but it still felt too early to ask. Admittedly, though, it was hard to know how long was an appropriate length of time to wait before asking somebody about a monster eating their heart.

She heard Vas cry out when the rock that had struck her boat a moment ago got his next. She shot back a dirty look, but the tunnel was far too dark for him to notice. Thisby didn't care that he was scared, but did he have to be so loud about it? The last thing she wanted was to attract unnecessary attention. There was no way to know what was lurking beneath the water, or in the shadowy nooks as their boats drifted ever forward along the never-ending river.

Thisby was relieved when the boats came out of the narrow passage and into a wide, dark cave and she could stand upright again. Her knees popped as she stretched her legs.

"Mingus," she whispered, and he grew brighter.

It was the same cave where she'd seen the catoblepas what felt like a lifetime ago. The gamekeeper in her was initially happy to see that the algae she'd spread in the water had proliferated quickly and formed a nice, nutritious scum on its surface, but just as quickly she realized that it'd only grown so well because there was nothing around to eat it. The catoblepas had all disappeared. Without asking permission from the others, Thisby rowed her boat over to where the beasts had been previously.

There were huge lacerations on the side of the cave that reminded Thisby instantly of the rock golem that she had seen. She thought of the hodag they'd encountered near where she and Mingus had found the rock golem but didn't think it was responsible for this. Its claws weren't big enough, for one. But whatever it was, it'd chased off an entire herd of catoblepas.

"What did this?" asked Vas, pulling up alongside her. He ran his fingers along the walls of the cave, feeling the grooves cut into the solid rock.

"I don't know," said Thisby.

Thisby leaned in close and examined the lacerations. The marks were old. Mold spores had already begun to collect on the freshly exposed rock, and tiny spots of green fuzz sprang up in the cracks. She ran her fingers over the soft, fuzzy mold and sighed before dipping her oars into the brackish water and paddling away from the empty catoblepas chamber, farther up the Floating River.

They found a place to camp for the night as the second day drew to a close. A bit of dry riverbank where the tunnel widened out. On the back wall of the shallow overhang against which they'd prepared to rest, Thisby spotted some strange flowers growing through the cracks in the wall. She touched a yellow one beneath her fingers and was so lost in thought that when Vas spoke to her from behind, she flinched.

"Sorry, I didn't mean to startle you. I'm just curious. Seeing flowers like that . . . so deep below the earth," he said.

"We must be on the other side of Elphond's Escape. The magic, it spreads like a weed, through cracks in the walls. Sometimes I wonder if it'll eventually take over the entire dungeon. Can you imagine? Walking into the Black Mountain to find a world full of life. Plants and sky and rivers and animals. How would you even know you weren't still outside?"

Nearby, lying in one of the three glass boats they'd dragged ashore, Bero had already begun to snore. The walls of the boat amplified the noise in an almost comedic way.

"It's wonderful," said Vas.

"Yeah. It is," said Thisby.

She sat down with her back against the wall, staring out over the sad embers of the small fire Bero had conjured before falling asleep. Without him left to tend to it, the light was quickly dying. Mingus was no help, either, falling fast asleep as well and returning to his nonluminous dull gray color. Apparently, that was the natural color of a pewder sér. Which was another thing that Thisby hadn't yet had a chance to properly process.

"I never planned to make it out of the dungeon alive," said Vas.

If this was his attempt to fill the silence, he'd chosen an interesting technique. Thisby looked at him but wasn't sure exactly what to say, so she looked away. She suppressed a strange instinct to apologize.

"I came here to die, I mean," he said as if misunderstanding was the reason for her silence. The fire crackled a response of its own, and Vas continued.

"My father wanted me to enter the Wretched Scrattle because he wanted me out of the way. He was afraid that I'd replace him in his old age. He was right, I suppose. That's the way things go. But he had me pegged all wrong. I don't care about money. Not like he does, at least. It doesn't really matter."

Thisby kept her eyes fixed on the orange glow of the dying fire to avoid looking at Vas. Bero's snoring filled the silence.

"Do you ever feel like all that stuff is just a distraction from something bigger? That there's something impossibly huge hiding under all these layers of country and money and business and war, something that you know is there but you can't quite put your finger on? Something that you think if everybody would just look at it, if everybody could just touch it, hold it, feel it, it would erase all that other stuff?"

Thisby felt a bit embarrassed by what he'd said, but she was moved by his conviction nonetheless. She was reminded of Iphigenia and how her role had been thrust upon her as well, just like Vas. They both had so much and yet they also seemed completely incapable of appreciating it. Just as Thisby's mind had wandered off, she felt Vas's hand close over her own and give it a squeeze.

Thisby sprang to life as if somebody had dropped a live mindworm down the back of her pants. She bolted for the rowboat, crossing her arms and muttering something about how it was late and they had a big day tomorrow. She lay down in the beached boat underneath the seats, curled into a ball, closed her eyes as tightly as they would go, and tried hard not to think about anything other than making it to the castle. After several minutes, she held her breath and peeked over the stern of the boat, but it was too dark to see anything now that the last embers of the fire had finally surrendered to their inevitable fate.

# CHAPTER 16

The edge of the dagger pressed against Thisby's throat.

"You make a sound and you're dead."

Her eyes adjusted to the dark in a hurry, spurred on by the adrenaline pumping through her body. The hooded man squatting over her had an ugly face with a squashed-in look to it.

"Get up," he commanded.

He grabbed Thisby by the arm and dragged her out from beneath the overhang. Without Mingus's light, she could barely make out two other figures standing several yards away by the edge of the river, looming above lumps she guessed were probably the bodies of Vas and Bero. She hoped they were still breathing, but it was too dark to tell.

She was led down to the water, where two adventurers stood in front of Bero and Vas, who were tied up at their feet. One of the adventurers could've been the younger brother of the man who'd grabbed her, and the other was a woman who didn't fit in at all with the others. She had a long braid of hair the color of fire and could have been mistaken for royalty if she wasn't wearing the armor of a seasoned adventurer.

"They're alive," she said, before Thisby could ask.

Upon seeing that Thisby was seemingly no threat, the woman sheathed her sword.

"If you don't cause any trouble, you'll live, too," she said.

Thisby watched as the younger man lifted Vas like a sack of potatoes and placed him in one of Bero's magic glass boats.

"What's your name?" asked the woman.

Thisby studied her and said nothing. The man was still grabbing Thisby's arm rather roughly, but when the woman gave him a nod, he let go and moved over to help the younger man lift Bero into the same boat in which they'd placed Vas.

"Thisby," said Thisby.

"Thisby," the woman repeated. "My name is Elfriede."

Thisby didn't respond.

"Do you want to tell me why you're worth ten thousand gold, dead or alive, Thisby?"

Thisby said nothing, so the woman pulled out a scroll that had been rolled up and tucked into her belt. She unrolled it and handed it over.

Sure enough, there was a drawing of Thisby's face floating above a promise of ten thousand gold as reward for either her capture or proof of her death. It was what the Master had been warning her about before the incident at Giant's Crossing. He'd been trying to tell her that Marl had placed a bounty on her head.

Her thoughts spun around the one inevitable truth that must be at the center of this turn of events: Marl knew that she was competing in the Wretched Scrattle and was terrified that Thisby was going to win.

"I don't know," said Thisby.

Elfriede stepped closer to Thisby and squatted down so they were eye level with each other. She smiled.

"I don't like games, Thisby. I won't play them. Do you believe me?"

Something in her voice told Thisby that was the absolute truth. She nodded.

"Good. Now I will tell you the truth. I don't want to kill you or your friends, but I will. I will do it without hesitation if you don't answer my questions honestly. Since I'm being honest with you, it only seems fair. Nod if you understand."

Thisby nodded.

"Wonderful. Now I'm going to ask you that question again. Only this time, if you don't answer, one of your friends dies. If you don't answer again, the other dies. If you don't answer for a third time, you die. That's all there is to it."

Elfriede paused to let that sink in.

"Now why would somebody offer ten thousand gold for you?" she asked.

"I'm the gamekeeper of the Black Mountain," said Thisby. "The Overseer, Marl, doesn't want me to win the Wretched Scrattle."

"Why?"

"I'm not sure."

"Think harder," said Elfriede.

Thisby considered what she knew. Marl had imprisoned the Master and put a bounty on Thisby's head, which could mean only one thing.

"She wants the dungeon for herself," said Thisby.

"And?" asked Elfriede.

"And if I win, that complicates things."

"Fair enough," said Elfriede, standing up. "Thank you for your cooperation."

Elfriede waved for her partners to come over, and they obeyed.

"Tie her up," she said, motioning toward Thisby.

The men closed in and grabbed her by her shoulders.

"Wait! What are you doing?" Thisby demanded, trying to wriggle free of the men.

It was a pointless struggle, as the far larger men managed to hold her down with relative ease and bind her hands behind her back.

"We're taking you to the Overseer. To collect our reward. Just be thankful I've decided to deliver you alive. For now."

The younger man carried Thisby to a boat and tossed her in. She tried to lift her head to get a look at the other boat holding Vas and Bero, but she couldn't see over the edge.

"Stop!" she yelled. "You can't navigate the river!"

"With your help we can," said Elfriede, climbing into Thisby's boat.

She pulled Thisby upright so she could see and sat her at the prow of the tiny boat. There was barely room for both of them in there. Looking back over her shoulder, Thisby saw that the older man with the squashed face had grabbed Bero's pack of spell books as well as their other supplies and Mingus, who Thisby was sure was doing his "inanimate object" routine.

Mingus's last-ditch tactic when captured by enemies involved popping out his fake eyes and staying completely still, refusing to glow. When he did this, it was easy to mistake him for a jar full of weird jelly, although explaining why Thisby would carry such a thing around with her could be tricky. Thankfully, her kidnappers didn't seem to be asking too many questions that didn't pertain to the reward for her capture.

In the boat behind him, she could see Bero and Vas tied up on the floor of the boat, with the younger man standing over them, using his paddle to push off into the water. Thisby hoped they were all right but knew it was probably herself that she should be worried about. If Elfriede managed to hand her off to Marl, there was no telling what the

Overseer would do to her. If the bounty was any indication, it wouldn't be good.

Elfriede jabbed Thisby in the back with the paddle.

"Eyes forward," she commanded. "You need to concentrate."

Thisby turned around and looked down the river. There was a fork up ahead. She'd seen it when they'd landed. To the left, the tunnel was coated in fine moss. To the right, the tunnel was moss-free and she felt a cold breeze blowing down it.

"Which way?" demanded Elfriede.

"Left," said Thisby without hesitation.

"Are you sure?" asked Elfriede.

"Positive," said Thisby.

Elfriede asked no more questions and turned her boat toward the right.

"I said left!" shouted Thisby, but it was too late.

"I know you did. Which is why I went to the right," said Elfriede. "Do you think I'm so stupid as to fall into a trap?"

Thisby was glad for the darkness as they passed into the tunnel. She would've hated for her captor to see her smile.

So far, the group had managed to navigate the Floating River without encountering anything more dangerous than a pair of dire otters, which Elfriede and the other two had successfully chased off by slapping their oars against the water and yelling. It made for quite a scene, but considering the sorts of monsters that dwelled along the river, Thisby knew that they'd been incredibly lucky.

Unfortunately, she still had no way of knowing how far they were from Castle Grimstone without her maps. If she'd had them, they could've made the journey from Long Lost Lake to where the Floating River crested near the top of the Black Mountain in a day's time, and from there it was only another half a day's journey on foot. That part, at least, she was certain she could navigate even without maps. There was no way Marl had managed to change enough of the top quarter of the dungeon so that Thisby wouldn't recognize it. She'd spent her whole life in that part of the dungeon and knew it as well as anyone would recognize their childhood home. Just because somebody had put the toilet in the kitchen didn't mean she'd be tricked into taking a bath in the sink.

Before they'd been captured, they'd already spent one night along the Floating River, which meant that at some point they'd gone off course from the most direct route. Even on an indirect course, Thisby was fairly certain they'd arrive at the top of the river by the end of the day. What she couldn't be sure of was that they'd be the first to arrive. It was possible, she supposed, that somebody had already won the Wretched Scrattle. For all she knew, they could be coronating a new Master right now. All she could do was hope she wasn't too late.

"Again?" griped Elfriede, scolding her extinguished torch.

Every time she lit the torch, moments later it was extinguished by a cold breeze blasting through the tunnel strong enough to rock their entire boat.

"I keep telling you, I have a lantern," said Thisby.

Elfriede relit the torch, and Thisby watched her face bloom to life in the darkness.

"And I keep telling you it's broken," said the older man with the squashed face, who Thisby had learned was named Rathburn.

"It's not broken, it's magic," Thisby insisted. "It only works for me."

"We ain't fallin' for that, girl," chuckled Rathburn.

"Just give it to me and I'll show you! You can hold your dagger to my throat if you'd like! I won't try anything funny, but I also can't navigate these tunnels without being able to see!"

On cue, a stiff breeze blew out Elfriede's torch again. Thisby heard her cursing in the darkness.

"Oh, just give her the stupid lantern!" snapped Elfriede.

Thisby felt their boats bump together in the darkness, and they fumbled around until Mingus was placed on the floor of the boat in front of her. The slime glowed softly, enough for them to see, and Thisby smiled.

"See?" she asked. "I told you. Now untie my hands so I can use it."

Elfriede laughed. "Not going to happen. Give it here."

Elfriede jerked the lantern out of Thisby's hands, and they

were all immediately plunged back into darkness.

"It only works for me," said Thisby. "It's magic. How many times do I have to tell you that? Bero, please explain it to them."

Through the dark, she heard Bero's soft voice from the far boat. He sounded much closer than she'd realized.

"It's true. The lantern is soul-bonded," he said.

Elfriede muttered more curses, and Thisby felt the cold steel of her knife searching around her wrists. With a flick that seemed far too confident to perform in the pitch darkness, the rope around Thisby's wrists was cut and fell away. Mingus started to glow as soon as Thisby picked up the lantern.

"Don't try anything stupid," said Elfriede.

It was good advice but also too little too late. Thisby had done something stupid, but it had happened hours ago when she'd tricked Elfriede into taking the wrong tunnel.

The boats rounded a corner and began to gain speed as they headed through a long tunnel covered in ice, glittering blue in Mingus's light.

Thisby's boat slammed into a chunk of ice and spun around 180 degrees. Another chuck of ice struck the stern, and this time the shock was enough to knock her out of her seat. Thisby landed on all fours in the boat and watched through its glass bottom as chunks of ice drifted past. Rathburn yelled something, and although Thisby couldn't clearly make out the words, when she glanced back over her shoulder, it seemed likely that it had to do with the river ahead ending abruptly in a thick wall of ice.

There was no way Thisby could stop her boat now, not that she wanted to. Taking a deep breath, she dove in. She hit the water, and the shock to her system felt like she'd just hugged an electric snail. Frigid water rushed up around her, filling her nose and mouth. When she bobbed back up above the surface, it was just in time to watch her boat slam into the wall and capsize, spilling Elfriede out as well. Still clutching Mingus, Thisby swam ashore, her arms aching from any exertion in water this cold. She was coughing and shaking when she heard the others behind her.

"Stop her!" yelled Rathburn.

Wet and freezing cold, Thisby ran without looking back. For now, she'd have to hope that Vas and Bero were okay with their captors. She was the real prize and hoped they'd take the bait. It was her only shot.

As she ran, she felt her clothes warming as the tunic dried itself off. If she survived this, she was going to have to find a way to properly thank Iphigenia for her gift.

Thisby turned down a narrow tunnel which ended in a great, vaulted stone doorway, the kind you might see leading into a cathedral, only here there was no door. Instead, the entrance was almost completely frozen over with ice. That "almost" was all she needed. Thisby was already halfway squeezed through the only remaining fissure in the frozen doorway, her nose squished up against the ice, when she heard the sound of the others coming down the tunnel behind her. If it was a tight fit for her, there was no way for the others to get through without chipping away the ice first, and Thisby knew from experience what a chore that was.

Elfriede's fingertips brushed against Thisby's sleeve just as she squeezed through into the room, but Elfriede couldn't hang on. Thisby could hear Elfriede and the others shouting on the other side of the crack, but for now she was free, for as long as the ice would hold.

"Nice work back there," she said to Mingus.

"Ditto," he said. "*Pfft!* Magic lantern!"

"You're kinda like magic, I guess," she admitted.

Mingus slid his eyes back into place. He tended to feel self-conscious without them.

"You're my magic lantern," she teased.

"How dare you," he said. "I'm a pewder sér."

Thisby tapped on his jar playfully. "Yes. You. Are."

"It looks empty," said Mingus, looking around.

The room they'd entered looked like an old throne room, only everything was covered in a layer of ice. For that reason, it was shockingly well-preserved compared to the rest of the rooms in the dungeon. The tapestries were intact, untorn, their colors still shining out brightly from beneath a crystalline coating of ice. The forms and figures of the furniture and decorations were warped and distorted by the way that light hit the curves in the ice that surrounded them, but otherwise it all made for a rather idyllic setting.

Thisby cupped her hands over her mouth like a megaphone and shouted, "Hello," over and over. There was no response.

"Hey, what are you doing?" said Mingus.

"Hello?" bellowed Thisby again.

"Something's going to hear you!" scolded Mingus.

Thisby turned with an annoyed look. "That's the entire point of saying hello."

"I mean something . . . bad," said Mingus.

"Hello?" repeated Thisby, ignoring his warnings.

There was still no answer.

"Where are they?" Thisby asked, to nobody in particular.

Mingus replied regardless. "Who are you looking for anyway?"

"Ice wraiths."

"Of course you are," said Mingus.

Thisby made her way to the back of the chamber. There was a raised platform upon which sat three grand thrones. The one in the middle was larger than the other two, just as the one in the middle had been in the throne room of Nth when Thisby had visited. It was a perfect reminder of the ubiquitous vanity and pettiness of all kings everywhere. Whether they lived in the wealthiest city in the world or buried deep within the Black Mountain, some things were universal.

Thisby was just about to shout hello yet again when she noticed something behind the center throne. She made her way behind it and stared at a large hole in the wall, easily as wide as three of herself laid head to toe.

"What is it?" asked Mingus.

Thisby ran her fingers around the edge of the hole, which had been smoothed over with ice.

"I don't know," she said. "But we're going to find out."

With some effort, she climbed up into the hole. Inside, the hole became a long tunnel, twisting into darkness up ahead. She passed Mingus's light around the entrance to the hole and saw deep, angry gouges in the tunnel's walls, huge claw marks that set off a primordial warning in her brain, a basic evolutionary signal practically begging her to run away. She ignored it.

"Claw marks," said Thisby. "Like the ones we saw in the rock golem and the catoblepas's cave. Like the ones we've been seeing around here ever since the Wretched Scrattle began."

"Maybe we should go?"

Thisby could hear the tremor of fear in his voice.

"Something happened here," she intoned, trying not to betray the same weakness.

Her steps echoed down the tunnel as she walked farther in. An unslakable curiosity was drawing her in, deeper down the tunnel—at least, that was what she hoped it was. She felt powerless to resist. She had to know what was doing this.

Back behind her, she could hear Elfriede and the others still chipping away at the ice wall, but it seemed so far away that it didn't matter. They'd get through eventually, but it would take a long time. Right now her best option was to keep moving forward.

As she ventured farther on into the tunnel, Thisby noticed the ice melting and spotted a trail of footprints in the wet, muddy earth. Icicles dripped into them. They were strangely familiar. Up ahead she heard the sound of crunching and slurping. A dim light shone around the next bend of the tunnel. She stopped. It was right around the corner.

She had no weapon to draw, no backpack full of tricks to get her out of trouble. It was just her and whatever was lurking around the corner. Mingus was silent, frozen in terror. Thisby took a step forward. Then another. The crunching grew louder.

When she saw it, she couldn't explain what "it" was. Only that it was somehow wrong. There was a jumble of parts put together incorrectly, like a Deep Dweller. Long tentacles and arms and legs and teeth that seemed to have been hastily assembled onto the body of something that seemed far too human. It had long, dark hair and looked almost like a boy but it was far too large, easily the size of a troll. It huddled in the tunnel, stooped and miserable, holding on to a skeletal figure clad in gray robes that could only be the missing ice wraith. When the creature turned its head, she wasn't prepared for what she saw.

"Ingo?" she said as if she were dreaming.

The Deep Dweller with Ingo's face screeched at her,

*When Thisby saw it, she couldn't explain what "it" was.*

dropped the ice wraith, and took off the opposite way down the tunnel as fast as it could run. The abomination retreated from the light, and Thisby stood there staring after it until it had vanished completely.

After some incomprehensible amount of time, the ice wraith moaned and Thisby snapped back to reality.

"He's dying," she muttered.

Thisby stared at the wounded ice wraith, but her thoughts were elsewhere. She couldn't help it. There was no way to explain what she'd seen. It was as if Ingo had come back from the dead as a Deep Dweller and had been let loose in the dungeon. Or maybe he'd never died at all. They'd never found his body. Still, none of it made any sense. You didn't just turn into a Deep Dweller. You were either born one or you weren't. Right?

"What about me? Can I touch him?" Mingus asked. His voice startled Thisby as if she'd forgotten he could speak at all.

"I don't . . ." She trailed off.

"The flame that never goes out. The light of the stars itself. That's what Bero said about pewder sérs. I can do this," said Mingus.

"No," said Thisby. "Absolutely not. It's too risky."

"I saved Iphigenia. I can save him. What makes one life more important than any other?" said Mingus.

Thisby held Mingus up in front of her face and looked him square in his button eyes. He shaped his jelly into a wobbly smile and glowed a comforting gold color. Thisby sighed.

"I'm not your master. It's your choice," she said. "You sure?"

"I'm sure," he said.

Thisby held her breath, opened his jar, and set him down onto the wounded chest of the ice wraith. The moment he touched the heaving chest of the creature, a horrible hissing sound made Thisby wince, but when she opened her eyes, Mingus was glowing. Slowly the ice wraith's wounds healed shut, and when Mingus was done, Thisby helped him slide back into his jar.

"I'm not sure if you're brave or just stubborn," she said lifting her friend's jar and tightening the lid back on.

Mingus smiled back, a bit worn out from his expenditure of energy. "Can't I be both?"

"Both it is," said Thisby.

They watched the wounded ice wraith begin to regain his bearings, the dim blue light returning to his undead eyes. The wraith didn't sit up as much as he floated upright until he hovered several inches above the ground. The wraith adjusted his crown and looked down at Thisby and Mingus, still a bit disoriented after everything that had happened.

"*Yoooooou saaaaaaaved meeeeee . . . ,*" said the ice wraith once his breathing returned to normal. "*Hooooow caaannnnn I eveeeerr repaaaaayyyy yooooooou?*"

"It's nothing. Really," said Mingus.

The ice wraith disagreed. Once they were back in the throne room, the ice wraith insisted on dumping a handful of precious gems into Mingus's jar, most of which absorbed into his body, where they floated around like marshmallows in jelly. After his debt was repaid, the ice wraith took a seat on the center throne, and Thisby approached him with the appropriate formality.

"We need your help," said Thisby with a small bow.

"*It wooooooould beeeee myyyyy honooor, Mssssss. Thessssss-toooop.*"

"Is there another way out of here?" asked Thisby.

She noticed that Elfriede and the others had given up on chipping their way through the ice wall. Without the proper tools it would've taken too long, and by then they must've figured Thisby would be long gone. They may not have been the nicest people in the world, but they weren't stupid. Thisby could only hope that they wouldn't harm Bero or Vas. She wished there was more that she could do for them, but since they hadn't been harmed so far, she couldn't see why Elfriede would do so now.

The ice wraith gave the best directions to the castle that he could, while Thisby took diligent notes on a scrap of cloth with some makeshift charcoal they'd made from a pointy stick and some ash. It was the first time in too long that she had taken any notes, and doing so brought her a profound sense of relief. It felt good to get back to basics. Writing things down. Organizing information into something useful.

There was a power in that. A sense of control she hadn't felt in too long. It was a welcome sensation with how chaotic everything else had been over the past few weeks.

Thisby knew it was silly to ever consider a dungeon full of monsters "safe," yet that was close to how she'd felt before the Wretched Scrattle. The dungeon had been her home. It was her safe place . . . even when it wasn't. But ever since the Wretched Scrattle, the dungeon hadn't felt very safe at all, and if she was being totally honest, it hadn't felt much like home, either.

Outside the ice wraith's den, Thisby was relieved to find that Elfriede and the others hadn't been waiting. If it really was all about money, perhaps they'd thought that winning the Wretched Scrattle was more valuable than the ten thousand gold reward for Thisby's capture. Whatever it was, it seemed obvious that they'd decided to go on without her, and she was thankful for that. She didn't let her mind linger on the thought too long, but she was also relieved that she didn't find Bero and Vas outside the den, either.

If Thisby stuck to the ice wraith's path, she should arrive at the gates by evening, and despite her other anxieties, the news practically made her heart sing. The Wretched Scrattle had been taxing, and the knowledge that it would soon be over warmed her as she left the chilly ice wraith's den behind and continued on her journey. She even allowed her mind to wander.

What was she really going to do when she won the

Wretched Scrattle? She didn't want to be Master, but she supposed she would have to take the position, at least for a while until they figured things out. Would she have to sleep in Castle Grimstone from now on? The thought of leaving her bedroom behind made her feel a kind of homesick queasiness that she hadn't expected. The only thing that gave her any solace was the hope that she could pass the job off to Grunda quickly. If she insisted, she was sure there was no way Grunda would say no.

It would all be over soon enough. She'd win the tournament, kick out the Overseer, and then there'd be plenty of time to figure out the rest. Plenty of time to get everything back to normal. Back to how it should be. Thisby as gamekeeper. Feeding the trolls and watering the wereplants and scraping the gnoll pits. Everything would be back to normal soon.

The air grew warmer, and somewhere nearby a cave cricket chirruped.

Decades after the Wretched Scrattle, after the history books had all been written, revised, rewritten, thrown away, and written again by someone who'd never lived through the events in the first place, the proprietor of the Rat-Upon-a-Cat inn in the small village of Three Fingers would post a sign on the front of his property that read, "Visit the room where Queen Iphigenia declared war on Umberfall." It was false advertising. What she actually said was:

"I'd like to stay here and see where this goes."

Admittedly, that didn't have the same ring to it.

"Is that a request? Or your official word?" asked General Lillia Lutgard. The General sat across from the Princess, eyeing her like a jeweler searching for imperfections in a gemstone.

"It's my official word," said Iphigenia.

"You sound sure."

"I am."

Lillia nodded as if to indicate no imperfections had been found.

Iphigenia continued, "If Umberfall has snuck an agent into the Wretched Scrattle, then I believe there's a good chance of invasion regardless of whether they win or lose. War is inevitable. That means we'll need an organized defensive front here at the base of the Black Mountain to hold them off. I would rather lead them myself, here, at the front, than from a hundred miles away, safely hidden behind the walls of Lyra Castelis. I'll require your help, of course, General."

"Very well," said Lillia. "I'll send word to the castle at once." She paused. "Although it's you who'll have to deal with your father, not me."

There was something winking and conspiratorial about how the General said that last part that made Iphigenia fight back a smile. She nodded, stood up, and dismissed Lillia.

After the General left, Iphigenia summoned Oren, the soldier who'd informed them of Umberfall's plans. He'd been tasked with sending scouts into the Black Mountain to head off Vaswell Gandy before he could make it to the top of the mountain, as well as opening a line of communication with Overseer Marl if possible, to warn her about what was happening. This was assuming she wasn't involved. The idea that Marl had been compromised during her time in Umberfall while working as a spy for Nth nagged at Iphigenia. Mostly because if that was true, then there was nothing left for her to do. There would be a war, and the Black Mountain would be stuck in the middle—Thisby would be stuck in the middle.

This was the last bit of information she'd asked Oren to gather from the Black Mountain, as a personal favor. She needed to find out if Thisby was okay. And as much as Iphigenia refused to admit it, that was the first question on her mind when Oren entered her room. Not if he'd figured out whether Marl was working for Umberfall to bring down the Black Mountain, not if he'd heard whether Vaswell Gandy had succeeded in his mission, but if Thisby was okay.

Oren bowed quickly and Iphigenia nodded in return.

"What have you heard?" she asked, dispensing with formalities.

"Nothing yet. Our scouts haven't returned from the mountain. It could be days before they return."

Iphigenia's heart sank. It was still early. She knew that. But she'd hoped for something. Even if it was just a rumor.

"There's something else," said Oren. He seemed nervous but then again, he often seemed that way. Especially around the Princess.

"Go on," she coaxed.

Oren stepped aside from the doorway, and in hobbled a tiny, knobby old goblin.

"Hello, dear."

"Grunda!"

The goblin smiled.

"Hah! Good to know that the Princess of Nth remembers my name," she said with a playful snort.

Grunda invited herself in, and Iphigenia waved her over toward a vacant chair. Thankfully, Iphigenia had managed to secure a second chair from the proprietor of the Rat-Upon-a-Cat. It was quite the luxury.

"How have you been?" asked the Princess, but the goblin waved her off.

"Never mind the small talk . . . let's get down to it!" said Grunda as she grunted and settled into her seat. Old goblins, like old people, do a lot of grunting when they sit.

"Yes, let's," said Iphigenia with a smile.

Grunda's demeanor was a welcome change from the way Iphigenia noticed the soldiers had been treating her. Even Lillia was guilty of being overly formal at times. Iphigenia often found herself missing the way Thisby spoke to her. As if she were a regular person. It was refreshing to hear the goblin do the same.

Grunda turned in her seat to face Oren, who was standing by the door, looking bewildered. "You can call off your scouts, if you want. I can tell you exactly what's going on in the Black Mountain."

"Please do," said Iphigenia.

Grunda turned back to the Princess, who in turn nodded for Oren to close the door.

"First of all, Thisby's all right. She's doin' her best and it's hard. But she's all right."

Iphigenia felt her eyes get a little watery with relief. That Grunda had known it was her first concern, that she hadn't had to ask or put on airs, was almost as much of a relief as the words themselves. Iphigenia nodded appreciatively.

"Second, you're right that there's a spy from Umberfall making a mess of things. Only I'm not so sure you've got the right guy."

Oren made a face. "I beg your pardon?"

Grunda turned to look at the soldier and then back to Iphigenia. "Why are the pretty ones always so slow?"

"Excuse me!" said Oren, turning red, but Iphigenia waved him to be quiet.

"Go on," said Iphigenia.

"That kid, Vaswell Gandy, I'm not sure he's your spy. His father has dealings with Umberfall, but I'm not so sure about the kid."

"And how would you know?" demanded Oren, speaking out of turn.

Iphigenia shot him a dirty look, but he was right. It was a fair question.

"I've got eyes and ears on the inside," said Grunda.

"There's a barrier preventing magical beings from entering the dungeon during the Wretched Scrattle, correct? How can you get inside?" asked Iphigenia.

"I can't," said Grunda. The goblin grinned, revealing a mouthful of crooked yellow teeth—perfectly natural for a goblin—and reached into a leather satchel that Iphigenia hadn't noticed until now. She pulled out a jar covered by a lid with airholes punched in it. A large red worm was curled up around the base of the jar. From its head, twelve eyes glittered like rubies back at Iphigenia, studying her, and she suddenly had the feeling that someone was rooting around inside her brain like it was a trash bin.

"What is it?" asked Iphigenia.

"Mindworm," said Grunda. "Incredible creatures."

The mindworm wriggled around, and Iphigenia couldn't help but thinking that, yes, mindworms truly *were* incredible creatures. Perhaps she should elect a mindworm to a position of power? Grunda unscrewed the top of the jar and sprinkled in something that looked like ground-up leaves, and as the mindworm began to eat contentedly, Iphigenia felt her thoughts return to normal.

Grunda tucked the jar back into her satchel as she continued, "They're all over the dungeon. And they can relay messages to each other over thousands of miles, so when one is apart from the rest . . . they're still quite together."

"You're using them to keep an eye on the dungeon," added Iphigenia.

"You might say that . . . ," she replied, but trailed off. "The important part is that Thisby is okay. She's still going to win the Wretched Scrattle, thanks to your help. But what I need from you is not to be too hasty."

An uncomfortable sensation crept into the room like an imaginary spider. Iphigenia motioned for Oren to leave, and he gladly obeyed.

"What do you mean? Don't be too hasty?" said Iphigenia after the door had latched shut and she was certain they were alone.

"Don't take this the wrong way, Princess, but you need to stay out of the affairs of the Black Mountain. Focus on the affairs of Nth instead."

"The affairs of the Black Mountain *are* the affairs of Nth."

Iphigenia refused to flinch. She knew that most goblins believed the Black Mountain should be fully independent of Nth. She wasn't surprised Grunda felt the same; however, after all they'd been through together, she'd hoped that the old goblin would show her a little more deference. That was clearly not the case.

"This is about more than politics. It's about more than a war between men. More than a squabble over land or money. The fate of the world . . . the Eyes in the Dark . . ." Grunda trailed off.

"The Eyes in the Dark is locked safely away in a prison you built, need I remind you," said Iphigenia sharply.

"There's no such thing as 'safe' where the Eyes in the Dark is concerned!" snapped Grunda.

"We're on the same side!" insisted Iphigenia, no longer fully convinced of the words herself.

"Are we?" asked the goblin. "You humans are all alike! Playing a game where you don't even know the rules! Why do you think I've done everything that I've done? To keep the Eyes in the Dark at bay! To keep the dungeon safe!"

Iphigenia was shocked to see that tears were beginning to form in the old goblin's huge dinner-plate eyes.

"It will be safe. It will. When Thisby is Master—" began Iphigenia.

"You're right," Grunda interrupted. "When Thisby is Master. When Thisby is Master, things will be different."

"What do you mean?" asked Iphigenia.

"Wait and see," said Grunda.

And with that, the goblin vanished.

# CHAPTER 17

Marl stalked around the blackdoor machine with her hands twisted behind her back, her mind racing. She hadn't slept in days, hopped up on red tea and unable to pry herself away from the flickering screens, watching the mayhem unfold below.

The gamekeeper was still out there somewhere. The last time the Overseer had managed to spot her was when she'd encountered the cuco in the tunnels behind the ice wraith's den, but soon after that she'd lost her trail. It'd been one of her most profound disappointments that the creature had chosen to run away instead of finishing the job and making her life easier, but that had been the problem with the cuco since she'd first introduced it to the dungeon: it was highly unpredictable.

She'd bought it from a monster trader who specialized in exotic creatures, with the idea that one cuco could easily take the place of a hundred other monsters, since it could take nearly any form. Marl had been hopeful that it was finally about to earn back what she'd paid for it by finishing off the irritating girl, but for some reason it ran away. The cuco had been a spectacular waste of money, mostly just killing other monsters and doing very little else. Still, there were other things to be optimistic about.

So far, Marl had seen fourteen people make it to the gates of the castle, and not one of them had gone a step farther. That was something. There were still hundreds of adventurers left in the dungeon, though, and it could take weeks to clear them all out. However, if the nagging feeling in her gut was right, the end would come much sooner than that.

The Overseer hadn't left the blackdoor machine room since she'd taken the Master and tossed him into prison. And why should she? From here, she could watch over the entire dungeon. As far as she was concerned, she should've insisted that the blackdoor chamber be her office from the moment she'd arrived at the castle. Only the Master never would've allowed that. He was so set in his ways. Fortunately for her, he was rotting away in jail now while she was free to do whatever she pleased . . . with one impossibly irritating exception.

Marl had long since given up on attempting to use the

blackdoor machine to create actual blackdoors. She could load up scrying spheres and watch events unfold, but creating actual blackdoors, let alone blackdoor beads, was far beyond her comprehension, and she'd been the best student in her class at the Grand College of Arcanology—*go, Werewolves!* What really drove her crazy was how someone as clueless as the Master had managed to figure out how to work the machine.

The Master had no intention of sharing his secret. Marl had tried to have some ghouls "extract" the information the hard way, but as simpering and pathetic as he might appear, the Master knew the value of this information, and Marl quickly become convinced he'd die before he ever gave it up. She decided to try again after the Wretched Scrattle was over, but for now she'd have to make do with just being able to watch.

A ghoul entered with her red tea and set it down by the door. Before Marl could even stand, he was gone. Too many times she'd flung the tray in his face for not having it the proper temperature or it not being sweet enough until they'd reached a sort of armistice that involved them never coming within twenty feet of each other or making direct eye contact. The ghoul would simply leave the tray by the door full and come back later to find an empty teacup. So far, the arrangement had worked fairly well for both parties.

Listening to the ghoul's footsteps as he scurried away back to the kitchen, Marl came over and grabbed the tray. Not only had she not left the blackdoor machine room since the Master's imprisonment, but she also hadn't bathed or slept. She'd barely eaten, either. Tea had been her primary source of nourishment, and it was a poor one at that. Yet she hardly noticed her hunger with all the other things going on in the dungeon.

Every screen was a constant reminder of her abject failure as Overseer, but never was it worse than when she realized the gamekeeper was still alive. When Marl realized that Thisby had paired up with a conjurer, she'd broken a dozen scrying spheres in a fit of pure rage. That she'd made the mistake of omitting conjurers from the contest rules was infuriating. That Thisby had teamed up with that conjurer was more than she could handle. Marl didn't believe in fate, but it was hard for her to shake the feeling that the plucky little gamekeeper with the big nose was destined to undo her. What Marl couldn't figure out was why fate had it out for her to begin with.

After all, what had she done as Overseer that was so bad, really? She'd tried to bring a little law and order to the dungeon. So what? She'd hosted an event that brought more people to the Black Mountain than ever before. Was that a crime? Sure, she'd planned on robbing them blind, but she hadn't done it yet. And if she was being fair, she was still planning on taking the dungeon by force and selling it off to the highest bidder, but that was just business. It wasn't anything personal. Why shouldn't the kingdom that paid more have the better army?

Marl paced around the chamber, looking at the bags of

gold coins that she'd stockpiled. They lay around the black-door chamber like sandbags hoping to keep out the tide. She'd taken to using them for furniture, for all the good they were currently doing her. The time to cut and run had long passed. She had too much gold now to remove it from the mountain without the use of blackdoors. She was going to have to see this thing out to the bitter end.

On the screen above her was the scrying sphere that showed the path to Grimstone Castle. Marl sighed deeply as she watched Thisby walk on-screen.

"This is it," she said to herself.

Marl knew there was nothing to do now but watch the end play itself out. She hoped it would at least make for a good show.

If Thisby made it through the gates, if the gamekeeper won, she knew that her career as the Overseer would be, well, over. Anyone else, she may have been able to manipulate into keeping her around. With Thisby there would be no convincing. It would be risky and possibly lead to a full-blown revolt, but if she found the opportunity there was always murder, she supposed, if it came to that.

*You will not kill the gamekeeper,* said the voice that had become all too familiar since she'd come to the Black Mountain.

Marl finished the last sip of her tea and scowled at the bottom of her empty cup.

"Oh, go away!" she screeched "You and your bad advice!"

She cursed and threw the teacup against the blackdoor machine, where it shattered into hundreds of tiny pieces, before she sat down on a pile of gold coins to feel sorry for herself.

Thisby stood at the base of the tall ladder that led up three hundred and four rungs to the wooden gangway. If she followed the gangway to the right, she would end up at her bedroom, and if she followed it to the left, there was a path that would take her straight to the castle. By the time she reached the top of the ladder, it was all she could do not to follow the gangway to the right, to open her bedroom door, to crawl into bed, get good and snugly, and fall fast asleep. But there was still work to do. After she became the Master of the Black Mountain, there'd doubtless be even more.

Despite her better judgment, Thisby had allowed herself to fantasize about what it meant to become the new Master. She knew that her only real choice was to abdicate the title to Grunda, but there was no harm in daydreaming about what it might be like to have some real power for once. Maybe it'd be nice to boss people around. Unfortunately, she knew that wasn't true. The little taste she'd had of being a boss under Marl's new rules had been a miserable experience. It might've been a nice thing to dream about in theory, but the reality was something else entirely.

She was still toying with the idea, however, when they approached the gates into Castle Grimstone.

The gleaming skulls cast mocking grimaces out from between the twisted spikes as Thisby tried to open the door. Unsurprisingly, it was locked. She knew the odds of the door being unlocked was roughly a bajillion to one, but you never knew unless you tried. Thisby was a firm believer in always trying the obvious thing first. She shrugged and started looking for another way in.

She combed the area. The only thing that struck her as odd were the thousands of char marks on the floor and walls. Little ones. Like someone had sprayed the walls with fireworks. She followed the path where they seemed most concentrated and discovered a pile of ash in the corner of the room that'd previously gone unnoticed, as it had blended in with the mottled gray floor.

Thisby kicked the ash with her toe.

"What is it?" asked Mingus.

"I don't think you want to know," said a familiar voice.

Thisby spun around to see Elfriede. She held Bero with one arm, the other being used to point the tip of her dagger at his Adam's apple.

"Where's Vas?' asked Thisby.

"Dead," said Elfriede.

"She's lying!" yelled Bero, but she pressed the dagger into his throat and he shut up. A thin ribbon of blood began to trickle down his neck.

"You're ruining my fun," she sighed. "He's with my men. He's safe. For now."

"Thisby! She's a traitor!" blurted Bero.

"Another word and you die," rasped Elfriede.

"Leave him alone!" said Thisby.

"I will. When I'm done," said Elfriede.

"You're from Umberfall," said Thisby.

"Don't be stupid, girl," said Elfriede. "I just need him to open this door. If he helps me, he lives. It's not complicated."

"Why do you need him?" asked Thisby.

"Think about it. You said it yourself when we first met. The Overseer doesn't want anybody to win the Wretched Scrattle. So why do you think she excluded magic users?"

Thisby took another look around at the chamber. She was no wizard, but she could practically smell the magic in the air. The entrance into Castle Grimstone had to be a trap that could only be solved with magic.

"You need him to open the door," said Thisby.

"There it is. Now you're using your brain."

Elfriede prodded Bero forward.

"Step back or he dies," Elfriede commanded.

Thisby did as she said.

Elfriede marched Bero across the sooty floor until they reached the door, where she motioned to a small skull that was inset, like a button, to the right of the door.

"Press it," she ordered. There was no waver in her voice.

Bero did as she said, and a loud buzz filled the chamber, followed by a voice that sounded like two sheets of metal rubbing together.

"What is the secret of magic?" it asked.

"Well, what is it?" demanded Elfriede.

Bero remained silent.

"Say something, curse you!" she shouted.

There was a mechanical clicking sound, followed by dozens of tiny balls of light flooding into the chamber. The first one that whizzed by Thisby made the air sparkle with electric heat and the second one actually touched her cheek, causing her to cry out in pain. Thisby dove for the floor as more balls of light zoomed into the room.

"Wisps!" Mingus yelled over the intense buzzing noise.

"Say something right now or you die!" screamed Elfriede.

More wisps shot by Thisby and stung her with their electric jolts as several smacked into the wall, leaving behind tiny scorch marks where they made contact with the stone. She flinched away from their stings, which were growing more painful by the second.

Everything around her was a swarm of glowing light as the wisps zipped around the chamber, stinging her. The only thing she was able to focus on was Mingus, who for some reason was as visible as ever through the chaos. Distracted as she was by the pain of the stinging, it took her a few seconds to figure out why.

"Mingus! Ow! They're avoiding your—ow!—light! Glow—ow!—brighter!"

There was a burst of intense light from her lantern, and

*"Mingus! Ow! They're avoiding your—ow!—light! Glow—ow!—brighter!"*

the wisps scattered. The light that emanated off him was so bright that Thisby couldn't look at Mingus directly. She had to shield her eyes as she and Mingus parted the sea of wisps and made their way back to the door.

"I can't keep this up for long!" shouted Mingus. "We need to run! The other way!"

"I can do this!" said Thisby. "I have to!"

Mingus's light faded a bit, and the bubble of wisps around them constricted. There was no way to see Bero and Elfriede through the swarm. They could've been right next to her for all she knew. Thisby pushed through the swarm toward the door.

Mingus's light faded, and the bubble of light grew smaller. The wisps drew close. Thisby reached out her hand blindly through the chaos, feeling around for the button near the door. At last her fingers found it, and she pressed the button a second time. Barely audible over the din of the room was the metallic voice.

"What is the secret of magic?"

Mingus's light faded a bit more, so only a thin layer of space separated them from the wisps, who swarmed like hungry piranhas around the legs of a cow fording a river.

This was it. She had to think. Magic was always some sort of riddle. A logic problem. Last year, the spell on the Darkwell had been broken because something passed through an impassable gate. It was about opposites. What was the opposite of the secret of magic?

Mingus's light gave out, and the bubble of wisps collapsed. They singed Thisby's flesh and burned holes in her tunic. She was dizzy with pain, nearly delirious, when something popped into her head. It was stupid. It was illogical. It was something only a wizard would come up with.

"There is no secret of magic!" Thisby shouted at the top of her lungs.

As quickly as they had arrived, the wisps vanished back into the wall.

The room went silent and Thisby collapsed, dropping Mingus. His lantern rolled a few feet forward and bumped into the door, which had slowly begun to open.

Thisby lay on the chamber floor, her skin hot and tingling from the wisps' stings, for a full minute before she pulled herself to her feet. She picked up Mingus and surveyed the damage. The entire room was covered in ash, and Elfriede was lying motionless in the center of it all, at least what was left of her. She was darkened and skeletal, but Bero was beneath her, seemingly having used her body as a shield.

There was nothing to be done for Elfriede, but Bero still seemed to be breathing, if just barely. Thisby pushed Elfriede off and knelt down beside Bero's body.

"Mingus, can you . . ." She trailed off.

"I'm weak but I'll try," he said.

Thisby slid the barely glowing Mingus out of his lantern onto Bero's badly burned body. The conjurer was so covered with welts that it was hard to tell where to start. Mingus glowed faintly as he passed over the worst of it. He was just as surprised as Thisby when after a few minutes Bero opened his eyes.

His speech was garbled, but Thisby could've sworn he asked for Donato.

"No. It's Thisby," she said.

Mingus was so exhausted that he could barely maintain his shape. He was practically a liquid when Thisby scooped him into his jar. Bero seemed to be coming to his senses.

"My spell books," he said faintly.

"They're not here," said Thisby.

"Small one. Belt," he said.

Thisby checked his belt pockets and discovered he was correct. There was the small leather-bound pocket-size spell book. The cover was a bit burned, but it was more or less intact. She pulled it out and tried to hand it to him, but he refused.

"You need . . . to read it," he wheezed.

Thisby exchanged looks with Mingus, who sloshed around in his lantern, barely able to hold himself together.

"I can't," she said. "I'm not magic."

Bero let out a laugh that quickly turned into a cough.

"There's no . . . secret . . . of magic," he rasped.

Bero closed his eyes momentarily, and Thisby flipped frantically through the book, looking for a healing spell. She nudged Bero awake and showed him pages that looked like they might be right.

"This one?" she asked.

Bero shook his head.

"How about this one?" she asked, turning the page.

He shook his head again.

Finally she found a spell that had a picture of ice crystals at the bottom of the page. Maybe it would help with his burns. She showed Bero the page, and he nodded.

"Read the words in your head," he mumbled. "Place your hand . . . on your chest."

"Not on you?" she asked.

He shook his head no again and closed his eyes.

"Hurry," he said.

Thisby took a deep breath, placed her hand on her chest, and read.

She'd never tried to read magic before, and it was far more difficult than she realized. The words seemed to change as she read them, as if they were trying to escape her understanding. It was more than reading, it was like the words were a wild animal she was trying to corner. She had to restart twice, but on the third attempt she felt something slide into place in her mind. She'd cornered the meaning at last, and now it slid into her brain fully formed. It was a frightening thing to comprehend.

Thisby froze. Not out of panic but because something had gone terribly wrong.

Every muscle in her body had locked in place. Even the small ones, the little ones that she didn't even know had been moving automatically until they no longer could. She couldn't move her mouth to yell for help, she couldn't even blink her eyes. All she could do was stare, her eyes fixed straight ahead at a permanent focal distance of about two feet in front of her face.

In her periphery, she saw Bero struggle into a sitting position and pluck the spell book from her numb hand. He opened it, recited something that she couldn't comprehend, and then climbed to his feet, looking much better than he had a moment ago, his fresh wounds fading into old scars before her eyes.

Bero disappeared from her view. After what felt like an eternity, because now every moment she couldn't move felt like forever, he returned with his bag of spell books and stepped out in front of Thisby with a wide smile.

"I'm actually sorry about this," he said, his voice sounding alien and distant.

"I suppose that was the last test then," he continued. "The fail-safe. I assumed there'd be one. Only someone who truly understands magic could open the door, yet nobody who understands magic was allowed to enter the tournament. It has a simple elegance, I suppose, but it's far from foolproof. After all, you figured it out, right? And you didn't even know enough about magic not to cast a paralysis spell on yourself."

A single tear rolled down Thisby's cheek, only it wasn't from sadness or anger but from not being able to blink.

"Crying? Really?" said Bero mockingly, followed by a

*tut-tut* clucking noise that made Thisby want to scream and punch him in the face, neither of which she could do for obvious reasons. "Don't worry. You're not going to die. You'll wake up soon enough. In fact, come tomorrow morning you'll carry on as gamekeeper. Just like you always wanted. Only you'll do so under Umberfallian rule. Under my rule. It won't be as bad as you think. You might even learn to like it. If everything goes according to plan and you play along nicely, there's even room for promotion. You won't be Master, but those are the breaks, I suppose. Again, I'm truly sorry I had to do this to you. It'll all be over soon, though, and then everything will be back to normal. You understand, right?"

Thisby was red-hot with anger.

"By the way, I just wanted to let you know, Vas didn't have anything to do with this. His father hired me and Donato to help him win the Scrattle. Can you imagine? Anyway, I changed the plan. He was never meant to be Master; he never even wanted the job. I did. So it goes. Goodbye, Thisby. I'll see you in the morning."

With that Bero faded out of focus as he walked into Castle Grimstone.

The Wretched Scrattle would be over soon. Bero would win. Umberfall would win. And once they claimed the dungeon in the name of Umberfall, a war with Nth would be inevitable. The Black Mountain was doomed.

Thisby felt herself begin to drift into something between sleep and passing out. Her immobile eyes began to darken as the world softened into nothingness. Her last waking thought was that this was exactly why you should never trust a wizard.

There was still no answer. Annoyed, the Master snapped his scrobble closed and stuffed it back into his pocket next to the now mostly empty bottle of facial moisturizer—prison, it turned out, was very dry. But that wasn't even the worst of it.

Prison was also cold and it smelled bad and the Master was convinced that he was due to go crazy from boredom at any moment. There was a way out, but he'd been putting it off with the vain hope that Thisby might still come through for him, though it was seeming less likely by the minute.

The Master picked up the chunk of loose stone he'd pried from the back wall and weighed it in the palm of his hand before setting it down again. He'd give her one more chance to answer. Maybe two.

There were footsteps down the hall.

"Hello?" called the Master, nudging the chunk of stone under his mattress with the toe of his boot. "Are you coming to let me out? I'm very bored."

There was no response.

"And my skin is dry," he added.

Still nothing.

The Master walked over to the bars and peered down the hallway into darkness. The footsteps were growing closer, but there was no torchlight. Whatever was coming this way apparently didn't need light to see. Something else was wrong, too. There was only one way into and out of the hold, from the stairway down at the barely lit end of the hall, but the footsteps were coming from the other direction. The Master's pulse began to quicken.

"Marl?" he asked, knowing full well it wasn't.

"No," said a familiar voice from the darkness.

A shape began to swim out of the void, and the Master felt his breath catch in his throat. He opened his mouth to speak, but no words came out.

"How do I look?" said the figure.

The Master peered out from the bars at the last thing he'd expected to see: himself.

"Awful, I suppose," said the creature who'd taken his shape.

There was one notable exception in the otherwise identical version of himself that made it possible to tell the two of them apart—aside from knowing which side of the bars they were on. This duplicate had a set of horrible yellow eyes with slits like a lizard. They were the kind that the Master had seen before in countless visions since coming to the Black Mountain. They belonged to the Eyes in the Dark.

"Impossible," said the Master.

The Eyes in the Dark laughed. It was the Master's own laugh, and it was strange to hear it coming from someone else.

"Is it now?" said the Eyes in the Dark.

"You're not really him," said the Master. "You're

something else. A doppelgänger. No. A boogeyman, is that it? Perhaps a cuco. Some creature that can take the form of its victim's fears? Stop me if I'm getting warm."

The Eyes in the Dark approached the bars, and the Master backed away.

"If you say so," he said with a grin.

"The Eyes in the Dark is locked away in the Deep Down."

"Perhaps," said the Eyes in the Dark. "But not forever. Our time is coming."

"I won't have this conversation with a mirage," said the Master.

The Eyes in the Dark pressed his face between the bars of the Master's cell. The Master stepped back, watching in horror as the creature began to ooze between the bars, a copy of his own face stretching grotesquely, his body compressing like melting wax until it re-formed on the other side, on the inside of his cage.

The Master tripped backward over his own straw mattress and hit his head against the wall as he fell. He clutched the back of his head, feeling his hair growing warm and wet and sticky with blood from where it'd struck, while the Eyes in the Dark walked slowly forward toward where he sat.

"The end is coming. First for you. Then for the dungeon. Then for everyone," said the creature, his yellow eyes shining.

The Master reached beneath his mattress and grabbed the chunk of stone, knowing it was now or never. Taking a deep breath, he slammed the stone into the right side of his mouth. The creature took a step back.

Fishing around in his mouth with two fingers, the Master removed a black tooth, shiny and wet with blood. He spit on the floor of his cell as he stood up, facing the bewildered creature.

"I was hopin' I woodna' hafta do dat," he mumbled.

The Master threw the tooth against the back wall as hard as he could, and with a popping fizz a blackdoor portal ripped open.

The monster was still staring in disbelief when the Master jumped through the portal and disappeared from the dungeon for good.

"Thisby! Thisby!"

". . ."

"Oh, no. You're still frozen, aren't you?"

". . ."

"I'll take that as a yes. Okay, I'm going to try to get out of my lantern. Don't move."

". . ."

"That was a joke. Never mind."

". . ."

"Well, I thought it was funny."

". . ."

"Okay, I'm out! I'm gonna climb up your arm now."

Thisby saw what she could only assume was Mingus

sliding mere inches in front of her face. With her focal distance stuck beyond where he was, he looked more like a bluish blur than anything.

"I'm going to try my slime healing magic, okay? Although I guess I should call it 'star jelly' healing magic, huh?"

He paused.

"You don't think Bero was making *that* stuff up, do you? Because he's evil and all? Nah, probably not. I can't think of a reason why he would. Never mind."

He paused again.

"Oh, and Thisby? You're really not going to like this. After it's done, I think it'd probably be best if we never spoke of it again."

The bluish blur disappeared from her vision, and for a while there was nothing.

The first sensation that came back to her was the feeling of choking. Then her vision returned and she felt warm all over as blood rushed back into her skin. Thisby collapsed to the ground and felt herself start to vomit up something warm, only it wasn't bile that came out of her mouth but Mingus, slimy and wet and blue and screaming as loud as he could.

"Ahhhhhhh, I hate that!"

She coughed and rolled over, gasping for air.

"You taste terrible!" she yelled, spitting to get the taste from her mouth.

"It was no treat for me, either!" shouted Mingus, sliding as quickly as he could back into his open jar. "I really wish we could go one full year without somebody coughing me up like a hairball!"

"I'm sorry. Thank you," said Thisby after she'd regained her composure.

"The real thanks will be us never talking about that again. Now come on, we have to stop Bero before he gets to the top of the castle!"

Thisby took a deep breath and entered the castle, the mocking skulls that adorned the giant doors frozen in silent laughter as they closed slowly behind her.

"I hate magic," she muttered under her breath.

Castle Grimstone swallowed her whole as the door shut, locking automatically with a cacophony of grinding gears and clanking mechanics. From the threshold of the castle, the impressive blackness of it was overwhelming. The tile, the walls, the ceiling, the decor, everything in the castle was as black as the night sky and dripping with an abundance of shapes and textures, which in the low light created an optical illusion that made Thisby feel as if she were floating in space. She gave her eyes a moment to adjust—after the intense brightness of the wisps, she was still seeing spots—and as soon as she was able, she stepped forward into the castle.

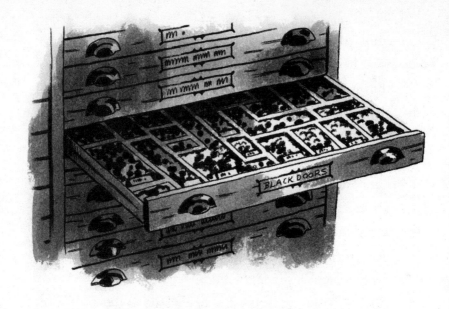

# CHAPTER 18

The last time she'd been here, Thisby had needed Jono's help to find her way to the Master's room. With any luck, Bero was experiencing the same problem. It was her only hope.

Castle Grimstone was designed to be intentionally confusing to anybody who didn't live there, and to this end, it was incredibly effective. There were winding hallways that doubled back on themselves, dead ends, and stairs that went up for four flights only to let out into a broom closet. Combined with the sheer amount of stuff—the cumulative legacy of generations of trophy-happy Masters—the castle was positively labyrinthine. Thisby's best hope at finding the Master's chamber was to combine the few bits and pieces that she could remember with a healthy dose of good old-fashioned luck.

Mingus's green light guided the way as Thisby moved briskly through hallway after hallway. She passed libraries, bathrooms, bedrooms—even one children's bedroom, which struck her as odd—before she heard cursing coming from up ahead. Mingus dimmed his glow, and Thisby crept along as quiet as a particularly stealthy mouse, rolling her feet the way Grunda had shown her all those years ago to avoid making noise. The cursing grew louder. It was coming from a room up ahead.

"Who needs this many bedrooms?" grunted the voice.

"Bero!" whispered Mingus before Thisby could shush him. They both knew who it was. There was no reason he had to say it out loud.

Thisby crouched low and crept close enough that she could peer through the crack in the bedroom door, where she caught the reflection of Bero in the mirror.

"Hide!" whispered Mingus. "You don't want him to see you!"

"Of course I don't want him to see me! There's no reason to say it! You're just going to get us caught if you keep saying things!" she whispered back angrily.

"Thisby? Is that you?" asked Bero, turning around.

He asked the question despite clearly recognizing Thisby's voice. Apparently, it was just the day to say obvious things out loud.

Bero stepped cautiously away from the bed and pulled out

the small spell book that was tucked into his belt. Thisby had no choice but to abandon stealth and run.

Bero sprang from the doorway and shouted an incantation. A bolt of lightning shot past Thisby's head and exploded an old grandfather clock at the end of the hall. She turned the corner and heard another shot miss.

It was the first time since losing her backpack that Thisby was thankful she didn't have it with her. Over the years of carrying it, she'd built up quite a lot of leg strength, so now, she was remarkably fast without it. There were more flashes of light and more explosions, but she could hear his voice recede as he chanted the incantations from farther and farther away. She was losing him. The two of them were essentially polar opposites; Bero was big and slow and Thisby was small and quick. If he hit her with a single spell, she was done for, but as long as she could keep her distance, she might be able to outrun him all the way to the Master's office—assuming she could find it.

Thisby turned to find a long hallway lined with suits of armor clearly not designed for human use; they were far too big and had far too many limbs. At the end of the hall was a set of double doors. When she had a moment of weakness and looked back the way she came, a lightning bolt nearly blasted her in the face for her troubles as Bero rounded the corner, firing at will. There was only one option left. She'd have to hope the double doors at the end of the hall didn't lead into a dead end.

There's an old expression that goes "hope in one hand, poop in the other, and see which fills up first." Well, that's the polite version (as polite a version as you can get, anyway). Thisby hadn't heard that particular expression, but she understood the spirit of it better than most people her age, which was to say that she didn't put a lot of stock in hope. And when she burst through the double doors to find herself in a sort of strange armory, her hopes, short-lived though they were, were immediately dashed. There was no other exit. The room was a dead end. Thisby knew full well which hand had filled up first.

The walls of the armory were lined with more inhuman suits of armor that leered menacingly at her as she entered. From Mingus's swaying lantern, the armor almost seemed to move of its own accord, dancing in the blue-green light. Thisby reminded herself it was just an illusion and pressed on.

The middle of the room was divided into four long rows of glass display cases, which contained an incredible variety of rare and exotic weapons that were hard to imagine being functional in battle. Thisby ran her fingers over the glass as the curiosities contained within seemed to call out to her, mesmerizing her with questions. A sword-whip hybrid designed to look like a snake sat next to a crossbow that fired bolts forward and backward simultaneously. Two sets of barbed claws rested on a shelf above what appeared to be a helmet designed for a monstrous bird, far larger than anything of its kind Thisby had ever seen in the dungeon. She realized she'd let herself get momentarily distracted by the room's oddities when she heard the doors open behind her, and she bumped into a rack of crooked arrows that went clattering to the ground.

"I'm impressed," said Bero from back near the entrance. "That spell should've held you for hours. You're far more clever than I assumed."

Thisby stepped quietly, deeper into the rows of display cases, trying to keep as much distance as possible between herself and his voice.

"First the riddle at the gates and now here you are. You would've made a fine wizard. Or a conjurer, I suppose. All those terms! They're too confusing, aren't they? Wizard, conjurer, mage, warlock, blah, blah, blah! They're all different ways to do the same thing! I read spells. Wizards memorize them. Sorcerers internalize them. Warlocks tattoo them on their skin. Isn't that weird? Most people just say 'wizard' because it's easy to remember."

He mumbled a spell and the room lit up. It was the same one he'd used earlier, in the lindorm's chamber.

"You know, people look down on conjurers. That's why we were forgotten when they were writing the rules of the Wretched Scrattle. It's the reliance on books, I think. It's a real shame. In a way, you rely on books, too, don't you? I've seen your little notebooks. Without them, what are you? Without my spell books, what am I? The truth is, I don't know."

His steps were getting closer. Thisby ducked into the next row.

"You can still have the job, you know? If you give up now, I'll let you stay on as gamekeeper. I don't mind your ambition. I actually respect it."

Thisby was tempted to respond, to tell him that she'd never work for him, maybe even to ask him why he was doing this. But she knew that was what he wanted. He was trying to goad her into talking, into giving away her position. Besides, what did she care about why he was doing this? Maybe Bero was just loyal to Umberfall. It didn't matter. The only thing that mattered now was that if Thisby didn't beat him to the top of the castle and become the new Master of the Black Mountain, the dungeon was doomed. Perhaps all of Nth by the time Umberfall was done with it.

She heard his footsteps echoing around the room as he searched the first row of shelves. She crept silently into the last. Unlike Thisby, Bero had never had a goblin teach him the art of moving stealthily. If the tables were turned, she'd have been able to find him easily.

The last row contained items behind glass that hardly seemed like weapons at all. There were about a dozen short, carved wooden sticks brightly painted and engraved with runes. Next to those were seemingly mundane items; a pair of boots, a jeweled crown, a bag of seeds. Near the center of the row were several wooden crates overflowing with items that had not yet been sorted into the displays. It was impossible to tell how long they'd been sitting patiently, waiting to be sorted and hung, but from the thick layer of dust that caked them, Thisby would have guessed it was far longer than she'd been alive.

From two rows over, Bero let out a frustrated snort.

"Fine. If you want to play hide-and-seek, let's play," he said, and followed it up with more arcane mumbling.

Thisby peeked out from behind the display case on the end of the row to see him reading another spell from the small book, which still bore the damage from their encounter with the wisps. Not that it mattered now, but the burns in her tunic had healed quite nicely. When Bero was finished, he waved his hands and with a burst of pink light, two wolves—taller at the shoulder than he was—appeared by his side. He whispered something inaudible into their ears, and the wolves began to stalk away, along opposing walls, their hackles raised. They were hunting. And Thisby had nowhere left to run.

"Well," said Bero, breathing a sigh of relief. "This is where we part ways. I'm going to go win the Wretched Scrattle now. If by some miracle you survive this, please report to my office first thing tomorrow morning. There are a number of changes to be made in the dungeon, and I'd like to get started as soon as possible. Goodbye, Thisby."

Thisby could hear the low, rumbling growl of the wolves getting louder as they stalked down the ends of the rows. Beyond that she heard the sound of the door—the only way out—closing. The long shadows of the wolves swayed against the back wall of the armory as they stalked toward her down the aisles. Mingus looked helplessly to her. Thisby wished she could offer him some sort of comfort, but how? There was no way out.

The wolves were closing in. Thisby looked around, desperate for the miracle Bero had mentioned. The closest she could find was noticing that one of the crates full of unsorted items had a loose lid, which perhaps she could hide under. It would only delay the inevitable, but considering what the inevitable was, delaying it wasn't such a bad choice. Just as the wolves' muzzles crested beyond the edge of the display case and Thisby caught sight of their slavering jaws, she pulled the lid shut on top of her.

Inside, the crate was filled with wood shavings hiding something big and soft, which Thisby prodded with her foot, but it was too dark to see without Mingus's light. Outside, she could hear the sniffing of the wolves and the soft pads of their feet as they turned down her row, closing in. Thisby felt her heart pounding in her ears.

The inside of the crate was swelteringly hot and almost entirely devoid of air. Thisby struggled to hold on to the little amount of breath that she could find. She buried herself below the wood shavings so that only her face was exposed and listened as hard as possible.

First there was more sniffing, the beasts practically tasting the air through their long noses. This was followed by the nudging of the crates, including her own. Through the narrow slit between the lid and the crate, Thisby could see their large, leathery noses and catch flashes of the wolves' bared yellow teeth. Her heart raced. She felt more trapped than she'd ever been. Even when she and Iphigenia had been trapped on a bridge between hungry wyverns, at least then they could've jumped. Sure, the fall would've smooshed them flat, but it was still nice to have options.

To keep her pulse steady and her breath from getting erratic, Thisby fought to think happy thoughts. She thought about Iphigenia and the time she'd spent at the castle. She thought about Grunda and how nice things had been in the dungeon for that short time between terrible events. She thought about Mingus and even Catface for some reason.

The wolves paused on her crate. For a moment, their sniffing stopped, and then they began to growl furiously. It was the sound that signaled the end was coming. The sound of death. They'd found her. She tried to keep happy thoughts in her mind as the crate tipped over and crashed to the floor.

Thisby found herself suddenly upside down and buried beneath a pile of wood shavings. She tried desperately to make sense of what was happening. It was hard to breathe, and she tasted blood in her mouth. The crate had remained intact, for now. But there was something else confusing her senses. Giant paws scratched at the upturned crate, snapping boards and bouncing her around as she clung to the sides like a turtle hiding in its shell. The growling and scratching was unbearably loud and making it harder to think . . . about what? Something was wrong. There was a sensation that didn't fit the rest. Her hand!

More boards splintered as Thisby realized that there was a cool breeze on her left hand that didn't fit the rest of what was happening. Through where the wolves had broken the crate, tiny streams of light shone on its contents: a backpack. It was almost as big as the one she'd lost but far fancier, and it took her a moment to realize that her left arm had gotten inside it. Only it wasn't. From outside the backpack, her arm somehow wasn't there, but yet it was. She wiggled the fingers of her left hand and reached out to touch the inside of the backpack, only it wasn't there. Her hand felt nothing but the cool breeze.

She rolled head over heels again as the wolves batted the crate around. Thisby tried to hold on to the loosened lid, but the jolt as the crate collided with a wall made her lose her grip. Without anyone to hold on to it, the top popped horribly open and sent her tumbling out onto the floor with the backpack still wrapped around her arm up to her shoulder. For the first time, she saw the wolves in their entirety. They were even larger than she'd imagined, their yellow eyes watching her as she stood up.

The wolves made a move for her, and Thisby did the only thing that made any sense—despite it not making any sense at all. She raised the backpack over her head and let it fall over her, swallowing her completely.

*The wolves made a move for her, and Thisby did the only thing that made any sense—despite it not making any sense at all.*

Thisby tumbled down a short staircase and into a dimly lit room, where she landed on a very soft and probably considerably expensive rug. It hurt a bit, but when faced with the alternative of being devoured by wolves, the fall didn't bother her at all. It did confuse her, however.

She was relieved to see that she'd held on to Mingus despite being rolled around by the wolves and was comforted when he began to glow a pale yellow.

"Where are we?" he asked.

Thisby stood up and looked around. The room in which she stood resembled a library, with rows and rows of intricately carved wooden shelves and drawers. In her immediate vicinity was a living area with a desk, tables, and chairs, and a small kitchen. Everything was meticulously placed and designed, like the set of an elaborate play, lit by a large stained-glass ceiling through which shone a pleasant, soft light. However, far and away Thisby's favorite feature of the space so far was its lack of giant wolves.

"It's somebody's home," said Thisby, but that didn't feel quite right.

"Inside the backpack?" Mingus asked.

Thisby shrugged. "Inside the backpack" was definitely where they were, but she didn't have to like it. The presence of any magic in her life at this juncture was a bit unwelcome, even if it'd just saved her life and came with the pleasant smell of incense and old books.

She walked up to a round door at the top of the small staircase and opened it a crack, but it was too dark to see out. When she poked her head through, she found herself face-to-face with the curious muzzle of one of the wolves. The wolf stopped what it was doing and lunged at her, but Thisby managed to withdraw in time. A moment later, the wolf's snapping muzzle was poking into the room, thrashing wildly, filling the entire doorway and sending Thisby tumbling down the short staircase for the second time today.

From her spot on the rug, she could smell the stink of the wolf's hot breath, but it was firmly stuck in the doorway. As angry as it was, there was no way the wolf could fit its entire head into the room, and after watching it struggle ineffectively for a few minutes, she breathed a sigh of relief. When her mood eventually transitioned into anger, Thisby grabbed a poker from in front of the fireplace and whacked away at the beast's nose until it withdrew itself with a whimper and she could slam and lock the door.

"I guess we're stuck here," she said.

It wasn't ideal. She was happy to be uneaten, but every moment stuck in the backpack was another moment that brought Bero closer to the finish line. Thisby sat down in one of the surprisingly comfortable chairs around the kitchen table.

"Now what?" she groaned, setting Mingus down on the table. "I guess eventually most spells wear off. The wolves should de-spell at some point, but it might take days. Or longer. We don't have that kind of time . . . Mingus?"

Thisby looked to her friend, but he was clearly distracted by something else. Something on the ceiling.

"Thisby, look."

She craned her neck up to look at the stained-glass window. She'd been so distracted before that she hadn't even noticed what it was: a depiction of two people, a man and woman locked in an embrace. Behind them was a tree, which wrapped around the frame entirely, and upon its branches were inlaid the words, *To My Beloved Ulia. With Love, Elphond.*

"Elphond the Evil? The first Master of the Black Mountain? Ulia? Where do I know that name from?" Thisby muttered to herself.

"Did Elphond make this place?" asked Mingus. "He made the Escape, so I guess a place like this isn't a stretch."

Thisby tried to shake the name "Ulia" from her mind, but it stuck to the sides. She looked at the woman's face. She was beautiful. Elphond wasn't so bad himself, actually. Being so used to the current Master of the Black Mountain, Thisby had assumed all Masters were stocky bald men with cruel faces, but apparently, that wasn't the case.

"Maybe there's something here we can use," said Mingus.

Thisby nodded.

Grabbing Mingus, she walked back into the shelves and was relieved to find that they were labeled and alphabetized. Everything was organized outstandingly well. It was as good a job as she could've done herself.

"Ant Lion Glands, Anthracite, Antivenom . . . ," she read aloud as she walked down the long row of drawers. "This is stuff you find around the dungeon. Stuff like I had in my own backpack."

"Stuff a gamekeeper would have," Mingus added, finishing her thought for her.

When she made it to the *B*s, her eyes lit up.

"Mingus! Look! Blackdoor Beads!"

She pulled out the big flat drawer and there it was. An entire drawer full of blackdoor beads, divided into neat little sections that were each well labeled and bore the names of the locations where they let out. Thisby's heart was positively soaring now. This was it. This was the stroke of luck she'd so desperately needed.

"Darkwell, Giant's Crossing, Long Lost Lake, Castle Grimstone Gates, the Hold, the Blackdoor Machine Room . . ." Thisby trailed off as one of the names caught her attention.

"Jono's room?" she said, scrunching up her nose.

Then it came back to her. She remembered where she'd heard the name Ulia before. When she'd first met Jono in the castle and told him she was the gamekeeper, he asked if she knew Ulia. Thisby's mind raced as she put the pieces together. Elphond the Evil and Ulia were in love, and this backpack, the stained glass, this whole place, based on the inscription, must've been some kind of gift to her because . . . why?

"Ulia was the first gamekeeper. Elphond must've used his

magic to make this backpack for her. Much nicer than what the Master got me for my first day on the job."

"Which was?" asked Mingus.

"Nothing," she said.

"I think Elphond might've liked this Ulia more."

"I think he might've loved her," said Thisby.

It was either that or he was just the nicest boss to ever have "the Evil" as his official title. If she was right and Elphond and Ulia were romantically involved, was it possible that Jono was . . . their son? Maybe, she supposed, but there was no way to be sure. She'd have to show the backpack to Jono when this was all said and done. Perhaps it might jog his memory and then she'd have her answers. In the meantime, she had work to do.

"Come on," she said, grabbing a bead from the Blackdoor Machine Room section, since it seemed as if that was the closest one to the top of the castle.

Moments later, Thisby's head peeked out of the backpack on the floor of the armory. Thankfully, enough time had passed and the wolves had lost interest. There was the sound of snoring from somewhere in the chamber.

Thisby crawled out of the backpack, put it on, and threw the blackdoor bead at the ground. When the gate popped open, the snoring stopped, but before the wolves could make it back to her, she was through the portal and quickly closing in on becoming the new Master of the Black Mountain.

★ ★ ★

The blackdoor machine was asleep when Thisby stepped into the room. Its arms hung limply at its sides, its screens were dark and empty. Aside from the crackling noise of the blackdoor portal closing behind her, the room was completely silent. Thisby resisted the urge to say, "Hello?" Mingus did not.

"Hello?" he called.

Thisby shushed him, but it was too late. There was a pathetic groan from the other side of the machine, and Thisby realized with a sinking feeling in her gut that they weren't alone.

"Hello? Who's there?" called Thisby.

"Oh, so it's okay when you do it?" grumbled Mingus.

They walked around the blackdoor machine on full alert, expecting to find yet another in a string of seemingly endless obstacles; perhaps it was the monster that looked like Ingo, or another giant wolf, or maybe it was Bero waiting to zap them with a lightning bolt, but they were surprised instead to find a crumpled, pathetic figure, curled up like a cat atop a bed of gold coins and beneath a worn blanket. Trays and teacups were littered everywhere, still stained red. Apparently, the ghoul in charge of removing her empty teacups had finally had enough.

"Overseer?" asked Thisby.

"Mmmm," grunted the pile.

"Are you okay?"

The thing beneath the blanket sat upright. Coins jingled

across the floor. Overseer Marl peeked out, her eyes sunken and purple, almost bruised. Her green hair was wet from sweat and flat, her lips and teeth were stained a deep ruby color. She looked sick, or worse.

"Mm, okay. Okay, dear," she said, and then looked confused. "Wait. Who said that?"

Thisby was almost sure Marl was talking to herself.

"I did but I didn't," Marl continued. "I don't know when my words are mine. Oh, shut up and quit being such a baby. Just drink the tea."

Thisby understood the command wasn't meant for her.

"Fine. Fine. If it'll shut you up," said Marl, and she crawled on all fours over to a pot of tea that apparently wasn't completely empty and tipped the whole thing into her mouth, swallowing whatever remained at the bottom in big gulps and letting the remainder spill out the corners of her mouth. When she was done, she sat back and closed her eyes, smiling contentedly. When she opened them again, she was like a different person. Somebody familiar.

"Hello, dear," said Marl.

"Marl?" asked Thisby.

"Oh, no. This is very confusing, isn't it? But it's not Marl. It's Grunda."

"Grunda? How?"

"Bit of a long story. I don't feel like telling it right now, to be honest, but I know you, and you need to know how everything works, so let's just get this over with."

It definitely sounded like Grunda, despite what Thisby's eyes were telling her.

"It's the tea," said Marl—or perhaps, more accurately, Grunda. "It's made from mindworms. An old goblin recipe. I've had my friends inside the castle feeding it to Marl ever since she arrived. It's quite delicious, but it has a nasty little side effect . . . it turns whoever drinks it into something of a puppet, if you know how to use it right. Which I do. Using another mindworm, I can communicate directly to Marl over a great distance whenever she drinks the tea. I can make suggestions. Plant ideas. Pull her strings. Just like a puppet."

Marl paused and looked a bit sad.

"What I have to tell you next might be hard to hear. Please, come," said Marl as she patted the ground in front of her, indicating that Thisby should sit down.

Thisby exchanged worried looks with Mingus but obeyed anyway, sitting down with her legs folded across from Marl.

"I was the one who gave Marl the idea for the Wretched Scrattle," she said.

Thisby's jaw dropped.

"What? Why?" she blurted.

"Sometimes you have to risk the things you love in order to save them. I know that's hard to understand, but I've been around a long time. A long time. I know what's best."

Thisby felt betrayed. How could Grunda have done something so careless? Something that had caused the deaths of so many monsters and people alike?

"What are you talking about? That's crazy!" shouted Thisby.

"Would you just be quiet and listen?" snapped Marl.

Marl took a deep breath and regained her composure. Her face softened.

"The moment that the King appointed an Overseer, it was the beginning of the end, Thisby. In that moment, the dungeon lost its freedom and became a tool of Nth once again. It's happened before, although you weren't around. The current Master of the Black Mountain wasn't going to stand up for us, for the dungeon. He had to be replaced. At least that was something both Marl and I agreed on. First, though, I had to ensure that this little experiment with the Overseer was a complete disaster. Otherwise they'd continue to appoint Overseer after Overseer until the dungeon was nothing more than a tool for Nth. Everything had to get worse before it could get better. There was no other way."

Thisby wanted to argue, to say that there was always another way, but she'd begun to doubt it herself. It was an awful thought, endangering the lives of the dungeon's creatures to accomplish her goals, and she felt terrible for even considering that it may have been the right thing to do. She'd learned a long time ago that even if something sounded like a good idea, if it made her feel terrible, it probably wasn't. It was easy enough to trick her brain into justifying bad behavior, but her gut was too smart for that. Either way, Marl took her silence as acceptance and continued.

"So I pulled the strings. I gave Marl the idea for the Wretched Scrattle, and her greed did the rest. I had her write that note that Jono found, the one telling you where to meet Iphigenia. And I pushed for Iphigenia to come to meet you in Three Fingers. I knew it was the only way you'd agree to enter the tournament. You trust her too much, Thisby."

Thisby felt her ears get hot.

"Because she's my friend!" she snapped.

"No, she's not! That's what you don't understand! She's one of them! Do you think that the King cares about the dungeon? Nobody cares about the dungeon except those of us who live here! It's why we need to be free of the crown, free of all of it, once and for all. It's why I needed you to become Master."

Marl paused and sighed.

"I need you to be Master so we can declare our independence. No more 'Royal Inspections,' no more interference from Nth or Umberfall. They're both our enemies, Thisby. It's time we start treating them as such."

"Iphigenia's different. When she's Queen—" started Thisby, but Grunda cut her off.

"Nothing ever changes! Don't you see?" yelled Marl. She grabbed a handful of coins and threw them angrily across the chamber. "She might be your friend now, but when she asks you to bow down, when she asks you to kiss her ring, when she asks you to go down into that dungeon and kill the monsters that've grown too big and too dangerous for the kingdom to risk having them escape, what are you going to do then?"

Thisby felt tears welling up in her eyes but fought them back.

"I don't know," said Thisby. "We'll figure it out."

"The dungeon needs to stand on its own two feet. You saw what happened last year when the royals interfered in our business. They almost freed the Eyes in the Dark, Thisby. I'm not letting that happen again. It's time we end this, once and for all."

Marl looked at Thisby as if she were trying to read her expression.

"I need you to win the Wretched Scrattle. I'd do it myself, but if a goblin were to take over, the King would march his army in here right away. They'd wipe us out while we were still depleted from the Scrattle. If you take over, they'll trust you. You can do what I can't do alone. Together, we'll free the dungeon. We'll set things right."

"But why?" asked Thisby. "Why now?"

Marl reached out and put her hands on Thisby's shoulders. Thisby thought she could probably count on one hand the number of times Grunda had shown her any sort of physical affection, and it had always been followed by terrible news. Doing so now, with Marl's face, made it all the harder.

"The Black Mountain grew from the body of the Eyes in the Dark. If the dungeon were to fall into the wrong hands and he escaped, it would likely mean the end of the world.

Your 'friends' the Larkspurs nearly freed him last year. I can't take that chance again."

Thisby shrugged Marl's hands off her shoulders. "No."

Marl looked stunned. Tears had begun to stream down Thisby's cheeks, but she hadn't noticed when they'd started.

"You're wrong," she said. "Iphigenia's my friend and we can make it work. Together. There's no reason humans and monsters can't coexist. We'll find a way. We'll figure it out."

"They'll ruin everything! If you trust the humans, the outsiders, they'll destroy this dungeon and free the Eyes in the Dark! Thisby, be reasonable!"

Thisby turned away.

"I have to go," she said. "Bero can't win the Wretched Scrattle."

"And what'll you do when you win?" demanded Grunda.

"I don't know," said Thisby.

"You're either with me and the monsters, or you're with them!" demanded Grunda. "It's time for you to pick! Whose side are you on?"

Thisby's heart was broken. That was the only term for it. It was the exact opposite feeling of the first time that you held someone's hand and knew that you were going to be with them forever. It felt as if her heart had put on a pair of cold, wet pants.

"I'm on my own side. I'm going to win the Wretched Scrattle and become Master," said Thisby. "After that, I'll do what I think is best."

"Thisby, be reasonable," said Marl. "There's too much at stake."

"I have to go," said Thisby, walking away.

"Thisby, stop! Right now!" shouted Marl.

Thisby turned.

Marl had pulled out a small bottle of purple liquid and held it out in front of her threateningly. "Don't make me do this, Thisby."

Before Thisby could respond, Marl shook her head as if she was waking up from a dream.

"Thisby?" said Marl. "What's happening? Is the Wretched Scrattle over? Are you here to kill me? No! Stop!"

Before Marl-Grunda could decide what to do, Thisby snatched the bottle from her hand and took off running as fast as she could for the door. The sound of Marl arguing with herself faded into the background as she dashed out into the hall.

It was a pleasant surprise to find she recognized where she was. She was close to the Master's quarters. She tore up the stairs with her blood thumping in her ears. Mingus was trying to say something from where his lantern was cradled in her arm, but she wasn't listening. Not to him, not to Grunda, or Marl, or whoever that was. She'd come here to win the Wretched Scrattle, and that was what she was going to do.

At the top of the stairs she found a long hall lined with ornate black sconces atop which danced bright purple flames. The hall ended in a set of double doors, which Thisby knew led into the Master's chambers and to the end of the Wretched Scrattle.

With a crack and a flash, the doors blew open, shards of smoldering wood flying everywhere. Thisby turned to see Bero huffing and puffing up the stairs behind her, holding a spell book in one hand and throwing lightning bolts with the other.

"You're not going to take this from me!" he howled as another bolt ripped past her head and crashed into the back wall of the Master's now open chamber.

There was nothing left to do but run. Her legs were turning over as fast as they could when Thisby realized that her new backpack not only contained an entire room within it but was also much lighter than her previous one. It was not entirely lightning-proof, however, and when the next bolt struck her backpack, the force sent her sailing forward, sliding down the long marble hall toward the Master's room.

Thisby clambered to her feet as another bolt narrowly missed her. She was close now. Close enough that she could see the tall, empty chair towering behind the Master's desk. When she burst across the threshold and into the room, a disembodied voice called for her to sit. It seemed to be emanating from the chair itself. That was it. The last task. All she had to do was make it to his chair and then this would all be over.

She leapt over a pile of smoking rubble as more lightning exploded around her. Nothing was going to stop her now.

Her heart was racing, her body was singing, she was positively bursting through her skin. She was going to make it better. She was going to fix everything. She was going be the best Master this dungeon ever had. She was going to make everything okay.

Something pulled at her ankle. Thisby looked down to see a viscous purple goo begin to crawl slowly up her leg.

"No! No! No!" she screamed.

The bottle had broken when she fell. The purple ooze spread rapidly and began to harden, locking her legs completely in place. Thisby looked behind her to see Bero charging red-faced toward her, and more importantly, toward the chair. He was yelling something, but Thisby could no longer hear clearly as the ooze spread up around her head. Right before it covered her eyes, the last thing Thisby could see was Bero sitting down in the Master's chair.

# CHAPTER 19

Thisby Thestoop wiggled her toes, placing her pinky toe over the toe-which-comes-next-to-the-pinky-toe. There was something on top of them. Something scratchy. A blanket. And not a nice one. She opened her eyes and sat up.

"Thisby?" said a familiar voice.

"Iphi?" she replied, straining to see against the impossibly bright light streaming through the window.

She felt her friend before she saw her. Two warm arms wrapped around her neck, and somebody soft and pleasant-smelling pressed against her cheek.

"What's going on? Where am I?" she asked.

The world was coming into focus now. She was in a

small inn room, mostly barren except for the bed in which she was lying, a small dresser, and a single chair facing the window.

"You're in Three Fingers," said Iphigenia, her face becoming more detailed by the moment. Her big eyes and dark hair, falling in loose ringlets that framed her face.

"What happened? How did I—"

"Marl brought you here. Through a blackdoor. It was the strangest thing," said Iphigenia. "She showed up with you, and you were encased in a sort of purple crust. It took hours to pry it off. I wanted to thank her for her service, but she left before I had a chance."

"I don't think that was Marl," said Thisby. "Not exactly."

Iphigenia patted Thisby on the shoulder and guided her back to lying down.

"How are you feeling?" asked Iphigenia.

Now that it was all coming back to Thisby, she didn't know how to answer that question honestly.

"What happened to the dungeon?" she asked.

Iphigenia sighed.

"It's been claimed in the name of Umberfall. The flags rose this morning."

Thisby felt an incredible weight on her chest. Her mind raced through every creature who was stuck inside with them, from Catface to the lowliest ooze. Her heart went out to all of them. The thought of how they would be treated at the hands of the Umberfallians made her queasy.

"The Master is likely dead," added Iphigenia.

"I wouldn't be so sure," said Thisby. "He has a knack for surviving."

"I'm not sure which I'd prefer at this point," said Iphigenia with a slight smirk.

"Me neither," said Thisby.

Iphigenia got up off the edge of the bed and went to the window, cracking it open. The fresh breeze was wonderful for Thisby's lingering headache, and she could even hear a few birds chirping. It was such a relaxing moment that it felt at odds with the terrible news she was receiving.

"What happened in there?" asked Iphigenia.

"Grunda planted the seeds for the Wretched Scrattle," said Thisby. "Marl was just a pawn. A greedy pawn who put a bounty on my head, but a pawn nonetheless. Grunda was trying to make me the next Master. Unfortunately, some Umberfallians snuck in and screwed it all up."

Iphigenia could hear the hurt in Thisby's voice.

"Are you . . . okay?" she asked.

Thisby nodded. She hesitated, wondering if she should mention the rest of what Grunda had said. About the dungeon's independence and warning her not to trust Iphigenia and Nth. She couldn't bring herself to say the words out loud.

"I'm as good as I can be . . ." She let her voice trail off as she remembered something she'd forgotten to ask about. She felt like a terrible person. "Wait! Where's Mingus?!"

Iphigenia laughed in a comforting way.

"He's fine! He's fine! Sam has him over at the shop. Last I saw him, he was looking at some new lanterns he might like to try out."

Thisby's racing heart slowed.

"Oh. Good," she said.

They both grew silent and listened to the birds singing outside the window. Thisby didn't know enough about birds to know what kind they were. In the dungeon, she could tell the difference between the cooing of a cockatrice and a basan without hesitation, but here she was out of her element. She sat up in bed again and watched Iphigenia, staring out the window like a proper queen overlooking her kingdom.

"What now?" asked Thisby.

Iphigenia didn't take her eyes off the horizon.

"There will be a war. There's no other way my father can respond. Umberfall has invaded the Black Mountain, and in doing so they've invaded Nth."

Thisby's stomach twisted. As much as she hated to admit it, Grunda's words had crept back into her head at hearing Iphigenia refer to the Black Mountain as part of Nth. It was an ugly thought, and she swallowed it back down.

"Thisby, you need to be prepared for what's coming. Umberfall has no mercy. They'll turn the monsters of the dungeon into weapons. They'll unleash them on towns. Whatever comes next, it's going to be bad."

"And what do we do?" asked Thisby.

"We?" said Iphigenia, turning away from the window at last. "We'll stop them, of course. Together."

Thisby climbed out of bed. Her legs were a bit wobblier than expected, but she managed to hobble over to the window, where she supported herself on the back of the chair.

"Thisby, I . . ." Iphigenia paused before continuing. "I want you to know that I made a promise. Before I left the castle to find you. I swore that I'd protect the dungeon, no matter what. And I don't go back on my promises."

"I know," said Thisby.

"Not just the dungeon," added Iphigenia. "But you as well."

Thisby smiled. "I thought I was the one who saved you from monsters."

"True. But we're not in the world of monsters anymore."

Thisby watched outside the window as life went on as usual in Three Fingers. Farmers herded pigs, men rolled barrels, a mother scolded a child. Iphigenia was right. They certainly weren't in the dungeon anymore.

"It's going to be hard to get used to life outside the dungeon," said Thisby.

Iphigenia smiled and nudged her in the ribs with her elbow.

"Too much fresh air and sunshine?" she asked.

"Exactly," said Thisby.

It was hard to say how much longer they stood there before either of them spoke again.

★ ★ ★

Big green waves churned and crashed into the shore, tossing about tall ships like they were toys in a bathtub. The man who stood watching the show from the docks with his cloak pulled up over his head thought this was a particularly cruel irony, since he hadn't been able to take a bath in weeks.

The wind ripped at the sails and his cloak, and when he could take it no more, he turned away from the docks and stumbled into the nearest bar, which was alive with both music and the yells of people trying to be heard over that music. The interior was composed of the parts of crashed ships, which was perhaps a bit of gallows humor for the sailors who drank there every night. The man fought his way forward to the bar, purchased a drink, and then fought his way back toward the emptiest corner of the room—whose emptiness turned out to be due to a rather horrible smell—and took a seat.

It'd been a rough couple of weeks, but he was here now. Here at the end of the world. The Nameless Sea. He'd tried out the joke about giving it a name on a pretty young woman at a different bar last night, and it hadn't gone well. She'd probably just heard that one before, he'd told himself.

The man threw off his hood and drank deeply of something that tasted like sewer water but made him pleasantly warm inside. He was staring into the bottom of his cup when he heard the chair across from him being pulled out. It made an awful sound against the wooden floor.

*It'd been a rough couple of weeks, but he was here now.*
*Here at the end of the world.*

"Seat's taken," he mumbled.

"It is now," said an obnoxiously familiar voice.

The former Master of the Black Mountain sighed and set down his cup. A small old goblin woman was sitting across from him. She set down her drink as if she were joining an old friend.

"What do you want?" he grunted.

"You can't outrun what's coming," said Grunda.

"I can try," he spat back.

The former Master upended his cup and finished whatever was left. It tasted terrible, but he was ready to do anything to make this conversation less painful.

"I thought nobody was going to win the Wretched Scrattle?" the goblin said with a grin.

"It's not my fault Marl's rules didn't include conjurers!" he snapped, defensively. "My riddle should've been—"

Grunda burst into laughter. "Your riddle? You mean the Secret of Magic? Don't tell me you're still using the Secret of Magic? You use that same dumb riddle for everything! You know you're not supposed to do that? You really should change your passwords!"

The former Master's face grew beet red. "Did you come all the way here just to mock me?"

Grunda's eyes grew dark as she leaned forward.

"Of course not. You know why I'm here. The wheels are in motion, and I think you know that better than anyone. The Eyes in the Dark—"

"Stop!" he interrupted. "Just stop, right there!"

He slammed his empty cup down on the table.

"I don't care about the Black Mountain. I don't care about the Eyes in the Dark. Frankly, I don't care if and when this whole world burns. When it finally happens, you know where I'm gonna be? Sipping fancy, fruity drinks on a beach on the other side of the Nameless Sea, that's where. Save your breath. I'm done with this. Forever. There's nothing you can say or do that will change my mind."

The former Master stood up to leave but didn't start walking. Grunda sat perfectly still, wearing a wide, smug grin.

"What are you smiling about?" he said, immediately regretting he'd asked.

"I'm happy because you're wrong," she said. "There is something I can say that can change your mind."

"Go on then, say it! Say the magic words that'll make me stay. You better hurry up, because the second I walk out that door, I'm not coming back."

The former Master threw up his hands and began to stomp away.

"Your son's alive. Well, technically he's undead, but you get the idea."

The Master froze in his tracks, still turned away from the goblin.

"Where?" he demanded.

"In the dungeon. Right under your nose this whole time," she said.

The Master sighed and turned around. He had his shoulders slumped in a look of mock defeat, but there was something else in his eyes. Something hopeful.

"Thanks for waiting until now to tell me," he said.

"His name is Jono now. You've actually met him," said Grunda.

The Master trudged back to the table.

"Then you know . . ." The Master trailed off.

"What, about you and Ulia? Or do you mean that I know who you really are? Of course I know. Admittedly it took me a while to figure it out, though . . . Elphond." She grinned.

Grunda took an annoyingly long drink while the Master struggled to find a response. She finished her drink and set the empty cup down on the table emphatically.

"Come now, Elphond. We've got a lot to discuss," she commanded.

Elphond the Evil sighed. He supposed it had only been a matter of time before somebody figured it out. The fact that it was her, however, only proved his earlier theory. Fate was trying to punish him.

"Where are we going?" he asked.

"To help save the world, I guess," she said.

"Do I have to?" asked Elphond.

"Yes," said Grunda.

Elphond sighed so long that he was still exhaling when the doors closed behind him. He stepped out into the street.

The night was alive with the sounds of crashing waves and snapping flags over the muted din of the revelers inside. On the horizon, the sky was green and stormy, and somewhere in the distance a raven laughed.

# Books by
# ZAC GORMAN!

**HARPER**

*An Imprint of HarperCollinsPublishers*

www.harpercollinschildrens.com • www.shelfstuff.com